Dig

A Morgue Mama Mystery

C. R. Corwin

Poisoned Pen Press

First Edition 2005
Large Print Edition 2005

10 9 8 7 6 5 4 3 2 1

Library of Congress Catalog Card Number: 2005928749
ISBN: 1-59058-204-7 Large Print

Poisoned Pen Press
6962 E. First Ave. Ste. 103
Scottsdale, AZ 85251
www.poisonedpenpress.com
info@poisonedpenpress.com
Printed in the United States of America

Dig

A Morgue Mama Mystery

Also by C. R. Corwin

Morgue Mama

To Carol, for believing
when the odds were unbelievable.

Murders don't make the front page in Hannawa anymore. Not unless the victim is somebody famous. Not unless the circumstances are ghastly or bizarre. And Gordon Sweet was not famous. He was just a silly old college professor. And the circumstances of his death? A single, everyday gunshot to the back of his head, resulting in a single, everyday four-inch stick of copy on an inside page of Sunday's metro section, under a puny headline that read so matter-of-factly:

`Body Found At Landfill`

Is it any wonder my tired old eyes had passed right over it?

Dolly Madison Sprowls
Head Librarian
The Hannawa Herald-Union

1

Monday, March 5

The obituaries are the best part of my day. I get to the newsroom right at nine. I make my first mug of Darjeeling tea. I settle in at my desk with a crisp copy of that morning's paper. And I read the obits.

My assistant Eric Chen thinks it's the funniest thing in the world. "You just want to make sure you're still alive," he says, "so you can go about your earthly mission to make everybody else's life miserable."

"Poop!" I snarl back at him. "I'm just being nosy."

Anyway, the only person I made miserable reading the obits that particular Monday morning was me. "Good gravy," I gasped. My stomach was rolling like I'd swallowed ten pounds of baby snakes.

Eric's desk bumps right up to mine. He was drinking his first Mountain Dew of the day. "Somebody you know, Maddy?"

I answered in a whisper so faint I barely heard it myself. "Somebody I used to know very well."

I clutched the loose skin on my neck and read:

Gordon Sweet

Gordon E. "Sweet Gordon" Sweet, professor of archaeology at Hemphill College, died this week. He was 69.

He was born June 5, 1934, in New Waterbury to Archibald and Ruth (Berghoff) Sweet.

He attended Hemphill College from 1952 to 1958. He received a Ph.D. in archaeology from the University of Michigan and returned to Hemphill College in 1961. He was a member of the Society for American Archaeology, the Society of Professional Archaeologists, the Archaeological Institute of America, the Archaeological Society of Ohio and the Meriwether Square Baked Bean Existentialist Society.

He is survived by his sister, Gretchen Gitlin of Captiva Island, FL, and a nephew, Michael Gitlin of Harper's Ferry, W.Va.

He was preceded in death by his parents, and his brother, U.S. Army Lt. Walter Sweet.

A memorial service will be held at 11 a.m. Saturday at P.W. Leech

```
Unitarian Universalist
Chapel, 185 Goodhue
Ave.
```

When I looked up I found Eric leaning over the front of my desk on his elbows. He'd been reading along with me, upside-down. "His name was Gordon Sweet and his nickname was Sweet Gordon?" he asked. "How cute is that?"

I did not like him referring to my old friend in the past tense. I did not like hearing myself do the same. "We called him Sweet Gordon because that's the way his name always appeared on college grade lists," I said. "Sweet comma Gordon."

Eric slipped back into his chair. "Better than Morgue Mama, I suppose."

He was referring, of course, to me. My name is Dolly Madison Sprowls. I'm 68 years old. I'm short, a little dumpy, and I haven't changed my hairstyle since college. For the past 33 years I've been the head librarian at *The Hannawa Herald-Union*. In the newspaper business they call the library the *morgue*. It's where we keep the stories that have already run—the dead stories if you will—from the big political scandals on the front page to the PTA bake sales buried deep inside. When one of our reporters needs background for a new story they're writing, they come to me. "Maddy," they say, "I need everything you've got on so and so." And I go digging through the files.

The problem is that reporters are always asking for information they don't need. That's why I go out of my way to be a royal pain-in-the-ass. So reporters won't bother me unless it's absolutely necessary for their stories. And that's why—behind my back—they call me Morgue Mama.

Anyway, Eric could see I wasn't in the mood for his teasing. He apologized by acting interested. "So you and Sweet Gordon were buds in college?"

I tried to force a smile on my face. And failed. "We were the best of friends for a long time. He went on to become a professor. Right there at Hemphill. In archaeology. He specialized in some kooky field called *garbology*—digging up old junk to see how people really lived."

"Well—sounds like he was an interesting guy."

"He was an eccentric old fool," I said. "I wonder how he died?"

Eric's eyes sagged with dread. He pulled the huge Sunday edition off the top of his computer terminal and shook out the Metro section. He turned the first page timidly, as if pulling the sheet off the face of a corpse. His eyes drifted down the page. "I knew that name rang a bell," he said. Now I was the one reading upside-down. BODY FOUND AT LANDFILL, the tiny headline said.

Those baby snakes in my stomach had grown into a ton of pythons. Gordon Sweet had been murdered.

> HANNAWA—The body of 69-year-old Hemphill College archaeology professor Gordon Sweet was found Saturday at the abandoned Wooster Pike landfill in Durkee Township.
>
> Police said he had been shot once in the head.
>
> The body was discovered shortly before noon by a graduate assistant who told police he had been looking for Sweet since he failed to show up to teach his Friday morning class.

> The body was found in high grass a few yards from the gravel driveway, police said.
>
> The graduate assistant, Andrew J. Holloway III, told police Sweet had been conducting an archaeological dig at the landfill for the past four summers.
>
> Police said they have found no motive for the shooting and are continuing their investigation.

I'd read the Sunday paper at home. From front to back. As I always do. But it was such a small story, stuck at the bottom of an inside page, next to an inky ad for truck tires. The headline must have passed through my eyes and out the back of my head without my groggy, Sunday-morning brain taking notice.

I pulled the metro section from under Eric's elbows. I cut out the story with the big, black-handled scissors I've been using since my first year at the paper. (I call them my black-handled scissors even though the black paint has been worn off for ages.) Then I cut out the obit from that morning's paper and stapled the two together. I read them again and again. There was more information in those two little columns of print than my mind—or my heart—could digest. Yet I wanted more. I wanted every horrible detail. I wanted to know that the bastard who killed Sweet Gordon was already in jail, hanging from the ceiling by his big toes.

One thing I did know was that the story in Sunday's paper hadn't been written by Dale Marabout, our regular police reporter. It had been written by one of the general assignment reporters in metro, whose turn it was to work the weekend. Pestering that reporter for more information on Gordon's death wouldn't do me a bit of good. The weekend people don't physically go to the central police station downtown the way Dale does during the week. They call from the desk. They jot down what the cop on the other end tells them. They pound out the shortest story possible. So if I wanted more information on Gordon's murder, I'd have to wait for Dale to come in, and hope he had something new to tell me.

I knew I should put Gordon's murder out of my mind and get to work. Louise Lewendowski would be drifting in at noon and I'd promised her all the old stories we had on the Hannawa Zoo—she was writing some dreadful puff piece on the zoo's 75th anniversary—and knowing Louise she'd almost certainly have a little sack of her delicious apricot kolachkys for me. She bribes me with bakery the way house burglars carry raw meat in their pockets for big nasty dogs. But how could I not think about Gordon that morning? About the young Gordon I knew in college dancing madly in smoky jazz clubs, or slumped against the trunk of a big oak discussing poetry or politics? Or about the old Gordon I still bumped into occasionally at the supermarket, sprawled out dead in the high, soggy grass?

"You would have liked him," I said.

Eric *had* gotten to work. He was clicking away at his keyboard with all ten fingers and both sides of his brain. "That Sweet Gordon guy, you mean?"

When Editor-in-Chief Bob Averill decided to computerize the morgue some years back, he knew I was too much of a Neanderthal to handle the job. So he hired Eric as my assistant. And no doubt about it, Eric is a wiz on those computers. He is not, however, a wiz at real life. He is sloppy and absent-minded. He never loses a story in cyberspace but he is forever losing his wallet, or the keys to his pickup, or his heart to the wrong kind of women. "That's who we're talking about, isn't it?" I growled.

Eric gave the left side of his brain permission to pay attention to me. "What was that baked bean thing in the obit?"

"The Meriwether Square Baked Bean Existentialist Society—I was puzzled by that, too."

"So you don't understand it either?"

"Oh, I understand it," I said. "I'm just surprised to see it listed among all those real organizations."

"The Meriwether Square Baked Bean Existentialist Society isn't a real organization? Hard to believe."

I rolled my eyes in embarrassment. "It was the little group of beatniks we belonged to in college."

Eric stopped typing and focused both sides of his brain on me. "You were a beatnik?"

I retreated. "I shouldn't have said beatniks. Gordon hated that word. He said it was a made-up word by some smart-ass magazine writer that trivialized what we stood for."

"Which was what? Eating beans?"

As horrible as I felt I had to laugh. "We did eat

a lot of beans," I said. "But we also stood for looking at the world in a new way. That life wasn't all about making money and living in a big house."

He squinted at me over the top of his soda bottle. "You majored in library science. Was there any danger of you ever living in a big house?"

"We were young, Eric. The campus bohemians. Members of the beat generation. Maybe we weren't beaten down ourselves—we were just silly middle class kids with too much time on our hands—but we did relate to those who were. We wanted to purify America's corrupt, materialistic soul. So we listened to jazz, drank little cups of coffee and talked and talked and talked."

"And ate a lot of beans," he added.

Eric was only in his thirties. Even the 1970s were ancient history to him. I could no more expect him to understand the crazy excesses of my youth than I could understand the crazy excesses of his. "It was a long time ago," I said. "I just can't believe they put that in his obituary."

I sped to Dale Marabout's desk the minute I saw him sit down. I had the clippings in one hand, my mug in the other. "You know anything more about this?"

Dale put on his reading glasses, tilted his head back until the print came into focus. "Ah, yes—the dead professor. I'm following up for tomorrow."

"Have they arrested anybody yet?" I asked.

Dale handed the clippings back. "It's only been two days, Maddy."

"He was an old friend. From college. So whatever you have."

Dale pulled a reporter's notebook from his jacket. He squinted at his scribbles. "Single, small caliber bullet in the back of the head. Probably dead a couple of days when he was found."

"There's no way it could have been an accident?"

"Almost point blank."

"Or a robbery?"

"Still had his wallet and Donald Duck watch."

"No chance it was a suicide?"

"Not unless he used a biodegradable gun."

"So no weapon was found?"

"Not at the landfill or anywhere else."

"Definitely a murder then?"

"Yup—the professor is dead because somebody wanted him dead." He flipped the notebook shut.

I was disappointed. And angry. "Nothing more?"

"Just that the grad assistant who found his body also found his car," Dale said. "By the college ball fields. A good fifteen miles away. His name is Andrew J. Holloway III." He put a sarcastic, lilting accent on *the third.*

"Do the police consider this Andrew J. Holloway III a suspect?"

Dale searched his clutter for his coffee mug—it was hiding behind a stack of old newspapers—and headed for the cafeteria. "I gather he's piqued their curiosity."

I followed him. "Anything in particular pique your curiosity?"

"The Meriwether Square Baked Bean Existentialist Society—whatever that is."

"I know exactly who they are," I said. "In fact, Mr. M, I'm a charter member of that prestigious little gaggle of fools."

Dale and I chatted for a few minutes in the cafeteria. About Gordon Sweet. About Dale's son's chances of graduating from high school on time. Once upon a time Dale and I had been lovers. When I was in my horny forties. When he was a pudgy young reporter thrilled to be sleeping with anyone. It went on for five years, until a young kindergarten teacher named Sharon Saporito moved into his apartment building. Now Dale and I were just friends. Full of advice for each other.

"It wouldn't be the worse thing if your boy had to take a course or two in summer school," I told him. "It would be a good lesson for him."

"Now don't get crazy with this Gordon Sweet thing," he cautioned me. "Let the police handle it."

Then I rushed back to the morgue and the Z files. Louise Lewendowski got the old stuff she needed on the zoo and I got my little sack of kolachkys.

2

Saturday, March 10

Eric showed up at my house at ten-thirty, wearing an ill-fitting sports coat and the only necktie he owned, a bright red Cleveland Indians tie dotted with grinning Chief Wahoo faces. "Don't you look nice," I said.

I'd put on my navy blue funeral suit. I hadn't worn it in maybe five years. The jacket was a little looser in the shoulders than I remembered. The skirt a lot tighter around the waist. I hated to face it, but I'd reached the age when a woman shrinks and expands at the same time. Caterpillars metamorphose into butterflies. Women metamorphose into caterpillars—shapeless, low-to-the-ground lumps. "You're not looking too bad yourself," Eric said.

"We'd better get going," I said.

Eric offered to drive but there was no way in hell I was going to Gordon Sweet's memorial service in a pickup truck. Not that my old Dodge Shadow was any classier. We took Brambriar to Teeple, then turned east onto West Tuckman and headed toward Meriwether Square and Hemphill College. The sky was purple. Snowflakes as fat as my fake pearls were blowing in every direction.

To tell you the truth, I was glad that Eric was going with me. After all these years even my old college friends would be strangers. There was likely to be a lot of uncomfortable small talk. Inane comments about the hereafter I knew Gordon didn't believe in. It would be good to have company.

Eric was glad to be coming, too. "Are you kidding," he said when I'd asked him if he wanted to tag along. "How can I pass up a roomful of old beatniks?"

We reached the campus and the statue of the college's famous founder, Horatio Ellsworth Hemphill, pointing toward the future. H.E. Hemphill had been one of those indefatigable Renaissance men that nineteenth-century America produced by the bucketful: theologian, Civil War general, advocate for women's education, pioneer in rot-resistant seed potatoes for farmers. We took the brick circle to the right and turned north on Goodhue Avenue. We parked across the street from the P.W. Leech Unitarian Universalist Chapel.

Gordon's memorial service was nothing like I'd feared and everything I should have expected.

First of all, the music: It was not that dirgey organ music you usually hear at funerals, that squeals away at your ears like it's being played through the snout of a gerbil. It was jazz. Bebop jazz. Played loud and live by nobody less than Shaka Bop, Hannawa's answer to Charlie Parker. And it was not just Shaka Bop and his big silver saxophone filling the chapel. There was a drummer and a bass player. All three of them were wearing sunglasses and colorful African dashikis. Shaka was wearing a leather porkpie hat.

Second, the people in the pews: They hadn't come to mourn Gordon's death. They had come to celebrate Gordon's life. Crammed shoulder to shoulder, they were bobbing their heads and snapping their fingers, and whenever Shaka took off on some frantic run on his sax, they shouted, "Blow, baby, blow!"

Eric was thrilled by all this. I nudged him into a back pew. I resisted as long as I could, but as soon as Shaka's trio launched into Salted Peanuts my head started bobbing along with everybody else's.

I'd forgotten how good Shaka was—and how much I liked that kind of music.

The coroner hadn't released Gordon's body yet. So there wasn't a casket or urn of ashes to keep my eyes busy. There were just the people in the pews. What an odd collection! There were a lot of students, some so nerdy you just knew they had to be archaeology majors, others with tattoos and body piercings and brightly dyed hair that looked like a chimpanzee cut it. I figured they were the current crop of campus bohemians. There were lots of old hippies, too, middle-aged men with ponytails and pasty earth mother-types with long, straight Peter, Paul and Mary hair down to their sagging boobs. Professors, I guessed. Then there were the ancients, the folks my age. Most were dressed sensibly enough, although I did spot a beret or two.

Shaka Bop shifted to a surprisingly unjazzy rendition of Ebb Tide, a soothing old tune from the fifties. When everyone was mellowed out, the Rev. Bernice Wallenburg came to the pulpit. She was not a small woman. She was wearing a flowered dress that reminded me of my grandmother's drapes. She spoke for fifteen minutes on the ups and downs of life without once mentioning how Gordon's life ended.

She was followed by a small wiry woman with thick yellow lollipop glasses and hair so short you'd swear she was a lesbian if you didn't know she was anything but. "Good heavens," I whispered to myself, "that can't possibly be Effie."

But it was Effie. Fredricka "Effie" Fredmansky. We'd graduated the same year, both with degrees in library science. Like me, she was one of the charter members of the Meriwether Square Baked Bean Existentialist Society. Unlike me, she'd been quite popular with the college boys. That popularity had nothing to do with her looks. In the looks department she was as below average as me. But Effie had an extremely relaxed view of sex for those years. She flitted about as she wished, without guilt or emotional expectations. The last I'd heard Effie ran a used bookstore just off campus.

Effie had apparently remained very close to Gordon over the years. She told five decades' worth of wonderful stories about him. She talked about his good heart and his easygoing ways. It made me wish I'd stayed close to Gordon, too.

Chidsey "Chick" Glass was the next to speak. Like Gordon, he'd returned to Hemphill College to teach. Except for a few wrinkles and the curly, white hair hanging over his ears, he didn't look much different than he did in his college days. He was still skinny as the dickens. His nose still hung over his lips like the beak of a cockatoo. And he was still wearing a beret.

While Shaka Bop tootled softly in the background, Chick recited a poem he'd written for the occasion. It was in the old beat style we once considered so deep and dangerous, that was now, to tell you the truth, nearly impossible to follow:

"Man, wow,
Sweet Gordon
You vamoosed
So completely
So metaphysically
Without you and me
Resolving ever
That weighty question
That was such a thorny
Hang-up
That split us asunder
So un-copectically
Like Ti-Jean and the Howler
And now
You've split forever
And now that weighty question
That never mattered much

Matters not at all
And now I am bugged to the bone
Over the whole terrible ball of wax."

Eric was the only one who clapped. I stopped his hands. "Quit being so bourgeois," I whispered. "A beat never applauds. You show your appreciation with a slow nod and a faraway look in your eyes, as if you actually understood what he was saying."

The service went on for another half hour: kind words and funny stories by Gordon's old friends, praise and platitudes from his students, more wonderful tunes by Shaka Bop, a final prayer by Bernice Wallenburg that didn't once mention God. The only thing missing was Gordon's relatives. And I found that odd. Gordon didn't have a wife or children, but his obit did mention a sister and a nephew. And certainly he must have had cousins. Everybody has cousins. Didn't any of them have anything to say? Were any of them even there?

After the service we shuffled to the anteroom for cake and coffee. "Stay close to me," I told Eric. "I mean it."

"Sure," he said. Seconds later he made a beeline for a girl with a yin and yang tattoo on her bare midriff.

I retreated to the safety of the refreshment table. There was a big white coffee maker. There were stacks of Styrofoam cups rising from the white tablecloth like stalagmites. There were rows of white paper plates with squares of white cake with white frosting. There were white napkins and white plastic forks and spoons. Fortunately, there also was a white porcelain bowl of tea bags.

While I was making my tea, a shadow drifted across the table. With all that white staring me in the face, it was as ominous as a rain cloud. I looked up and found Chick Glass. "I figured that was you, Maddy," he said. He playfully flicked my Prince Valiant bangs with his fingers. "You haven't changed one iota, babe."

"And I see you still love those berets."

He sheepishly slid it off his head. "Actually I think they're silly. But for Gordon—and the poem—I thought what the hell."

He'd put such emphasis on *the poem* that I just had to lie and tell him I loved it. Chick had always fancied himself a poet. "Did you really dig it?" he asked.

"The most," I said.

He pulled a stack of folded Xerox copies from his suit coat and handed me one. "I ran them off just in case somebody wanted one."

He grinned at me like a love-struck circus clown while I pretended to read it. I folded it into a manageable square and slid it into my purse. "It's so good to see you again," I said. "If only the circumstances were different."

Chick was suddenly a very sad clown. "He was my best friend, Maddy. For fifty damn years."

I handed him a paper plate with a square of white cake. He didn't wait for me to hand him a fork. He took a huge bite, sadly wiggled his eyebrows like Groucho Marx, and walked away, plate in one hand, beret in the other.

His departure startled me. I was expecting to have a long talk with him—about the old days, about what each of us were doing now, about Gordon's murder. I finished making my tea. I nibbled on a piece of cake. I tried to get Eric's attention. He was finally talking to the girl with the tattoo on her belly. Then a sharp trill rattled my eardrums: "Dolly Madison Sprowls, I can't believe it's you!"

It was Gwendolyn Moffitt-Stumpf. She had her husband, Rollie, in tow.

Gwen Moffitt had been a year behind me in college. I have no idea what she majored in. She probably had no idea herself. She was one of those rich girls who went to college to find a boy whose potential equaled—and with a little luck surpassed—that of her father. The boy she found was Rollie Stumpf. Rollie was the son of a Pittsburgh steelworker. But his potential as a husband was dazzling. He had a brilliant mind and a malleable spine. How those two ever found their way into the Baked Bean Society I have no idea.

I do remember that Gwen was one of the few students at Hemphill with a car. It was a 1954 Buick Roadmaster convertible. It was a going-off-to-college gift from her father. A bribe so she'd still live at home. I have no interest in cars at all, but I sure remember that car. From the front it looked like an angry catfish. Like all Buicks back then it had those four nostrils on the front fenders. It was painted bright pink and had an enormous amount of chrome. It had white seats, a white canvas top and fat, whitewall tires that glowed in the dark. We Baked Beaners just loved riding around in it. We called it the Beat Buggy. Can you imagine it? The campus bohemians, sworn enemies of American materialism, crammed like sardines in that decadent car, cackling at our own hypocrisy?

"Gwen, Rollie," I said. "I figured you two would be wasting away in Florida by now."

"Not while there's still money to be made here in Hannawa," she said. It sounded like a joke but I knew from Rollie's hounddog eyes that she wasn't joking.

While Rollie fidgeted, Gwen and I took turns telling Gordon stories. Each one was funnier than the last. Each one made us a little sadder.

There was one story that Gwen and I artfully avoided. It was the one about the Halloween party at the Kappa Kappa Gamma sorority house, our junior year, when both Gwen and Gordon came as the Wizard of Oz scarecrow. The spiked cider was flowing and poor Rollie was busy bagging groceries at the A&P. As the night wore on, their silly, wobbly-legged dancing led to some serious cheek-to-cheek dancing, and then two hours of serious necking in the basement rumpus room. As far as I know it never went further than that, but they did keep their distance for the rest of the semester.

I'd no sooner pried myself away from Gwen and Rollie than I felt a finger drilling me in the elbow. I remembered whose annoying habit that was. I turned with the biggest smile I could muster. "Effie!"

"I figured that had to be you, Maddy."

"I really loved your talk, Effie."

"Sorry I don't have any Xeroxes."

Oh, how I howled at that. I'd forgotten what a wonderful sense of humor she had. Dark. Sarcastic. Always right on the button. "You still running that little bookstore?" I asked.

"Of course—and you're still at the paper?"

"Of course."

"You get married again after Lawrence?"

I shook my head. "How about you? You ever find time for a husband?"

She stood back and dramatically unfurled her arms. "Would I still look this good if I'd gotten married?"

We laughed. We ate cake. We talked about Gordon. "I saw him just three days before he was—before they found him," she said. "At the Kerouac Thing."

"The Kerouac Thing? You're still holding those?"

She smiled sadly and nodded. "Every year since 1959. Can you believe it?"

I could believe it. To members of the Meriwether Square Existentialist Baked Bean Society, Jack Kerouac's unlikely visit to Hemphill College was the first and second coming rolled into one. He'd visited the campus in late November 1956.

On The Road hadn't been published yet, but he was already well known among the little groups of beats sprinkled around the country. He only stayed for two days. He drank a lot of free beer and ate a lot of free food and slept on the sofa in Gordon's apartment. After 48 hours of mooching, he took the bus to New York and became famous. Three Novembers later the Baked Bean Society held its first party to commemorate his already legendary visit. We officially, and breathlessly, called it The Grand Kerouacian Anniversary Ball. By the second year we were simply calling it the *Kerouac Thing.*

"You had the Kerouac Thing in March?" I asked. "Whatever happened to November?"

"We stopped having it in November ten, twelve years ago. Finals and football kept getting in the way. Not to mention Thanksgiving. Half the time half the people couldn't come. So I finally said to Gordon and Chick, 'Jesus, why don't we just hold the damn thing when nobody's busy with anything.' March it was."

Lawrence and I were already two years out of college and married when the first Kerouac Thing was held. But we attended. And we continued to attend for the next several years. And those get-togethers were great fun. We'd read from Kerouac's poems and novels. Shaka Bop would play the bebop tunes Kerouac allegedly loved. We'd eat beans and drink cheap wine. We'd remember—and embellish—our precious personal minutes with the great bohemian bard himself. "You still have it at your place?" I asked.

Effie moaned like a seasick walrus. "Hell, no. I gave up that honor twenty years ago. We hold it at the Blue Tangerine."

"The Blue Tangerine? That's a little un-bohemian, isn't it?"

Now Effie laughed. "It's a lot un-bohemian. And I'm sure the great Mr. K is rolling over in his box. But time does march on, Maddy my love."

"That it does."

"We've sure missed you over the years," she said.

"After Lawrence and I divorced I guess I got busy with other things," I said. I could see that Effie was itching to ask me what went wrong between Lawrence and me. She'd once warned me not to marry a man that handsome and I did not want to reward her with the details of his infidelity. So I changed the subject. "You said you saw Gordon at the Kerouac Thing just three days before his body was found—did it seem to you that he was bothered by anything?"

Her eyes shifted back and forth inside her big yellow glasses. "No."

"It's just so hard to believe somebody would want him dead," I said.

"Yes, it is."

"And why that old landfill? Not that any place is a good place to be murdered."

"Maybe he was digging where he shouldn't have been digging," Effie said.

3

Thursday, March 15

I was a wreck all morning. That afternoon I'd be having lunch with Detective Scotty Grant. For better or worse Dale Marabout had let it slip to his sources at the police department that I knew Gordon Sweet. And now Grant wanted to see me. For what he called a friendly chat.

"I'd be happy to," I said when he called me Monday morning. "I'm in the morgue all day. Come by whenever you want."

He laughed so loud I had to pull the receiver away from my ear. "With a hundred reporters hovering around? I thought maybe you'd come to see me."

I'd never been to a real police station, of course, but I'd seen plenty of them on TV. I wanted no part of that testosterone-soaked lunacy. "Couldn't we meet on neutral ground?" I asked.

His laugh was kinder now. "I suppose."

We settled on Speckley's, that wonderful little mom and pop diner in Meriwether Square famous for its meatloaf sandwiches, glob of au gratin potatoes on the side. We'd meet there at two, after the lunch rush, when we'd be surrounded by empty tables.

So all morning Tuesday I made Eric's life a living hell—even more than usual—and then drove to Meriwether Square for my friendly chat with Scotty Grant. We both ordered the meatloaf sandwiches.

Scotty Grant looked more like a junior high school principal than a homicide detective. He was tall and doughy, comfortable in a suit that didn't fit very well. He had a high forehead and massive blond eyebrows that swooped across his brow like the McDonald's arches. He was closer to fifty than forty.

Grant and I had first met during our paper's investigation into the Reverend Buddy Wing murder the year before. The famous evangelist was poisoned on live television. As the weeks went by, and my suspicions began to bear fruit, Grant came to trust my instincts. I figured that was why he was having lunch with me now.

"So, you knew Gordon Sweet pretty well?" he asked.

"Years ago I did. When we were in college. We were all part of this little group called the Meri—"

He held up his hand like a stop sign. "I know about the little group."

I felt a flash of heat, from my ears to my toes. But it wasn't menopause—that bubbling cauldron of misery was long behind me. It was embarrassment. The Meriwether Square Baked Bean Existentialist Society was suddenly becoming a big thing in my life again. As if I'd once been a member of the Communist Party or something. "It wasn't a real organization or anything," I said. "It was just a bunch of—"

He stopped me again. "Have you stayed close to any of those people?"

I shook my head.

"So you weren't at that Kerouac Thingy-dingy the other night?"

"Good gravy, no. I haven't gone for years."

"So your relationship with Sweet and his friends is pretty much ancient history then?"

"Well, yes. I suppose so."

I could tell from the way Grant was nibbling on the ice in his water glass that he was disappointed. "Exactly when was the last time you talked to Gordon Sweet?" he asked.

"It could have been six months ago—or maybe a year."

"That memorable, was it?"

"It was just the usual small talk when you bump into someone. 'How you doing?' 'You're looking good.' That kind of thing."

"And was he looking good, Mrs. Sprowls? He didn't look troubled or frightened? Preoccupied with something?"

"Well, Gordon was always preoccupied with something," I said. "He was a very smart man and there was always a lot going on upstairs. But I don't have any memory of thinking something was wrong."

He put another spoonful of ice in his mouth. "You went to the memorial service, right?"

I nodded, wondering how he knew.

"You have a chance to talk to anybody?"

I told him who'd I talked to, Effie, Chick, Gwen and Rollie.

"Any of them say anything interesting?"

"Just the stuff everybody says. What a great guy Gordon was. How they're going to miss him."

"Nothing relating to his murder?"

"Well, Effie did say maybe Gordon was digging where he shouldn't have been."

Grant showed a smidgen of interest in that. "Was that *her* maybe or *your* maybe?"

"I'm pretty sure it was her maybe."

"So you didn't get any sense that she knew something?"

"Not really. But you do have to wonder if his dig had anything to do with his murder, don't you?"

The waitress brought our drinks. Grant had ordered a Diet Pepsi. I'd ordered hot tea. He watched me squeeze the goodness out of my teabag and I watched him take his straw out of the wrapper. I figured if he wasn't going to ask me another question, then I'd ask him a few of mine. "You don't have any suspects then?"

He bent the tip of the straw at a convenient angle and took a long suck of his Pepsi. "Every murder comes with a shitload of suspects, Mrs. Sprowls. Pardon my Vulgarian."

I waved off his apology. "But nobody you're going to arrest in the next day or two?"

He adjusted the angle on his straw and sucked again. "This one could take a while to unravel."

"What about that graduate assistant, Andrew Holloway III?" I asked.

One of Grant's big eyebrows arched higher.

One went flat. "What about him?"

"Dale said the kid found both Gordon's body and his car. Fifteen miles away from each other."

Grant stared at me for an uncomfortably long time. He was not thrilled that I knew that much about the graduate assistant, which meant he was not thrilled that Dale knew that much. Clearly somebody back at headquarters was going to get his ass chewed out for leaking that. "That's really all I know," I assured him.

"Let's try to keep it that way," he said.

The meatloaf sandwiches and sides of au gratin potatoes arrived. Like everyone who's ever eaten at Speckley's, we raved about how good it was all the time we were stuffing our faces. "I'm sorry I can't be more helpful," I said.

He put down his fork. Folded his fists under his chin. "That's not the only reason I wanted to see you."

I put my fork down, too. Fidgeted with my napkin. "Oh?"

"Let me ask you this—If you weren't that close to Professor Sweet anymore, why did you go to his memorial service?"

It was a good question. One I'd asked myself. I fumbled my way through a number of answers:

"I guess because he was such a nice man. And I had so many good memories of him. And to tell you the truth, I was curious to see who else might show up."

My use of the word *curious* made him wince, as if he'd just swallowed one of those bitter little gnats that buzz around over-ripe bananas. "You're not going to involve yourself, are you Mrs. Sprowls?"

"Involve myself?"

"You did a great job with the Buddy Wing thing. We never would have found the real murderer without you. We're very grateful. But that little snoopfest of yours was just a one-time deal, right?"

"Well, of course it was a one-time deal."

My assurance resuscitated his appetite. "That's good to hear," he said through a mouthful of slippery potatoes. "Because this case may have to be on hold for a while. And I don't want you out there causing trouble. For me or yourself."

"Heavens to Betsy, don't worry about that—what do you mean on hold for a while?"

"Not exactly on hold. But we only have so many detectives. And only so much time. And we're up to our boxers in this Zuduski thing."

He was talking, of course, about the murder of Paul Zuduski, younger brother of Congresswoman

Betty Zuduski-Lowell. He'd been missing for six weeks when his badly decomposed body was found in an abandoned factory on the south side. He'd been shot several times and duct-taped inside a Persian rug. He'd worked in his sister's Hannawa office, helping solve the everyday problems of her constituents.

"The good congresswoman is putting tremendous pressure on the mayor," Grant said. "And pressure on the mayor means pressure on the chief. Which means pressure on yours truly. But don't worry, Mrs. Sprowls, we'll get the sonofabitch who killed your friend sooner or later."

Of course I wasn't going to involve myself. No matter how many unanswered questions were eating away at me. No matter how upset I was that Detective Grant was putting Gordon's murder on the backburner while he figured out who killed the congresswoman's little brother.

Of course if I remembered something that might be important, I'd share that with the police. And if, as the head librarian of *The Hannawa Herald-Union,* I came across something interesting in my files, why, yes, I'd certainly pass that along. But involve myself? No way in hell was I going to involve myself.

4

Saturday, March 17

I knew right where to find Eric Chen—in the cafe at the Borders bookstore in Hannawa Falls. Eric spends every Saturday and Sunday there, from the minute the store opens until the manager sweeps him out at closing time, playing chess with the city's other dust-collecting geniuses. They're quite a bunch, I'll tell you. I suppose there are fifteen or twenty of them. Ethnically they're a real box of Crayolas: Whites, Blacks, Asians, Latinos, Iranians, just about one of everything. And almost all of them have an advanced degree in some difficult subject. They gather around the little tables like starved squirrels around a walnut tree. They play game after game after game. Fast, noisy games. They chatter and groan and slap their foreheads. They bang their chess pieces down and pound their timers. They giggle in Farsi and screech *Shit!* in Chinese.

Eric was sitting right in the middle of this mayhem, locked in battle with some unshaven old fart in a bowling shirt. I sat at an empty table and waited for him to notice me. When he did, I wiggled my fingers at him. He gave me the international finger signal for "just a minute." He played—and lost—three more games before joining me. "You know," I said, "if you and your little friends stopped wasting your brains on that worthless game, you could have half of the world's problems solved in about five minutes."

Eric was cradling a big, half-empty bottle of Mountain Dew in his arms. "Is there a compliment in there somewhere?"

"Actually, no."

"Good," he said. "I don't think any of us could take the pressure of being admired." He pulled out a chair with his foot and slumped into it. He held his Mountain Dew bottle up to the light and shook it until the carbonation bubbles were swirling like the snow in one of those worthless glass balls. "So, what brings you to Borders, Maddy? Trolling for a well-read man?"

"Trolling for a man who still reads comic

books. I need your help, Eric."

It took him two seconds to put two and two together. "Ah—Sweet Gordon. The police haven't arrested anybody yet?"

"From what Detective Grant tells me, that *yet* may be a long way off."

I was expecting him to put up a tussle. I'd forced him to help with the Buddy Wing investigation and that little adventure hadn't exactly gone well for him. But he just sat there, grinning at me like a toad that had just drilled itself out of the mud after a long winter. Post Traumatic Chess Disorder I suppose. I laid out my game plan before he came to his senses. "We'll have to look into his love life. From what I see on all those TV shows that's always numero uno. After that, relatives, other professors and his students. Anybody whose life is even marginally better now that Gordon's dead. But the big thing I'm going to need your help with is that awful landfill."

Eric screwed the cap off his Mountain Dew and took a long chug. He swished the liquid back and forth between his cheeks. He swallowed, scrunching his face as if he was drinking rat poison. "This isn't going to involve a shovel, is it?"

"Only your computer." I told him what I

wanted: "See what you can find out about the landfill itself. If anybody else has ever been killed out there. If anything else strange or controversial has happened there since it closed."

"Easy enough," Eric said. He took one of the ballpoints from his shirt pocket and wrote it on the paper napkin he carried in his pants pocket instead of a handkerchief.

I continued: "Second, let's see if anybody's missing from that part of the county—especially where the police expect foul play."

"Even easier," he said.

"This next one may not be so easy," I said. "There could be oodles of things buried out there that shouldn't be."

"Including a lot of poopy diapers."

"Illegal things, Eric. Something that would send somebody to prison for a long time if somebody found it."

"A body?"

"Maybe. Or maybe a murder weapon. Or a big wad of stolen money. Or a drug dealer's stash. Secret government documents linking Elvis and Lassie to the Kennedy assassination. Who the hell knows? An old landfill would be the perfect place to hide almost anything. But for the time being, let's concentrate on one thing—toxic waste."

Eric's eyebrows shot up until they were hiding under his shiny black bangs. "Ahhhh—Margaret Newman's series."

"That's right. Print out Margaret's stories for me. And anything else we might have on the subject."

Margaret Newman was *The Herald-Union*'s environmental writer. Several years ago she'd written a terrific series on a local chemical company caught burying some of its nastier stuff in the dead of night. "It's been a few years but I seem to remember that some of that goop was never accounted for," I said.

Eric had filled one side of the napkin and was now scribbling on the back. "The head honcho went to jail, didn't he?"

"I don't remember that much about it," I said, "but I think the guy hired to do the dumping is the one who went to jail. The *honcho*, as I recall, merely went missing."

"I see."

"No, you don't. And neither do I. It's just a hunch."

Eric launched into one of his irritating songs—this one sung to the tune of La Cucaracha: "Hunch about the honcho! Hunch about the honcho!

Deedee-deedee-deedee-dee!"

I put my fingers in my ears until he was finished amusing himself. "Now, you understand that this is not exactly a sanctioned project?"

"What fun would it be if it was?"

"Because if Tinker finds out we're snooping into another murder, he'll run us through the printing press feet first."

Tinker, of course, was Alec Tinker, the paper's managing editor. He was a sweetie, but a very nervous sweetie. There was no point bringing him into the loop until I knew that loop led somewhere.

Eric nodded that he understood the need for secrecy. "Anything else you need?"

"There is a feature Doris Rowe wrote for the Sunday magazine a few years ago," I said. "But I can find that myself."

Eric's eyes squeezed skeptically. "You sure about that?"

I wasn't sure. But I sure as hell wasn't going to admit it. "What am I," I exploded, "a sweet potato? If I said I can find it myself, then I can find it myself!"

Eric went back to his chess buddies. I drove to across town to Hemphill College, to see Chick Glass.

Chick, like a lot of his fellow professors, lived in one of the dark, old Tudors in the hills just west of the college. I parked on the street and waded through the snarls of pachysandra that filled his entire front yard. I climbed the broken stone steps. The door swung open before I could ring the bell. "Maddy Sprowls—where *have* you been?"

Chick stepped aside. I slipped into his narrow foyer. The table under the mirror was stacked high with junk mail. Only one of the three bulbs in the ceiling light was still burning. I let him kiss my cheek. He let me take off my coat by myself. "I had a meeting that went a smidge long," I said.

"Meeting on a Sunday morning? I didn't realize you were such an important woman."

I smiled and let him think anything he wanted to think. "It was nice of you to invite me for lunch."

"And it was nice for you to call me."

Niceties out of the way, we wound our way to the solarium at the back of the house. It would have been a lot sunnier if the window panels had been washed sometime in the past twenty years. "What a darling space," I said.

Chick grandly gestured for me to sit at the small wicker table. He poured two goblets of white wine and then trotted off to the kitchen. He returned with a huge bowl of tossed salad, heavy on the croutons, black olives and feta cheese. A second trip produced a pair of chilled plates, fancy silverware wrapped in cloth napkins, and four bottles of Kraft dressing to choose from. A third trip produced a pair of huge sourdough rolls stuffed with tuna salad. "Oh my," I said. Maybe Chick wasn't much of a housekeeper, but he'd certainly acquired some skills in the kitchen.

At first we talked about my life: How long I'd been at the paper and exactly what I did there; just where in Hannawa I lived and how I'd managed to stay unmarried after giving Lawrence the heave ho. Then we talked about his life: How he'd survived his two marriages and two divorces; what his three kids were doing; why he was still teaching at the rickety age of sixty-eight. To that last subject he said this: "A lot of that had to do with Gordon. If he wasn't taking the last train to Retirementville, why should I?"

"I'm not the retiring type either," I said. I told him about Editor Bob Averill's many failed attempts to show me the door.

"Anyway," he said, suddenly morose, "what would I do if I wasn't teaching?"

It was the opening I was hoping for. "What

about your poetry? I simply loved that poem you read at Gordon's service."

"Really?" His mood brightened as suddenly as it had dimmed. "Did I give you a copy?"

"Yes you did," I said, cracking a crouton between my molars like one of those chipmunks that have turned my backyard into Swiss cheese. "I've read it a dozen times. Not that I understand it any better."

Chick fell into that trap just as easily as the first. "What didn't you understand?"

I squashed the sourdough roll down with the palm of my hand, so I could get the end of it in my mouth. I paraphrased his poem: "That weighty question that split you and Gordon asunder like Ti-Jean and the Howler—whoever or whatever they are."

My ignorance simply thrilled him. "Don't you remember? Jack Kerouac and Allen Ginsberg."

"We called them that?"

"Everybody called them that, Maddy. Allen was the Howler, because of that famous book of his, *Howl*. And Jack, of course, was Ti-Jean."

"Of course."

"It's the nickname his mother gave him when he was a kid. It's French for Little John."

"Of course."

Chick pranced from the solarium like a barefoot boy running across a gravel driveway. I could hear his feet thumping up the stairs. Squeak across the ceiling. He returned out of breath with a photograph in a cheap wooden frame. "I keep it in my upstairs office," he said.

I licked the tuna salad off my fingers and took the photograph. It was a black and white glossy, an 8½ by 11, the kind someone who'd had a photography class or two would take. It showed a much younger Chick and Gordon sitting back-to-back behind a granite gravestone laid flush to the ground. They were both sporting grim, artistic faces. The inscription on the stone was large enough to read:

"Ti-Jean"
John L. Kerouac
March 12, 1922 – October 21, 1969
He Honored Life

Chick took the photograph back and cradled it in his lap. He smiled at it like it was a newborn baby. "Gordon and I visited his grave in the summer of 1970. The Edson Catholic Cemetery in Lowell, Massachusetts. We always talked about going back sometime."

Maybe I hadn't remembered their nicknames—assuming I'd ever known them—but I did remember a thing or two about Jack Kerouac and Allen Ginsberg. They'd started the beat movement in the late 1940s, when they were students at Columbia University in New York, along with William S. Burroughs and Neal Cassady and a troupe of other tortured souls. They bummed around the world together. They became living legends together. "So Kerouac and Ginsberg had some kind of falling out?" I asked Chick.

"Oh yes, a very famous falling out. Allen always thought Jack turned his back on the beat movement. And of course he did."

I got to the nub of my visit. "And apparently there was also some kind of *weighty question* between you and Gordon?"

Chick's face went pink with embarrassment. "Not all that weighty. We stayed friends right to—"

"The bitter end?"

Chick was suddenly interested in his sandwich and his salad, taking big mouthfuls of both. "We don't have to talk about it if you don't want to," I said.

He softened the food in his mouth with a long drink of wine and swallowed. "Like I said in the poem, it really didn't amount to anything."

"Enough for you to write a poem about it," I said, trying not to sound as interested as I was. "And then recite it at his memorial service—wearing that ridiculous beret."

Chick rubbed the bump on his cockatoo nose. "I'd forgotten what a pit bull you are."

"Too many people do," I said.

He leaned forward on his elbows, dug his fingers into the thick white hair hanging over his ears. An explanation was coming. "I guess you remember when Jack came to the college—"

"You and Gordon met him that summer in San Francisco at some poetry festival, and invited him."

"That's right. He stayed in Gordon's apartment. The one he had above the dry cleaning shop on Light Street."

"The one with the refrigerator in the living room?"

"That's the one. The night Jack left for New York, Gordon and I got carryout from Mopey's. You remember Mopey's—"

"It's a parking lot now, isn't it?"

He nodded. "And all three of us ordered cheeseburgers. Except that Gordon insists—insisted—that Jack had a plain burger. But it was a cheeseburger.

He wanted it smothered with mustard and piled high with pickle chips."

I waited for the rest of the story. But no more was coming. "That's it? That's the weighty question that split you asunder so un-copectically?"

"For forty-five years."

"But you remained friends."

"The best of friends. But it was always there. A tiny sore that wouldn't heal. Me insisting it was a cheeseburger, Gordon insisting it was a plain burger." He shook his head. "Sometimes we really got into it. It was all so damn silly."

"What do you mean by *into it*?"

His face turned even pinker than before. "The usual stuff grown men do. Yelling. Swearing. Making fun of the courses the other one taught."

"Like Garbology?"

He laughed. "Like the Forgotten Novelists of Western Indiana."

I laughed even harder. "You used to teach a course on the forgotten novelists of Indiana?"

"Western Indiana. I still do."

We concentrated on our salads and our sandwiches and the rain that was now rattling his rose of Sharon bushes. Then I brought up Gordon's murder. "Did you have any sense of his being worried about something? Or afraid?"

Chick refilled his wine goblet and tried to refill mine. I waved him off. "He was happy as a clam. Spring was coming. He had big plans for his summer dig."

"At the Wooster Pike landfill?"

I thought he was going to take a bite out of his goblet. Instead he took a long, noisy sip. "That God-damned worthless dump."

"Worthless?"

"I didn't mean worthless, Maddy. That garbology project was important to him. And important academically. But he was a wee bit obsessed."

"Obsessed?"

"It sounds selfish. But we used to travel together. Every July. Wonderful road trips all over the country. Wherever there were old ruins for him to crawl around on, and bookstores where I could buy the horrible, self-published novels of frustrated local writers. But the last few years, since he got permission to dig out there, he just couldn't pull himself away."

For twenty minutes Chick bored my pants off with their summer road trips. Halfway through an especially mind-numbing account of their drive across western Kansas, I changed the subject and asked him about the Kerouac Thing just three days before Gordon's body was found. "Just who was there, anyway?" I asked.

"The usual suspects," he said. "Me and Gordon, Effie and the Moffitt-Stumpfs. Other professors. Grad students."

"Shaka Bop?"

Chick used Shaka's real name, the name we all knew him by in the fifties, before his Black Panther days. "Sidney? No, Sidney wasn't there. He usually is though."

"And Gordon was okay that night?"

"Oh yeah. Of course he and I got into it about the cheeseburger. But we always did that." Chick finished his second goblet of wine and poured a third. He spoke derisively of himself in the third person: "What would a Kerouac Thing be without that crazy asshole Chidsey Glass having a nervous breakdown over some lousy four-inch square of American cheese?"

5

Tuesday, March 20

That morning I did something I hadn't done in thirty years. I called in sick. I didn't pretend to have a sore throat or the flu. I just called the newsroom secretary and said, "Morning Suzie, this is Maddy Sprowls. I'm taking a sick day." Suzie said "Okey-dokey" and that was that.

Then after a nice long breakfast while I watched Regis and Kelly, I drove to Hemphill College for my appointment with Andrew J. Holloway III, Gordon's graduate assistant, the young man who'd not only found Gordon's body at the landfill, but also his car, fifteen miles away.

To tell you the truth, I was more than a little surprised when Andrew agreed to take me to the landfill. He didn't know me from Adam. And to some degree or the other he was a suspect in Gordon's murder. I'm sure if I'd been up front about my motives, he would have treated me like one of those annoying telemarketers that call at suppertime—he would have slammed down the phone like he was dispatching a cockroach. Instead I'd gone on and on about how close Gordon and I had been in college—which was true enough—and how it would *do an old lady good* if I could see for myself the place that not only meant so much to his life, but also unfortunately meant something to his death. I think I even may have used that icky word *closure*, if you can imagine that.

So, Andrew agreed to show me the landfill and I felt just awful about my—what's that word Big Daddy used for it in *Cat on a Hot Tin Roof?*—my mendacity!

I pulled up in front of Menominee Hall, as we'd arranged the night before on the phone. I watched a skinny kid in a baggy unbuttoned pea coat trot down the granite steps toward my Dodge Shadow. His hands were planted in his pockets. His collar was pulled up around his ears. I lowered the window. He bent low so I could see his face. "Mrs. Sprowls?" he asked.

"Andrew J. Holloway III?" I asked back.

He got in and slammed the door so hard I thought my eardrums were going to burst. "Andrew is plenty," he said sheepishly. He had a narrow face and a huge, V-shaped smile that featured overlapping front teeth. He also had a thick streak of blue in his hair. I'm sure it was a fashion statement but it looked more like somebody had accidentally dropped a paint brush on his head.

I pulled away from the steps and looped back onto West Tuckman. "I don't remember seeing you at the memorial service, Andrew."

"I guess I'm not very good at those kind of things," he said.

"They can be awkward," I agreed.

I drove past the Puritan Square Shopping Centre, where I can't afford to shop, and then turned left onto Wooster Pike. We headed south through the low, rolling hills. When I first came to Hannawa, Ohio, in the early fifties, those hills were covered with cow pastures. Now they were covered with houses. "Gordon was a pretty good teacher, was he?" I asked.

"Yeah—Professor Sweet really had it going on."

Andrew had called me *Mrs. Sprowls* and now he had called Gordon *Professor Sweet*. He was an awkward, insecure, well-mannered kid. I just knew

I was going to get oodles of good information out of him. "Was this your first year as Gordon's assistant?"

"Second."

"You're close to getting your master's degree then."

"Just finish this semester and hand in my thesis."

"Then what?"

"Start on my Ph.D."

"Here at Hemphill?"

"Hemphill's too small to have a doctoral program. I'll have to go back to Ohio State."

"Back to Ohio State? You didn't do your undergraduate work here?"

"Wish I had."

We took the old iron bridge over Killbuck Creek. Gradually the housing developments gave way to open fields and thick stands of sugar maples. We were in Durkee Township now. "Quite a comedown coming to Hemphill, I guess."

Andrew finally showed some spunk. "Oh, no—Professor Sweet had built Hemphill's archaeology department into one of the strongest undergraduate programs in the Midwest. I couldn't believe he chose me."

"You must be a brainiac."

"When you're born with a Roman numeral at the end of your name, you have lots of time to study."

We both giggled. I liked this goofy kid. "Then you were here for his dig at the landfill last summer?"

"The summer before that, too."

"You and Gordon must have been pretty close."

He didn't answer. But I could tell from the absent way he was staring out the window that he'd felt very close to Gordon indeed. I thought about my Aunt Ruby, and how much I'd idolized her, and how when she died, during my senior year in high school, I couldn't bring myself to attend her funeral. I changed the subject before we both started crying. "I haven't been to the Wooster Pike dump in years and years," I said. "I'm dying to see it again."

Andrew knew the landfill's history better than I did: "For decades it was tiny township dump, going back to the 1920s. The city of Hannawa bought it from the township at the end of World War II, when the city's population was exploding. It was one of several dumps the city used back then. It served the Meriwether Square area, the college, some of the neighborhoods on the city's far west end. It wasn't expanded into a full-blown modern landfill until 1974, when the Environmental Protection Agency got on the city's back. It was Hannawa's primary landfill until 1996, when the Richland Hills facility was finally opened."

"Well, it was sure popular with students in the fifties," I said. "We'd come out from the college to see what kind of interesting junk we could find. Half of the dorm rooms were decorated with junk from that old dump. Half of the rooms smelled like the dump, too, as I recall."

Andrew flashed his overlapping teeth at me. "Professor Sweet used to tell us it was also where students came to drink and have sex."

"Well—in those days what passed for sex," I said.

We reached the road to the landfill. I pulled in and we bounced through the muddy puddles at the entrance. There was still a piece of yellow crime scene tape tied to the trunk of a tree. Andrew jumped out and unlocked the gate. We drove in. The road hadn't changed much in fifty years. It was still a narrow, gravel-covered lane cutting straight across a flat expanse of weeds and briars. For several hundred yards the ground sank ever lower. Then after a small brook it began to rise. The road wound through a series of knobby hills, finally ending in a small, gravel-covered parking lot.

We got out of the car. There wasn't a house in sight. "You can see why the killer wasn't afraid to shoot a gun out here, can't you?" I said. "It would just be a faint pop in the distance, if anybody heard it at all."

I didn't mean for it to be a rhetorical question, but Andrew treated it like one. He put his hands in his coat pockets and started walking toward the path that led up the side of a grassy hill. I trotted like a penguin to catch up. I tried again. "And you wouldn't have to worry about anybody else being around, would you?"

He didn't answer that one either. He put his head down and started up the hill. I followed. It was a dirt path but the ground was still hard from the winter. In a week or two, once the temperature climbed a bit and the spring rains started in earnest, it would be a soupy mess. "Exactly where did you find him?"

Andrew stopped and pointed into the brown, foot-tall grass, just a few feet to his right. "Right there."

"There?" I was expecting to find crime tape and footprints and ground stained purple with

Gordon's blood. But it was just grass, tall, dry and brown, nodding ever so slightly in the late winter wind. "So that Saturday you found him—did you see his body from the parking lot?"

"If I did, I didn't realize it was a body. I mean, you don't exactly expect to see a body, do you?"

Andrew was shaking. And it wasn't from the cold. I knew that because I was shaking, too. "No, I guess you don't."

"I started up the path toward the dig site, just like we're doing." He pointed again at the grass. "And there he was."

"Did you know right away it was Gordon?"

"He was face down. And the grass was kind of covering him. But I recognized his coat. He always wore this big denim barn coat."

"I know the police have already put you through this—and I know this is hard—but did you try to revive him?"

He shook his head, almost violently. "There was no doubt he was dead, Mrs. Sprowls. There was a hole in the back of his head. His face was all red and green and bloated. His eyes were—"

I waved off any further description. "What did you do then?"

"I ran back to my car and threw up. Right on

the door. Then I called 911."

I scanned the parking lot below us. "There's a pay phone out here?"

"Huh?"

I spotted the tiny leather case clipped to his belt and felt like a fool. I must be the only person alive who doesn't carry a cell phone. "Never mind," I said. "So did the police come right out?"

"A couple of sheriff's deputies first. Then a bunch of cars from the Hannawa police."

"I suppose they put you through the wringer."

It was an old expression from an old woman and it took him a few seconds to figure out what I meant. "I'm sure they think I killed him."

I pawed the air to let him know how ridiculous I thought that was. "I'm sure they even suspect me."

His eyes were cloudy now. "I loved the old guy, Mrs. Sprowls."

"Of course you did. We all did." I patted his shoulder until the sadness was gone from his smile. "Now, Andrew," I said, "what do you say we go see that dig site of yours."

We continued up the hill.

It was not a real hill, the kind made by God, time and the rumpling of tectonic plates. It was the outer rim of the man-made basin dug to hold

Hannawa's garbage. The slope was smooth and even, like the wall of an ancient earthen fort. We were on top in only a minute.

The landfill stretched out to our left—a prairie-like expanse of tall grass sprinkled with scraggly shrubs and trees. I'm no judge of space, but I bet it covered twenty or thirty acres. We turned to the right, toward a line of shaggy pines. As we walked, Andrew told me how the landfill had been constructed. "Landfills are like big bathtubs," he said. "The first thing engineers look for is a good hydrogeologic setting, a nice mass of unfractured bedrock that won't leak into the groundwater. They dig out a big bowl and put in a bottom liner, sometimes clay, sometimes high-density polyethylene, sometimes both. This site unfortunately has just clay."

As Andrew described the landfill, his entire demeanor changed, his voice and his eyes and the way he held his head. Maybe he was a goofy boy with blue hair on the outside, but inside resided a smart, serious, self-assured *man*. I could see why Gordon chose him over all those other candidates. "You really know your stuff," I said.

The boy in him blushed. The man in him quickly recovered. "As the garbage is dumped, it's covered with layers of clay, sand and gravel, and finally a layer of topsoil and grass—not just for aesthetic reasons, but to keep rainwater out. But of course water does get in, and picks up contaminates as it filters down. They call that contaminated water leachate. It's collected at the bottom of the basin in pipes and pumped out."

"It's hard to believe there's sixteen years of garbage bubbling away down there," I said. "It all looks so tidy on top. So peaceful."

My naiveté made him smile. "Despite all the science, and all the care, all landfills fail to some degree. This one included. Liners crack. Pipes clog. Roots and animals drill holes through the cover soil. People get lazy. Budgets get cut. Too much water washes in. Too much leachate leaks into the surrounding environment."

"Garbage in, garbage out?" I quipped.

"True enough," he said. "But then where would we archaeologists be without garbage?"

We reached the shaggy pines. And Gordon's dig site.

Just below the rim of the landfill was a dome-shaped mound, maybe 500 feet across. "That's the old Wooster Pike dump? I don't recognize it a bit."

"That's it," Andrew said. "The old dump road

you remember came along right where we're standing now. When the city built the new landfill they left the old junk right where it was. Covered it with dirt and threw a little grass seed around. Then they dug the new landfill basin alongside."

"They didn't make any effort to clean up the old dump?"

"Nope. They just covered it over and forgot about it. Which is great for us. There's a hundred years of wonderful old stuff under there. A real time capsule."

We headed down the slope and waded into the tall grass atop the mound. It was knee deep, cold and nasty, choked with the rotting stems of last summer's goldenrod. "Professor Sweet lobbied the city for three years to get permission to dig here," Andrew said. "He finally got it in 1999. But it was a couple more years before the dig actually started."

My foot hit something. I started to tumble. Andrew caught me. "Careful, Mrs. Sprowls. There's a stake every ten feet."

"Booby traps for nosy old women?"

"Grid posts for nosy archaeology students," he said. He dropped to his knees and pulled the grass away from the offending stake. It was about a foot high. Square. Marked with faded black letters and numbers that made no sense to me.

"What's that gibberish?" I asked.

"Coordinates. Archaeology is very precise. Where something is found is just as important as what's found. So before you start digging, you mark off the site in a grid pattern. You establish perpendicular baselines running north to south and east to west. Then along those lines you stake out digging squares. You excavate square by square, carefully recording what you've found, in what condition, at what depth, in what environment. Carefully boxing up the stuff you want to keep for later study."

We continued through the grass, Andrew high-stepping like a moose, me stepping very carefully, like a pink flamingo. "It would take forever to dig up the entire dump, wouldn't it?"

"Just about," Andrew said. "Professor Sweet only dug for twelve weeks over the summer—ten or fifteen students working in teams of two, each team hoping to finish one ten-foot block—so, yeah, it would take a while to excavate the entire site."

We reached the center of the mound and started down the other side. I could see now the twenty squares or so that had already been excavated and then re-covered with dirt. Lumpy and weedy. "It looks like my vegetable garden," I said.

He offered me a weak smile and continued: "Officially Professor Sweet was studying the eating habits of postwar American families. He called his summer course *Digging the Fifties: The Roots and Realities of Conspicuous Consumption*. But he'd joke that he was just an old beatnik reliving his wasted youth—at the expense of his students. 'Your parents' tuition money, your hard labor and my boyish joy,' he'd say."

"Do you think he was really joking—or really telling the truth?" I asked.

"I think he was really doing both," he said. "Archaeologists, if they can manage it, work in the historic periods that fascinate them the most."

The wind was picking up. I zipped my jacket as high as it would go and pulled in my neck like a snapping turtle. "You consider the 1950s an historic period, do you?"

He stuffed his hands in his pockets. "No offense, but, yeah, I do. Treating the recent past like the ancient past is what the field of garbology is all about." He gave me a primer on the subject: "The guru of the whole movement is Dr. William Rathje of the University of Arizona. He made his bones studying the burial sites of the ancient Mayan

Indians. Then in the early seventies he started the Garbage Project. He applied modern archaeological techniques to studying present-day waste in landfills. He studied what households were buying and discarding. What impact modern consumption habits were having on the nation's health and on the environment."

I felt a few sprinkles of rain on my face. I dug the plastic rain hat out of my pocket and pulled apart its accordion-like folds. I wrapped it around my head. I can only imagine how ghastly I looked. "Well, it sounds like a lot of fun," I said.

Andrew was much too young to carry emergency rainwear with him. He let the drops soak his hair. "It's also a lot of hard work. Tedious work. In order to get to the stuff from the fifties we have to dig down through the garbage from the sixties and seventies. And there was a lot of garbage in those decades."

"How well I remember."

My joke went right over his head. "And you can't just toss the stuff from the sixties and seventies aside," he said. "It's got to be sorted through and cataloged just like the fifties' stuff. The way you draw conclusions about one decade is to compare it to other decades."

"That makes sense."

He had more: "And the layers of garbage aren't predictable. Garbage was dumped and bulldozed. Older stuff pushed up, newer stuff pushed down. So it's easy to get decades mixed up."

I tried another joke. "You're telling me."

That one sailed as high over his noggin as the first one.

We circled through the excavated squares, as if there was actually something to see. The raindrops were getting fatter. "You think it's really necessary to burrow into stinky landfills to learn that America is happily eating itself into oblivion?" I asked.

"Perception is an important tool, but it can't hold a candle to a trowel," he said. "There's a big difference between what people consume and what they think they consume."

He was in teaching mode. I knew I'd have to stand there and listen no matter how waterlogged I got. "I suppose that's true."

"You bet it's true. For example, Mrs. Sprowls, what percentage of the waste put in landfills do you suppose is made up of disposable diapers, Styrofoam and fast-food packaging?"

I hate those kind of questions, don't you? No matter what number you guess, high or low, you'll be wrong and feel like an imbecile. "One hundred percent?" I asked sarcastically.

There was a flash of annoyance in his eyes. "Actually, it's just three percent."

I acted quickly to repair the damage. "That's amazing."

The rain was coming down harder. Without saying a word we agreed to head for the car. "So while plastic is a problem it's not the real problem," he said as we hurried along. "The real problem is paper. It makes up forty to fifty percent of the waste stream."

"Any idea how much of that is newspaper?" I asked.

It was an opportunity to get back at me and he took it. "Too much."

We reached the rim of the landfill and started down, once again past the spot where someone had skillfully put a bullet in the back of Sweet Gordon's skull. More than likely someone he trusted. "Tell me, Andrew, did you ever get the feeling that Gordon was digging for something in particular?"

"That may have gotten him killed, you mean?"

"Well, yes."

His entire body seemed to shrug. "I've been

wondering about that like everybody else."

"Everybody else, Andrew?"

"The police. Professor Glass. That woman from the bookstore."

"And just what do you tell them?"

The annoyance seeped back into his eyes. "Like I said, Professor Sweet was interested in everything from the fifties." Before I could apologize for my inquisitiveness, he conjured up a memory that made him smile. "Every day he'd walk from square to square, asking the dig teams the same question in that same Mr. Rogers way he had: 'Anything interesting today, boys and girls? Old soda pop bottles? Betsy Wetsy Dolls? Perhaps an old cocoa can or two?' We all knew it so well, we'd say it along with him, like a mantra."

We reached my car. We were soaked. By the time we reached the main road my threadbare car seats were soaked, too. We splashed through the puddles and headed north toward Hannawa. I was still full of questions: "You must have been frantic when you couldn't find him."

"Not really. It was odd that he didn't show for his eight o'clock class but—"

"Friday morning, right?"

"Yeah. I just figured he'd overslept or he was

sick or something."

"You were a student in that class?"

He nodded. "*The Making and Breaking of Archaeological Doctrine.*"

"So what did you do when he didn't show?"

"You know—the old ten minute rule."

"If the professor doesn't show up in ten minutes you take off like a P-92?"

I'd succeeded in baffling him again. "Take off like a P-92?"

I laughed at myself. "If I get any older I won't be able to communicate at all. It's an old saying, Andrew. The P-92 was a real fast airplane when I was a kid."

He said "Oh" and I said, "So where'd you take off to?"

"I figured I'd better check in with Karen, the department secretary. I thought maybe if he was sick he might've left word for me to teach his one o'clock."

"He wouldn't have called you directly?"

"He'd never missed a class before. I wasn't sure."

"So you were just being a dutiful graduate assistant?"

"Right—but Karen said she hadn't heard from him either."

"Was she concerned?"

"She'd figured he was in class."

The rain had slowed enough for me to put my wipers on low. "Is that when you started looking for him?"

"Sort of. I called his house and left a message on his answering machine. And then I hung out in his office for a couple hours and studied, in case he showed up. Then I had a quick lunch out of the vending machines downstairs."

"Then taught his one o'clock class?"

"Babysat was more like it. Then I taught my own two o'clock and after that I drove over to his house. The doors were locked and the porch light was on and his car wasn't in the drive."

"You try to talk to his neighbors?"

"No—I still didn't think anything was wrong."

"But you *were* looking for him," I pointed out. "You must have been a little worried."

"I guess I was beginning to wonder if something was wrong. But who knows? Maybe he had a family emergency and had to leave town? It sure didn't occur to me he might be lying dead somewhere."

We crossed back over Killbuck Creek. The water under the bridge was brown and rising. That end of the county has a lot of low, flat valleys. If the rain continued—and it looked like it might—there'd be a flood story for someone to write that night. "When exactly did you find Gordon's car?"

"Not until the next morning. When I was running."

"So that's how you stay so skinny."

"You think I'm skinny?"

"I think you're skinnier than me," I said. "You didn't try to contact him Friday night then?"

"I did try to call Karen once more before going to work. But she'd already snuck out for the day."

"I didn't know you worked."

"I deliver pizzas on weekends. Papa John's on Fridays. Domino's on Saturdays. Sometimes on Sundays for Carlo's. It's amazing how much tip money you can make if you're willing to sacrifice your social life."

I took that to mean he didn't have a girlfriend. "So you saw Gordon's car while you were running?"

"That's why the police are so suspicious of me. They think it's all a little too neat."

"Have they actually said that to you?"

"Not in so many words. But they're sort of scientists, too, aren't they? They come up with a hypothesis and see if the evidence supports it.

So they're thinking, 'Hey now! How convenient is that? The kid first finds the professor's car and then his body. Maybe it's part of some wily plan to make himself look helpful instead of guilty.'"

I figured it would be better to drive in silence for a while. Good gravy, what if Andrew Holloway III did kill Gordon? What if his finding Gordon's car and then his body was indeed part of a *wily* plan to hide his guilt? What if his agreeing to take me to the landfill was also part of that plan? To turn me into a collaborating witness? To show the consistency of his story? I pictured myself on the witness stand, some smart-ass assistant city prosecutor making me look like a total doofus. "Was he there for his Monday, Tuesday, Wednesday and Thursday classes?" I finally asked. "Assuming he had Monday, Tuesday, Wednesday and Thursday classes."

"He didn't teach Tuesdays and Thursdays. But I saw him that Thursday."

"That Thursday before he disappeared, you mean?"

"We met at Wendy's for lunch like always."

"Like always?"

"We met at Wendy's every Thursday at noon," he said. "We'd talk about the classes I was teaching and the classes I was taking. We'd talk about his plans for the summer dig. He liked their chili."

Finally I had an opportunity to ask a question I'd been itching to ask all morning. "That particular Thursday would have been the day after the Kerouac Thing. You go to that?"

"No way. I went the year before. It was really lame."

"Watching a lot of moldy oldies trying to relive their golden bohemian youths, you mean?"

He blushed. "Yeah. Sorry."

"No need to apologize. That's exactly why I stopped going."

"He was really into all that beat generation stuff. Professor Glass, too."

The next question came out of my mouth all by itself. "Speaking of Professor Glass—you know about their cheeseburger argument?"

"Everybody knows about the cheeseburger argument."

"Did Gordon bring it up at Wendy's? I understand they got into it at the Kerouac Thing."

"Not that I remember."

"He say anything at all about the party?"

"Just that I'd missed a groovy evening."

"He actually said *groovy*?"

"He was always using goofy words like that."

My mind drifted to all the wonderful late-night talks Sweet Gordon and I had in college. How the hip words of our generation sounded even hipper when he said them. How much I liked him, even though I was hopelessly in love with Lawrence Sprowls. "Did he seem okay to you that day?" I asked Andrew.

"A little wasted maybe. But for the most part he was his jolly old self."

We reached Hannawa and inched through the heavy, noontime traffic toward West Tuckman. "Where'd you grow up, Andrew? Your voice has sort of a southern Ohio twang to it."

"Circleville."

"Oh, the annual pumpkin festival! That must be fun!"

"It's a riot," he said. His voice that told me that he was not exactly proud to be from a town that celebrates pumpkins.

"I'm from LaFargeville, New York," I said in the same voice. "Three hundred people. Seven thousand cows."

I didn't take the same route back to the college. Instead I took the Indian Creek Parkway and wound through the bare oaks toward the athletic fields at the northern edge of the campus. It's a somewhat isolated area, flatter than a pancake, separated from the campus and its adjoining residential streets by the creek and a long shale ridge. There are soccer and lacrosse fields there, the practice fields for the track and football teams, tennis courts, a winding asphalt jogging path, and, of course, the four back-to-back baseball fields where Dale Marabout told me Andrew had found Gordon's car. Like the Wooster Pike landfill, it would be a perfect place to go unnoticed, especially in March when every day is shittier than the last. "I hope you don't mind," I said.

What could he say? We were already there, pulling into the parking lot alongside the baseball fields. "Where exactly was Gordon's car?" I asked.

He pointed. "In front of the restrooms there."

I drove up to the restrooms and stopped. We were a good two hundred yards from the jogging path, which presumably Andrew was using for his morning run. "You were able to recognize his car from quite a distance," I said. My question sounded an awful lot like a police question and I immediately wished I'd asked it less skeptically.

"Professor Sweet drove an old pea-green Country Squire station wagon, the kind with fake wood panels on the sides. Big as a battleship. Not too many of those on the road anymore."

It sounded reasonable. There weren't too many 1987 Dodge Shadows on the road anymore either. "I'm sure you were relieved to see his car."

"I figured maybe he was around here somewhere," said Andrew. "Using the restroom. Hiking along the creek or something. But his car doors were unlocked and the keys were in the ignition. And his briefcase was on the back seat. His whole life was in that bag."

"Now you got frantic?"

"I checked the restrooms—both sides—and yelled his name. I got in his car and started it—I thought maybe he'd had car trouble—and it ran just fine. Then I ran back to my apartment and got my car. I drove to his house again and then came back to the ball fields. I drove all over the place."

"And then you drove out to the landfill?"

Andrew's head bounced up and down like a basketball.

"I think I would have called the police first," I said.

He raked back his wet hair. "I almost did. But I felt a little foolish, know what I'm saying? Like I was overreacting. I thought maybe he'd arranged to meet somebody here and drove out to the dig with them. He was always going out there. Even in the winter. I just wanted to make sure he was okay."

Up to that point Andrew's story had made sense to me. Now I could see why the police were interested in him. Why would he think Gordon was at the landfill if his car was here? With the doors unlocked and keys in the ignition? With his briefcase on the back seat? Wouldn't Andrew suspect foul play by now? Wouldn't he call the police by now? Even the dopey campus police? No matter how foolish he felt? There simply had to be more to the story, even if this Andrew J. Holloway III was telling the truth. "I apologize for putting you through all this again," I said.

He tried to smile. "I know I don't have the greatest alibi," he said. "I can account for the hours I take classes and teach, and deliver pizzas, but I spend an awful lot of time alone in my apartment."

I drove him back to Menominee Hall.

6

Tuesday, March 20

After dropping Andrew off, I drove to Artie's for a few things. I bought a half-pound of smoked turkey breast, a few slices of baby Swiss, a bag of freshly baked croissants, and a big jug of laundry detergent. When I got home I put three strips of bacon in the microwave. While they shriveled, I sliced one of the croissants. I piled the bottom half high with turkey and cheese. I squeezed a thick squiggle of horseradish sauce onto the top half. I piled the bacon in the middle and carefully put the croissant back together, so the pointy ends matched. I searched the shelves in the refrigerator door and behind my sticky, almost-empty bottle of maple syrup found a lone pickle spear swimming in a jar of green juice. I poured myself a glass of skim milk. I put it all on a tray and headed for the basement. Not to do the laundry. To conduct an archaeological dig of my own.

In the old days the morgue was a sea of filing cabinets. Stories were clipped from the paper, dated, and stuffed into manila envelopes. The envelopes were stuffed into the cabinets, alphabetically, sometimes by subject, sometimes by people's last names. Finding what you wanted was always an adventure. Now we store everything in cyberspace. *Bink-bink-bink* on your keyboard and a story that might have taken you an hour to find in the old cabinets is hovering in front of your nose. Eric Chen, meanwhile, is slowly transferring all of the old files onto computer disks. As soon as he finishes with one of the old cabinets, that cabinet, files and all, goes straight into the back seat of my Dodge Shadow, and then down my basement steps. I bet I've got fifty of them down there. A few are painted an ugly green but most are what we used to call battleship gray. They are all exactly five feet high and 18 inches wide. They all have four deep drawers that require a determined tug to get open. Two or three nights a week—even when I'm not looking for anything in particular—I go down there and sift through the old clippings, remembering things

I'd forgotten, stuffing my brain with things I never knew. I know it doesn't say much about my social life but I just love it.

I put my lunch on the old chrome-legged kitchen table I keep by the dryer, pulled on the light, and headed for the D drawers.

Why the D drawers?

One reason was to see if any stories had ever been filed under *Dumps*, although that seemed unlikely. I couldn't remember ever filing anything under that category in my forty-odd years in the morgue. But I knew *The Herald-Union* had written about the David Delarosa murder. There would be plenty in the D drawers about that.

Andrew, you see, had pointed me in a direction I was already beginning to point myself. But it wasn't any of the interesting facts he told me about landfills, or archaeological techniques, or even the condition of Gordon's body that got my mind working. It was his *perceptions*—which was ironic given his high-minded declaration that "perception doesn't hold a candle to a trowel."

According to Andrew, Gordon never let on that he was looking for something in particular. Yet Andrew clearly suspected that Gordon's murder might be tied to something buried out there. "I've been wondering about that like everybody else," he said. As an old beatnik might say, Andrew had picked up a vibe.

And so had I.

And so all the time I was at Artie's, fighting my way through the aisles clogged with harried young moms, like some old salmon struggling up the rapids to spawn, my fertile mind was fixed not only on the fifties, but on the late fifties, and what might have happened all those years ago that touched Sweet Gordon's life enough to make him go digging now. David Delarosa's pretty face popped up again and again.

People are more ho-hum about murder these days. There are just so many of them. But back in the fifties, even in a big city like Hannawa, they rattled everybody. And David Delarosa's murder sure rattled us. I remember Effie calling me in a panic. It was April 18, 1957, the Thursday before Easter. "Somebody's killed Gordon's new friend," she said.

Just how Gordon met David Delarosa, I still don't know. But all of a sudden Gordon started bringing him to the jazz clubs, and inviting him to our parties. He didn't fit in and Gordon knew it. "Maybe David ain't the hippest cat," Gordon once told me, "but he's cool enough in his own way, don't you think?"

David Delarosa wasn't an intellectual. He wasn't artsy. He wasn't angry or introspective or full of high ideals. He was just a fun-loving kid from Sandusky on a wrestling scholarship. And boy was he good looking! He was lean and muscular. He had curly black hair, which he wore quite long for those years, and full pouty lips just like that actor Sal Mineo. Instead of having black Mediterranean eyes like you'd expect, his eyes were a cool, spooky gray.

Anyway, two days into the spring break, somebody threw David Delarosa down the stairway of his apartment building and then bludgeoned his pretty face with something hard and heavy until he was dead. As far as anyone knew, there was only one suspect, a local bebop jazz musician named Sidney Spikes, who was held for a few days, badgered relentlessly and then released. A decade later Sidney, as I've said, would change his name to Shaka Bop and become a major political force in the city.

Just as I'd expected, there were no stories filed under *Dumps*. But there sure were under *Delarosa, David.* I took them to the table, took a big bite from my sandwich and leafed through the clippings. The fat, black headline in the Friday, April 19, 1957 edition of *The Herald-Union* declared:

STAR HEMPHILL WRESTLER SLAIN

The headline in the Easter Sunday edition hinted at the difficulty police were going to have solving David's murder:

POLICE SCOUR CAMPUS
FOR MURDER WEAPON

On Wednesday, May 1, there was this frustrating headline:

SEARCH FOR CAMPUS KILLER DRAGS ON

Then on Tuesday, May 7, this one:

POPULAR NEGRO MUSICIAN
HELD IN DELAROSA MURDER PROBE

Oh my, how sick we were when we first saw that story! We all just idolized Sidney. He was the only *Negro* most of us fluffy, white slices of Wonder Bread knew. He was smart and funny and handsome. And could he play that saxophone! We simply could not believe he was a suspect.

I remember sitting that night with Gordon at Mopey's, nursing bowls of chili while the street outside filled with blowing snow. He yelled at his copy of *The Herald-Union* like it was God: "First you tell me David's dead. Then you tell me maybe Sidney did it. Man, what you gonna tell me next? That the moon's made out of cabbage?"

Three days later, on Friday, May 10, there was a happier headline:

NEGRO JAZZ MAN RELEASED

We were still worked up about David's murder—and the way the police were bungling the investigation—but the spring semester was slipping away and other things needed our attention. We took our finals. We graduated. Lawrence took his journalism degree and a 3.8 grade point average straight to *The Herald-Union.* I got a crappy part-time job at the city library scrubbing the sticky fingerprints off children's books. Gordon and Chick got jobs at a local factory to help pay for graduate school. Effie drove across country with a professor who'd just gotten his divorce decree. Gwen and Rollie had a huge church wedding. Lawrence and I took the bus downtown and got married by the mayor.

A full twelve months went by before the next story on David's murder appeared, on Sunday, May 17, 1958, in a black-bordered box across the top of Page One. The headline asked:

WHO KILLED DAVID DELAROSA?
One Year Later Police Admit They Don't Have A Clue

And that was the last of *The Herald-Union*'s stories on David Delarosa's murder. I read the headlines again. Then I read the stories themselves, and then re-read them, three or four more times, until my brain and my heart were filled with a dump truck-full of questions. I put the Delarosa file under my arm and carried my dirty dishes upstairs to the sink. I combed my hair and dabbed on just enough makeup to make myself presentable. I drove downtown to *The Herald-Union*.

Eric spun around on his chair when he saw me. He pretended to be disappointed. "I was hoping you'd died."

I threw my coat over the back of my chair and grabbed my mug. "So was I," I said, "but I guess the good lord wants both of us to suffer a while longer."

I went to the cafeteria and made myself a cup of tea and then sipped my way to Sports. Ed Boyer looked up from the funny pages he was reading. His chewing gum literally fell out of his mouth.

"Mrs. Sprowls—everything all right?"

You can understand his alarm, can't you? I regularly cut through Sports on my way to the cafeteria. But I never stop to chat. As far as I'm concerned, that ramshackle corner of the newsroom is a foreign country. They speak a different language. They have unfathomable customs. They wear bizarre native costumes. They eat indigestible things. "I was wondering if I could take a look at your old files," I said.

Ed's face went white with worry. "For?"

"I'm looking for information on a wrestler who was murdered many years ago—"

Ed was suddenly a statistic-spitting robot: "David Anthony Delarosa. Hemphill College. Wrestled in the 141-pound weight class his freshman year, 149 after that. Ohio Athletic Conference champ in fifty-four and five, All-American in fifty-six and seven."

I'd long ago learned that sports reporters know more useless information than anybody on earth. I was impressed nonetheless. "How the hell you know all that?"

"He's got a plaque in the field house," Ed explained. "Between the concession stand and the toilets. You see it every time you go for a wiz."

Ed led me to the storeroom by the back steps where Sports keeps its files. It was a filthy mess. "Do you have a plastic liner to catch the leachate?" I asked.

Despite all of my efforts, Ed never quite understood my joke. But he did know right where to find the file on David Delarosa. He accompanied me to the Xerox machine and chewed on his gum like a woodchuck while I made copies. I escaped to my desk just as fast as I could.

There was an inch of clippings on David Delarosa in the file but only one interested me. It was a column written by Ted Thomas, the paper's sports editor at the time. It was dated Tuesday, December 9, 1957:

WRESTLERS GRAPPLE WITH SLAIN CHAMP'S DEATH

By Ted Thomas, Sports Editor

Howard Shay says he doesn't feel like wrestling anymore, not since two-time All-American David Delarosa was brutally murdered just four days before Easter. But Shay, like the other young men on the Hemphill College squad, says he has no choice but to return to the mats this winter.

"I can feel him right next to me in the gym," Shay said with a sad grin, "threatening to haunt me for the rest of my life if I don't do my best to get the win."

Shay, an education major from Mallet Creek, who wrestles in the 197-pound class, was more than Delarosa's friend and teammate. For the two years they shared a one-room apartment in the off-campus building where Delarosa's body was found.

"We're determined to carry on," Shay told this reporter. "It's what he'd want us to do."

Indeed, at a prayer breakfast before the team's first match of the season, against arch rival Edinboro College, Coach Patrick Zemary dedicated the wrestling team's season to Delarosa's memory, saying, "David was an inspiration in life and he will remain an inspiration to us in death."

I went to the rack where we keep the phone books. I found the listings for Mallet Creek, a small town in neighboring Wyssock County. I found Howard Shay's number and dialed it. It rang four times before triggering one of those damn recordings: *"Big Howie here! Sorry I'm not there to take your call. I'm down in sunny Flor-ee-dah wintering away the kid's inheritance. Call back after the ground thaws!"*

There was no beep to leave a message. Just a quick click. Whatever I might learn from David Delarosa's old college roommate would have to wait. I took a deep breath and called Dale Marabout's extension. "Busy, Mr. M?" I asked.

"As a termite in a toothpick factory. What's up?"

"I just wanted to talk—about Gordon Sweet's murder."

I peeked across the newsroom and saw Dale glowering at me. I wiggled my fingers at him. "I know you told me to let the police handle it," I said, "but I think maybe I've stumbled onto something."

And so an hour later, after Dale had finished with his story for the next day's paper, he and I were walking down the hill, wet wind chapping our faces, toward Ike's Coffee Shop.

Ike's is located in the Longacre Building, one of the many empty office buildings in Hannawa's dying downtown. It used to house some of the city's most successful doctors and lawyers. Now it just houses Ike.

"Morgue Mama!" Ike sang out when we walked in. "Mr. Marabout!"

Ike is the nicest man. He's about my age. He taught high school math for 30 years before opening his coffee shop. He makes me laugh when there's nothing to laugh at. He drives me home when my car won't start. He maintains his high opinion of me no matter how cranky I get. He's earned the right to call me Morgue Mama to my face.

I should also explain that Ike's name isn't really Ike. It's Leonard, Leonard Breeze. He says he got the nickname because he was the only black man anybody knew who voted for Dwight Eisenhower.

Dale and I took a table by the window. We didn't have to order. Ike knew I'd want a mug of Darjeeling tea and Dale a regular coffee with room for a little half-and-half. He got busy pouring them.

"So what's this you've stumbled on?" Dale asked me, drumming his fingers on the table. "And more importantly, on a scale of one to ten how much agony is it going to cause me?"

I hate drumming fingers. I stopped them. "No more than a six," I said. "I just want you to do a little checking." I told him about my trip to the landfill that morning with Andrew, about David

Delarosa's murder all those years ago.

Dale connected the dots. "So you think maybe Gordon was looking for the murder weapon out there? That's a real stretch, don't you think?"

"I won't know if it is or isn't until you look into the status of the Delarosa case."

"It's been a billion years, Maddy. I'd say the status is that there isn't a status."

"I know the case is cold. But I thought maybe you could see if there's something in the police files that didn't make it into our stories. Was the murder weapon ever identified or found? Was Shaka Bop the only suspect ever questioned?"

I'd told Dale something he didn't know. "*The* Shaka Bop?"

Ike appeared out of nowhere with our drinks. "How many Shaka Bops do you think there are in Hannawa?"

Ike grinned at Dale. Dale grinned back at Ike. But they were not easy grins. Ike knew all about my history with Dale. And Dale knew that Ike knew. It was nice to have two men go grin-to-grin over me like that, but it sure wasn't going to help me get to the bottom of Gordon's murder. "Thanks, Ike," I said. "You're a lamb."

Ike retreated behind the counter and watched

us over the top of his espresso machine while he pretended to work.

"I'm sure I'm just tilting at windmills," I whispered to Dale, "but Gordon was pretty thick with David Delarosa and I remember how hard he took his murder."

Dale tipped his head and squinted, the way dogs do when they're trying to decipher the confusing sounds coming from the flat faces of their masters. "Are you saying Gordon was gay?"

"Good gravy, does everything have to be about sex?"

The second I said it I wished I hadn't. Sex was not a good topic for Dale and me. We were just friends now. He'd been married to Sharon for twenty years and I'd long ago lost what little physical appeal Mother Nature rationed out to me. But once upon a time Dale Marabout and I had been a couple of real bunny rabbits with each other, I'll tell you. So the S-word, in any context, always dredged up a lot of awkward feelings better left in the murky past.

And having those feelings dredged up in front of Ike made matters all the worse. Unfortunately, there was something more than friendship between Ike and me, too. Not that we'd ever acted on those feelings, of course. Good gravy! We were both closing in on seventy. He was black. I was white. He was a Republican and I'd once held a coffee klatch for George McGovern. No way were we going to mess up a wonderful friendship with foolishness. I started over. "Gordon's sex life is neither here or there. All that's important is why he was murdered."

Dale finished his coffee in a few great gulps. He was as anxious to leave as I was. "Okay, Maddy, I'll see what I can find. But this is not going to be Buddy Wing II."

"Absolutely not," I said. "This is the last thing I'm going to ask you to do."

We said good-bye to Ike and headed out into the evening. The rush hour was over. The streets were all but empty. It was even colder and windier than before. We climbed the hill to *The Herald-Union*. We said "See you tomorrow" in the parking deck, got into our respective cars and drove off to our respective houses.

I ran straight to Gordon's apartment that April afternoon in 1957 when Effie called to tell me that David Delarosa's body had been found. Literally ran, through a shower of cold rain that stung like

BBs. Effie was already there, making Gordon the only thing she knew how to make—canned soup. Gordon was sitting in the ratty, overstuffed chair he'd rescued from the dump. He was sucking on a beer and staring at the wall.

I don't remembering Gordon saying anything that night. Or eating his soup. I just remember Effie and me opening beer bottles for him.

Gordon drank for two more days and then on Easter morning took the bus to Sandusky for David's funeral. We all offered to go with him, but Gordon wanted to go alone. "Wowzers," Chick said in his best beatnikese as the Greyhound pulled out, "have you ever seen anything more appropriately beat in your life? Sweet Gordon bouncing along in a half-empty bus past soggy fields of broken corn, on a day when everybody else is celebrating life everlasting?"

I guess the reason I couldn't believe that Gordon was gay now was that it had never occurred to me then. Homosexuality wasn't something people talked about much in the fifties, not even us bohemian types, but we did know what it was, and surely we recognized it when we saw it.

Gordon returned from Sandusky just as depressed as when he left. He didn't say boo about

David Delarosa until that morning at Mopey's when we saw the story about Sidney being questioned by police. His sadness mushroomed into anger. And little by little that anger seemed to heal him.

When I got home I turned on *Jeopardy* and fell asleep during the first round. When I woke up Barbara Walters was interviewing the parents of sextuplets on *20/20*. I ate a bowl of grapes, paid some bills, and went to bed. I turned on my radio and waited for Art Bell to come on. While he interviewed a Wyoming man who'd been abducted nine times by time-traveling aliens, I thought about the men in my life who weren't in my life. I thought about my father, who'd died when I was eleven. I thought about my dead, philandering ex-husband Lawrence. I thought about Dale Marabout. I thought about Ike. And I thought about Sweet Gordon.

7

Wednesday, March 21

Eric appeared at my desk the moment I sat down with my morning tea. He was waving a folder in each hand. "Wooster Pike Landfill, toxic waste."

"Good boy," I said.

I wanted to plant my nose in those folders the second he handed them to me. But I was a woman with responsibilities. I put the folders in the top drawer of my desk, so I wouldn't be tempted. I got busy marking up that morning's paper, deciding which stories should be saved and under which categories. That always takes the better part of the morning. Then I looked up the information city hall reporter Mike Hugely needed on the Elmer Avenue bridge project. After that I was trapped in a one-sided conversation with Candy Prince about her five hairless Chinese cats. I self-medicated that twenty minutes of agony with a call to my niece in LaFargeville to wish her a happy fiftieth birthday. Finally at eleven-thirty I scooted off to the cafeteria with those two tempting folders and the Tupperware container of leftover chicken teriyaki I'd brought from home.

The folder on the landfill was filled with a lot of dry government stuff that was absolutely useless. Nor had Eric's search found any murders, missing person cases or other chicaneries in that part of the county that might require further investigation. I closed the folder. I couldn't decide whether to be relieved or disappointed.

I concentrated on my lunch then opened the other folder. There were oodles of stories on lead paint, asbestos and polluted creeks. There was a spellbinding three-part series on how the city was breaking its own rules on the disposal of used antifreeze and motor oil. There were several stories on Mayor Finn's failed effort to stop the federal government from trucking radioactive wastes through the city. I saved the best for last: Margaret Newman's stories on illegal dumping by the E.O. Madrid Chemical Co.

The nut of Margaret's stories was this: E.O.

Madrid was a small company on the city's industrial south side. It manufactured industrial solvents and adhesives. It prospered nicely for five decades under the long hours of its founder, Edgar Oliver Madrid. When a massive stroke whisked the still-working, 82-year-old Edgar off to his eternal reward in the summer of 1987, his 47-year-old son, Donald, moved into the big office.

Donald apparently had not inherited his father's attention span. He was much more interested in losing money on his minor league baseball team, the Hannawa Woolybears, than making money with the family business. And so in 1993, up to his shinbones in red ink, Donald decided to *out-source* the disposal of a toxic chemical called toluene. He hired an independent trucker named Kenneth Kingzette to make the toluene disappear.

And the toluene did disappear—into abandoned factory buildings, weedy ravines, old farm ponds, abandoned dumps. In 1995, when a fire broke out in an empty warehouse on Canal Street, firemen found several 55-gallon drums of toluene. The Ohio Environmental Protection Agency was called in. It did not take much of an investigation to trace the chemicals to the E.O. Madrid Chemical Co. Donald Madrid disappeared into the ether but not before fingering Kenneth Kingzette.

Kingzette's legal strategy was to keep his lips zipped and stare menacingly at the jury. It got him four years at the Southern Ohio Correctional Facility in Lucasville. Just as I remembered, the Ohio EPA estimated that an additional eighteen drums of the toluene was still out there somewhere. So I guess you know what I was thinking. Heavens to Betsy, wouldn't you be thinking that?

I know this isn't the least bit important, but it will help you understand just how small-town the big city of Hannawa, Ohio, is. Our minor league baseball team, the Woolybears, has nothing to do with ferocious, growling bears. Here in the Midwest, Woolybears are what we call those fuzzy brown and orange-striped caterpillars you find crawling all over your chrysanthemums in the fall. They are the larvae for a moth. They're about the width and length of a cheese doodle. We Midwesterners—with all seriousness—forecast the severity of the upcoming winter by how thick their coats are. The thicker the fuzz, the colder and snowier it's going to be. Honest to God we do that.

So we Hannawans are not only famous for having more television evangelists per capita than any city in America—as you know, we're known as the Hallelujah City—we also have a baseball team named after the larvae of a moth. Not a butterfly. A damn moth.

I wanted to talk to Margaret about her stories but I did not want Margaret to know that I was talking to her about her stories. It was dangerous enough that Dale and Eric knew I was snooping into another murder. If Margaret knew, the entire newsroom would know, and Bob Averill would finally have the ammunition he needed to force me into retirement

So a smidgen of subterfuge would be required.

I put on my coat and took the elevator to the pressroom. I borrowed the biggest screwdriver I could from the boys in maintenance and headed down the alley toward Charles Avenue.

Margaret Newman in my estimation is the best investigative reporter *The Herald-Union* has. She's won every journalism award short of a Pulitzer. Better yet, she's been sued for libel five times. And there's no better proof of a reporter's skill than having a lawsuit filed against them by some worthless weasel who's upset that the whole world now knows that he is one.

Margaret also has what people in our business call a built-in shit detector. And she can be a bit flinty at times. Two traits I normally admire. Two traits that would make my do-si-do around the truth anything but easy.

I reached Charles Avenue and headed down the hill toward the Amtrak station and the short stretch still paved with bricks.

You see, I'd decided to take a page from Louise Lewendowski. No, I wasn't going to seduce her with a sack of kolachkys. I'm afraid I wasn't born with the flaky pastry gene. I was going to give Margaret a ten-pound block of baked clay.

Only one passenger train a day stops in Hannawa any more, and that's at four-thirty in the morning. So I crossed the tracks without looking and started my search for the perfect brick.

Margaret for some unfathomable reason collects old paving bricks. She's got hundreds of them, from all over the country. She belongs to a paving brick club—the Northern Ohio Brick Bats. She attends paving brick conventions. She spends her weekends and vacations scouring abandoned brickyards. She's got so many of the blessed things in her garage there's no room for her car. Dale Marabout jokes that she's got so many of them in her bedroom there's no room for a husband.

Most paving bricks are just smooth blocks of baked clay. But the old-time brick makers, in order to advertise their wares, used to put their name on every 100th brick. So I was shuffling up and down the empty avenue, head down, fists on the small of my back, looking for one of those, in the hope Margaret would be tickled pink to get it. In the hope she would just yak and yak and tell me everything I wanted to know about Kenneth Kingzette.

I finally found what I needed, right in the middle of the avenue—a big red brick the size of a Velveeta cheese loaf, without a crack or a chip, bearing the etched image of an Indian chief. Under that in deep block letters was printed HANNAWA BRICK CO.

I waited for a UPS truck to rumble by, then carefully wedged the screwdriver between the bricks and wiggled it until the treasure I wanted came loose. I pried it out, wedged it in my coat pocket, and hurried back to the paper.

I kept my eye on Margaret until she clicked off her computer and pushed herself back from her desk. I grabbed the brick and hurried over there before she could leave. "Oh, Margaret," I said, "look what I found for you."

Her eyes got as big as dinner plates. "A Hannawa Brick Indian Head? Maddy Sprowls, where in God's name did you get that?"

Well, I sure wished she hadn't brought God into it. I'd stolen the brick from a city street and now, if I wasn't careful, I'd have to lie about it, too. I prayed that the Almighty wasn't eavesdropping. "You know, Margaret," I began, "I almost never go to garage sales. I just hate them. People pawing over other people's junk. But my neighbor Jocelyn just loves them. She's always asking me to go with her. And you know how I try to be a good neighbor. So, I saw this old brick and said to myself, 'I wonder if Margaret has one of these?'"

She took the brick and held it like it was the baby Jesus. "Well, I do," she said, "but I can always use another." She told me how rare they were. How she'd seen one just like it on Charles Avenue and how tempted she'd been to dig it out. "How much did you pay for it?"

I pawed the air. "It was a steal."

"I've seen them go for fifty dollars or more at auctions. Let me pay you."

"Oh, no. It's a gift."

"Well, God love you," she said.

As guilty as I felt, I'd succeeded in seducing the

better side of Margaret's nature. I let her go on and on about her brick collection until my toes were curling inside my Reeboks. "Well, you certainly live a more interesting life than me," I finally said. "You collect bricks, you protect the environment."

"I only write about people who protect the environment," she said.

This time she'd said just the right thing. "But you sure help them protect it," I said. "Like that illegal dumping stuff you did a few years back. You kept the pressure on with all those great stories. And that guy who dumped that stuff—what was his name?"

"Kenneth Kingzette."

"That's right. Kenneth Kingzette. He went to prison. How many years did he get, anyway?"

"Just four," said Margaret.

"That's all? From what I hear that stuff he dumped is pretty nasty."

"Toluene. And nasty doesn't begin to describe it. Even little doses can screw you up pretty good. Dizziness. Nausea. Impaired vision and speech. Exposure over a long time can permanently damage your liver and kidneys. Even your brain. Even kill you."

"Yikes. When's he getting out?"

"He was paroled in November."

"Well, I hope the police are keeping an eye on him. And you, too. On Kenneth Kingzette, I mean."

"He's working with his son," she said, lovingly brushing her fingers over the etched face of the Indian chief. "Some little rinky-dink moving company."

"Not here in Hannawa, I hope."

"Here in Hannawa."

"And they let him do that?"

"It's not against the law to make an honest living."

"But aren't some of the chemicals he dumped still missing?"

Margaret nodded. "And so is the president of the chemical company."

"Oh, that's right. Ronald or Donald something or other."

"Donald Madrid."

"Yes, Donald Madrid. I always figured Kingzette dumped him illegally, too."

"You and a lot of other people. But there was never any evidence of a murder. I think the police figure Mr. Madrid took off for tropical climes."

"And why would they figure that?"

"He ordered a shitload of stuff from Lands'

End a couple weeks before he disappeared—fancy set of luggage, several pairs of wrinkle-free chinos and one of those Indiana Jones hats."

"Any money missing?"

"Not from his personal accounts, but apparently Mr. Madrid was a regular Wolfgang Puck when it came to cooking the company books."

Margaret was watching the second hand on her wristwatch spin, a signal that I was wearing out my welcome. "Well, I've bothered you enough," I said. "I just hope you're happy with the brick."

She told me she was tickled pink with the brick, and before I could stop her, she dug a twenty-dollar bill out of her purse and stuffed it in my hand. "It wasn't any more than that, was it?" she asked.

I shook my head. I walked away wondering how many of the seven deadly sins I'd just committed.

8

Friday, March 23

I took a two-hour lunch and didn't eat a darn thing. Instead I drove to the college to talk to Bernard Murray. He teaches environmental science and was quoted extensively in a couple of Margaret's stories. He'd worked with the Ohio EPA that year they'd searched for the drums of toluene Kenneth Kingzette dumped for Donald Madrid. I was hoping that if there was any connection between Gordon's murder and the missing toluene, Murray would help me make the link.

When I called to make an appointment, I offered to take him to lunch. "Not necessary," he said. "Just pop in when you can." The second I walked into his office in the L.W. Hertzog Science Center I knew why he'd turned down the free meal.

He was the boniest man I'd ever seen in my life. The kind who eats a couple of celery sticks and then runs ten miles to burn off the calories. He was in his fifties, but the lack of meat on his face made it hard to tell just how far in.

"It's so nice of you to give me a few minutes," I said, sitting in one of the cheap, metal and plastic government office chairs lined up along the glass wall.

"I was a friend of Gordon's, too," he said. When he sat back in his huge swivel chair, the leather barely dented.

I explained my theory that Gordon may have been murdered to prevent him from finding something hidden in the dump. I told him I'd been reading old stories about the Madrid chemical case. "I know I'm probably tilting at windmills," I said, "but I can't help but wonder if there's a link."

Murray leaned forward on his elbows and pushed his fists into the thin layer of flesh under his eyes. "Actually, there just might be," he said.

I leaned forward, too. "You think so?"

He studied me, cautiously, I think to judge if I knew more than I was letting on. "When you called yesterday I thought maybe you'd already connected a few dots."

I gave my ignorance away. "I haven't even connected one dot yet."

He smiled grimly, as if he needed a swallow of Pepto Bismol. "Maybe you have now. Gordon worked with us on the investigation. As a volunteer. I recruited him, in fact. I figured his archaeological know-how would be helpful. Help us find ground that was freshly disturbed, that sort of thing."

"And was he helpful?"

"Yes and no. He loved poking around old farms and abandoned junk yards. But he seemed more interested in looking for arrowheads than drums of toluene."

"About those junk yards—was the Wooster Pike landfill one of them?"

"Oh, sure. We checked every old dump in a fifty-mile radius. We did find drums from Madrid chemical buried at the Hartville Road dump and in the dump in Morrow Township, but not the Wooster Pike site. Which frankly surprised me. The Wooster Pike dump would have been the perfect place for Kingzette. Accessible. Abandoned. Middle of nowhere."

"Did Gordon seem upset that not all the toluene was found?"

"We're all a bunch of tree-huggers around

here. We were all PO'd when the EPA pulled the plug."

I searched for the right words and couldn't find them. "Was Gordon's PO'd-ness more intense than other people's?"

He chuckled. "Did he jump up and down and vow to find those missing drums of toluene even if it killed him? I don't recall that."

"How about you? Did you jump up and down?"

He chuckled again. "I've been consulting with the EPA since my graduate days. They're always coming into a case too late and pulling out too early. They had enough to convict Kingzette and Madrid and they had other cases in other cities. They said they'd keep looking but they didn't, of course."

I'm sure Bernard Murray's atrophied stomach hadn't growled in years, but mine was beginning to sound like a wolverine in heat. "When exactly did you search the old landfills?"

He drummed on his bottom lip. "Let's see—May, June and July of '95."

"No more digging after July?"

"Nope."

I wanted to find the nearest fast-food drive-thru

window and order the biggest hamburger and French fries combo they had. But while I was at the college there was one more stop I had to make: the offices of the campus newspaper, the *Hemphill Harbinger.*

I knew *The Harbinger* was now housed in one of the massive old Victorians on the eastern edge of the campus. But I did not know which massive old Victorian. There were oodles of them. So I headed in that general direction, on foot, hoping I could get directions along the way. The first three students I stopped didn't have the foggiest idea. The fourth knew precisely where it was. Naturally she was yakking on her cell phone at the time. Without the slightest break in her important conversation—"That is so gross...That is so fantastic...How gross is that?"—she swung her index finger off her phone and pointed at the house right in front of us.

She walked on before I could thank her. I heard her mumble into her little phone, "Just some old woman who doesn't know where she's going."

I barked after her: "You're sure right about that, honey!"

I followed the uneven slate walk to the porch and climbed the lopsided steps. The door opened like an out-of-tune bassoon. I poked my head into the living room. It was a maze of messy desks and empty chairs. A real newsroom. Behind a huge, bright blue computer monitor I spotted a tiny girl with short, spiky, lemon-lime hair. She had two silver rings in each nostril. "I'm looking for the editor," I said.

She was feisty but friendly. "No—you're looking *at* the editor."

I told her who I was.

She'd heard of me. "Oh. My. Gawd! The same Dolly Madison Sprowls who found Buddy Wing's real killer? Oh. My. Gawd!"

"In the wrinkled flesh," I said.

She apparently liked the way I'd poked fun at my advanced age. Her eyes got dreamy. She reached out and shook my hand like a lumberjack. She told me her name was Gabriella Nash. She brought me a chair. She microwaved a mug of hot water for me and gave me a bowl of tea bags to choose from. She told me about her future career in journalism without stopping to think that I might be there for a reason.

"Well, I'm sure you're going to have a terrific career," I said. "In the meantime I was wondering if you'd let me look at some of your old morgue files."

She sprang out of her chair dutifully, as though I was Queen Elizabeth asking for another crumpet. "Is there a specific story you're looking for?"

I stood up slowly. "Well, it's a silly thing," I said. "I graduated from Hemphill College back in 1957—"

"Yes, I know."

"And so did my late husband. Lawrence Sprowls. He was a journalism major."

She tipped her head like a lop-eared puppy. "Oh—I'm so sorry."

I pawed the air. "He's been dead for fourteen years and we were divorced twenty-eight years before that," I said. "But I guess I've reached that age when a person gets the biological urge to reminisce. I was hoping I could rummage around a little. Maybe Xerox a few things."

She wrinkled her nose. "You know we had a fire, don't you?"

At first I thought she was talking about a recent fire. Then it hit me she must be talking about the fire in 1968 that destroyed the building that once housed the journalism department. It was one of five old wooden barracks built for soldiers on the GI bill after World War II. In April 1968, one night after the assassination of Martin Luther King Jr., those five old barracks, as well as a dozen run-down houses near the campus, were burned by students, both black and white, whose belief in nonviolence was blown to smithereens by their overwhelming anger. "Don't tell me all the old files were lost."

"I'm afraid so."

"You're sure? It happened before you were born."

"I know about a lot of things that happened before I was born." She said it with a smile but I could tell from the way her cheeks were quivering that I'd insulted her.

"I'm sorry—I guess I'm just disappointed."

She accepted my apology. "The fire's sort of a legend around here." She led me into the once-magnificent dining room. There was a row of battered filing cabinets along the wall. She pulled out a file and showed me a story published in *The Harbinger* two weeks after the fire. Said the headline:

FIFTY YEARS of history
go up in ANGRY smoke

"That's the oldest story we have," she said.

"What about the college library?" I asked.

"They don't even have this one," she said.

I drove back to work, right past a Burger King

and a McDonald's and two Wendy's. I was feeling much too empty to eat.

What had I hoped to find in *The Harbinger*'s old files?

For one thing, I wanted to see how they'd covered David Delarosa's murder. If they'd uncovered some interesting little morsel *The Herald-Union* hadn't. For another, I wanted to see if something else had happened back then, something that I'd forgotten about, or never knew about, that Gordon might have known about and might have remembered.

And, to tell you the truth, I also wanted to splash around in my own past a bit, just like I'd told Gabriella Nash that afternoon. Hemphill College was an important part of my life. I'd grown up there. Blossomed there. Lost all of my small-town virginities there. When you reach my age you're no longer interested in reliving your youth, but you do like to visit it occasionally.

I left the morgue right at five. Not to forage through my files in the basement. To pick up James' winter poop in the backyard, before the grass started growing in earnest.

James is my neighbor Jocelyn Coopersmith's American water spaniel. Of all the backyards in the neighborhood, James, for reasons only a dog could appreciate, likes to poop in mine the most. Even in the winter when the snow's a foot high he waddles back there to do his business.

I put on my worst pair of khaki slacks and an old sweatshirt that, if worse came to worst, I could deposit right in the trash can. I got my biggest garden trowel and a plastic garbage bag, wiggled my fingers into a pair of yellow kitchen gloves, and headed for the backyard.

I don't have much of a front yard—but boy do I have a backyard. It's as big as a football field. My bungalow was built in the late forties, when young newly married couples were leaving the inner city neighborhoods for, quite literally, greener pastures. The old houses in the city were huge but they had very small yards. The new houses being built on farmland at the edge of the city were just the opposite. To make them affordable, the houses were no bigger than a shoebox. To make them attractive to couples bent on producing a gaggle of antsy kids, the backyards were enormous. Lawrence and I bought my bungalow in 1963, four years after we were married. We planned to fill our backyard with antsy kids, too. But then Lawrence got that job doing PR for the autoworkers' union. A secretary with irresistible tits came with the job. His preoccupation with those irresistible tits put an end to our procreation plans. We divorced. Lawrence got the secretary. I got the bungalow. Which turned out to be the better long-term investment. Lawrence would marry three more times before he died.

I started at the back of the yard and worked forward. For a while I worked alone. Then Jocelyn let James out the back door. He came running, with all the grace of a duck learning to roller skate.

James is never going to win the Westminster. He's covered with wild brown curls. His sides stick out like he's swallowed a beach ball. His front legs are shorter than his back, so he's always going downhill. His ears dangle like ping-pong paddles and his tail looks like it was transplanted from an opossum. His tongue flops over his gums like a big, pink slice of Easter ham. He also has the most beautiful brown eyes you've ever seen. And I just love him to death. "Good afternoon, Mr. Coopersmith!" I sang out.

He circled me twice and gave me another plop of his neighborly love to pick up.

I laughed. And quoted Shakespeare. "Et tu, Brute?" He rolled onto his back and dangled his legs in the air. I peeled off my rubber gloves and scratched his big belly.

9

Tuesday, March 27

It had been a week since Dale promised to look into the Delarosa murder for me. A week since that uncomfortable episode at Ike's. Except for a few finger wiggles across the newsroom, a week since we'd had any communication at all. Half of me would have been perfectly happy to wait another week. But the other half—the half that almost always ends up winning—refused to wait another minute. I punched Dale's extension the second he got to his desk. "Up for a little lunch today, Mr. M?"

"Why not," he said.

So at noon we buckled ourselves into his red Taurus station wagon and drove to Speckley's. We were still waiting for the hostess to seat us when he clutched his chest and hissed, "Shit!" I thought he was having a heart attack. But it was only his cell phone vibrating. He angrily fished his phone from the breast pocket of his sports coat and pressed it against his cheek. His eyes narrowed and darted back and forth. "Okay," he growled into the tiny, candy bar-sized electronic wonder. "And send Weedy if he's available."

Weedy was Chuck Weideman, the photographer Dale always wanted with him on important crime stories. I started buttoning my coat. If Dale wanted Weedy sent somewhere, that meant Dale was going there, too. "You can drop me off on the way," I said.

The afternoon of misery that apparently awaited me made him grin. "No time for that, Maddy."

We got on the interstate and hurried north to Hannawa Falls, a once picturesque village now uglified beyond recognition with strip malls. Dale told me what he knew: "A man in a fifth-floor apartment apparently doesn't want to be questioned by police. He's got a rifle and a whole lot of bullets. He's already shot one cop in the foot and blown out a bunch of windshields. We get to hang around until he's arrested or dead."

We parked at the Home Depot and trotted against the sloppy March wind toward a large block of apartment buildings. A dozen silver cars with blinking blue lights were scattered about the street and adjoining parking lots. Cops in combat wear were jogging about with huge black shields. Yellow police tape was being strung between telephone poles. Behind us a trio of EMS trucks were inching forward without their sirens. The satellite truck from TV 21 was already there. Tish Kiddle, the station's cute-as-a-button crime reporter, was already preparing to go live.

We spotted Weedy and waved to him. He waved back and went about his business, looking for that one perfect photo that told it all.

Dale led me to a corner mailbox just a few yards from the police line. It was one of those big blue jobbies that look like a World War I battle tank. "We'll make this our office," he said. "We can duck and cover if bullets start flying our way."

"That likely to happen?"

"I've covered enough of these SWATathons to know anything can happen any second. That's why the cops take their good old time." He spanked the top of the mailbox. "And why we're going to stay close to Big Bertha here."

No sooner had he said that, than he started walking toward a gaggle of police officers. "I thought we were going to stay close to Big Bertha?" I squeaked.

He turned and grinned. "I've got a story to cover. See if you can find some coffee."

I pitied myself for a few minutes then let the wind blow me back toward the Home Depot. There was a Starbucks right across the street from it. I bought two blueberry muffins, a large coffee and tea to go. I also took the opportunity to use the ladies' room. I am a big believer in the preemptive strike.

It was a good forty-five minutes before Dale returned to the mailbox. He took a huge gulp of his coffee. "Cold as polar bear piss. Just the way I like it." He chewed on his muffin and told me what he'd learned: "This is going to be a good story no matter how it comes out. The shooter in the apartment is—lo and behold—a suspect in the Zuduski murder. His name is Kurt Depew. Apparently his brother Randy is a suspect, too. No evidence they're both up there, though."

The murder of Congresswoman Zuduski-Lowell's baby brother had been Page One for several weeks now. There'd been no leaks of possible suspects but the police had freely discussed how high on the hog 32-year-old Paul Zuduski had lived for a guy on a congressional staffer's salary. He had a pricey townhouse in Greenlawn and drove a $60,000 Humvee. Investigators learned he'd paid cash for both. He'd also taken a startling number of vacations to islands with palm trees.

Dale finished his muffin and started ogling mine. I preemptively gave him half. "The cops aren't saying much," he said, "but apparently the Depew brothers were young Paul's business associates. And when they went to Kurt's apartment this morning—presumably to inquire about the nature of their business with the late, rolled-up-in-a-rug congresswoman's brother—he welcomed them with a deer rifle."

I sipped sparingly at the last inch of my tea in my Styrofoam cup while Dale called Metro. He gave them what he had.

It sounds silly, but I could not keep my eyes off him. He was bald and jowly. His glasses were ten years out of style. But watching his brown eyes stare soberly into space while he dictated perfect sentences and paragraphs—well.

He pressed his cell phone against his chest and smiled at me. "You want someone from the newsroom to pick you up, Maddy?"

I shook my head no.

"I guess you know why I asked you to lunch."

"Sure," said Dale. "David Delarosa."

We'd been hovering around Big Bertha for two hours now, watching the police hover around their cars and the EMS teams hover around their trucks, watching Tish Kiddle hover around her hairspray can. "And?"

He yawned like a hippopotamus in a Disney cartoon. "And not much, Maddy. No weapon. No suspect. No motive. The investigation just petered out."

The investigation may have petered out. But I wasn't going to let Dale peter out. "Was the type of weapon ever identified?"

"Just that it was something heavy—and apparently blunt."

"Apparently blunt?"

"No major cuts. Just a faceful of small abrasions and big ugly bruises."

Reporters ask questions for a living. But when they're on the receiving end, they're as aggravating as everybody else. "Something like a hammer or a baseball bat?" I asked.

He yawned again. This time with his mouth shut. "From the size and shape of the bruises, the police surmised that the surface of the weapon was rather large and possibly flat."

I tried to think of all the large, flat things that could be used to bludgeon somebody. "Frying pan, maybe?"

"Actually that was one of the things police looked for. A big bloody frying pan."

I could feel my face scrunching. "That's right, there was blood. The old stories said it was splattered all over the walls and floor. Upstairs and down."

"More of a smattering than a splattering," Dale said, enjoying his way with words. "Delarosa's nose was smashed to smithereens. Police figured that happened upstairs, when he was first attacked."

"So the killer could have gotten blood on himself?"

"Bloody clothes were on the police search list."

"None found?"

"None found."

Dale now went on and on, quite cockily I must say, about how he'd talked the public information office at police headquarters into letting him see the Delarosa files: "I sure couldn't tell them I was trying to link Delarosa's murder to Gordon Sweet's. Shit, they'd stitch a big red N for nutcase on my chest and never let me get farther than the Mr. Coffee again. So I told them the paper was thinking of doing a series on cold murder cases. Which immediately got their sperm wiggling. There's no better PR than solving some difficult old case. Even if the media has to help. 'Well, we're just thinking about it,' I said. I asked to see a sample cold case file, to see what they looked like and how we might develop a story around it. And they bit. And I suggested the Delarosa case. You should have seen me, Maddy. I was almost as devious as you."

While Dale proudly described his deception, I tried to recreate David's murder in my head, matching what I already knew with what I'd just learned. It wasn't much but it did conjure up some very nasty images:

On the morning of Thursday, April 18, 1957, maybe just before dawn, David Delarosa, wearing nothing but socks and boxer shorts, came face-to-face with his killer in the hallway outside his off-campus apartment on Hester Street. Maybe they argued. Maybe they struggled a little. Then the killer swung something heavy at him. All I could picture was a big frying pan but almost certainly it was something else. Whatever it was, it struck him square in the face and apparently broke his nose, spritzing blood on the wall and the floor. Maybe the killer just struck him once upstairs, maybe it was a few more times or several more times, but clearly one blow sent David backward over the stairwell railing. He tumbled twelve feet to the marble floor in the lobby. You'd think the killer would flee at that point, wouldn't you? But he didn't. Either he knew the apartment building was empty or he was too enraged to care. He kneeled over David. He struck him again and again. "I guess it doesn't matter," I asked Dale, "but did David die from the battering or the fall?"

I could tell from Dale's smile that he liked my question. It was the kind of question a good reporter would know to ask, I guess. "Actually, the coroner was pretty clear on that," he said. "He died from the fall. It fractured the back of his skull and ripped his brain loose. His head quickly filled with blood and some of it trickled out."

"So the blood upstairs was from the frying pan—or whatever—and the blood downstairs was from the fall?"

"The coroner's opinion—"

"His opinion?"

Dale chuckled at my skepticism. "A coroner's opinion is not exactly the same as you having an opinion, Maddy."

I didn't care for the chuckling and I sure didn't care for his lack of faith in my deductive powers. "You think I'm going off half-baked here, don't you?" I hissed.

He had the good sense to retreat: "You're the most fully baked woman I know. What I meant is that the coroner's opinion comes at the end of a very thorough autopsy report. And the coroner's opinion was that the initial blow upstairs knocked him over the railing and while he was lying flat on his back, dying from a massive cranial hemorrhage, the killer smashed away at his face."

I thought my own brain was going to rip loose. It was filled with a swirl of grisly images: David sprawled helplessly on the cold floor while some fuzzy, faceless beast swung that big imaginary frying pan; Sweet Gordon climbing that grassy hill while an equally fuzzy beast raised a pistol and took careful aim.

Wouldn't you just know it, Kurt Depew chose that moment to poke the barrel of his rifle out his bathroom window and fire.

Everyone in Hannawa Falls ducked but me.

I heard Dale screech, "Will you get the fuck down?"

Well, I did get down. But it was a waste of time. There was only the one shot and it landed a million miles from us. By the time I pulled myself up Dale was already heading toward the police line. He was bent low like Alan Alda in the opening shots of a *M*A*S*H* episode, running toward that helicopter full of wounded soldiers.

I was only the paper's librarian. But when a big story like that breaks, you have to put everything else aside—your job description, your well-deserved reputation as an uncooperative old crone—and do what you can to help get that story covered. So I bent low and headed back to Starbucks for more tea and coffee. I'm sure I looked a lot more like Groucho Marx than Alan Alda.

"What about suspects?" I asked Dale. "There had to be someone other than Sidney Spikes."

It had been more than an hour since that shot sent everybody into a tizzy. Dale had gathered what little information there was and called it in.

Apparently Kurt Depew had just wanted the police to know he was still alive and kicking. He'd taken aim at a black SWAT team helmet sitting on the hood of a patrol car. Sent it bouncing like a beach ball. "They interviewed lots of people," Dale said, "but from the looks of their notes, Spikes was the only one they had much interest in."

"Any record of the police talking to a student named Howard Shay?" I wondered.

Dale checked his memory. "Yeah, that was one of the names I saw." His thoughtful frown twisted into a wicked grin. "Another name I saw was that of a young librarian—one Dolly Madison Sprowls."

My brain immediately went back to that day after Easter in 1957 when those two detectives appeared at my apartment door. They were both chubby, both painfully squeezed into threadbare blue suits. I remember thinking they looked like Tweedledum and Tweedledee in *Alice in Wonderland*. Anyway, they'd come at the worst possible time. I was trying to make the first poppyseed kuchen of my young marriage, using the indecipherable recipe my Auntie Edna had sent me from LaFargeville. They crowded around me in my tiny kitchen and peppered me with questions until I was ready to fly.

"One Dolly Madison Sprowls who didn't know diddly," I told Dale.

He laughed. "No, you didn't. And neither did anyone else."

"Including Sidney Spikes?"

Dale had long ago finished his coffee and was now tearing little pieces out of his Styrofoam cup and mischievously feeding them into the mail slot in Big Bertha. "Including Sidney Spikes," he said. "They tried their best to squeeze a confession out of him apparently. But Mr. Spikes stuck to his story: The night they said David Delarosa was murdered, he was ensconced most blissfully—and according to the interrogation reports those were the exact words he used, *ensconced most blissfully*—in the bedroom of a woman."

"And that woman backed him up?" I asked.

Dale nodded like Oliver Hardy. "And so did the people in the apartments adjoining hers, upstairs and downstairs and on both sides, who'd all suffered through a long night of noisy carnal excess."

We'd all been shaken when the police took Sidney into custody. We'd seen it as a racial thing, of course, the cops looking for the nearest black man to blame. There was a lot of that kind of justice back then, in Hannawa and everyplace else. But the fact of the matter is that the police had every reason to suspect Sidney.

You see, Sidney Spikes and David Delarosa had a very public fight the night before the murder. It was at Jericho's, one of the hole-in-the-wall jazz clubs that thrived in Meriwether Square back then. It was Easter vacation, today what they call spring break. Most of the students had gone home to be with their families, but there were still enough of us bohemian-types on campus to keep Jericho's jumping. In fact, the only Baked Beaners missing that night were my Lawrence and Gwen's unlikely beau, Rollie Stumpf. Both were in Columbus, at the state debate tournament. Rollie was debating. Lawrence was covering it for *The Harbinger.*

Well, anyway, Sidney that night behaved as Sidney always behaved. He played himself into a horny sweat during his hour-long sets and then during his breaks sought out as much physical contact as possible with the women in the audience. It didn't matter whether you were young or old, married or single, good-looking, or as ugly as a bread and butter pickle. And he'd readily admit it. "I'm the same with chicks as I am with my music," he'd say. "I'm always ready to go just as far as my abundant talent takes me. What can I say daddy-Os and daddy-ettes, I have been profoundly blessed, rhythmically and romantically, beyond the historic bounds of prim and proper behavior. I am such a *rascal!*"

That's how Sidney talked and that's how Sidney behaved. But Sidney was not really a rascal. Beneath all the huff and puff he was a gentleman. He never pushed his musicians or his women any further than they wanted to be pushed. And he was rewarded for his good manners with all the affection he needed, on stage and off.

And so Sidney was just being Sidney that night at Jericho's when he encountered David Delarosa's darker instincts. It was after his third set. He'd just finished a twenty minute version of Glenn Miller's "Little Brown Jug" which, to everyone's enthusiastic finger popping approval, didn't sound a bit like Glenn Miller's "Little Brown Jug." He jumped off the stage and started hugging the women, purring in their ears about how *gone* they were, suggesting they disappear out the back door with him for little *impromptu love-orooni.*

He propositioned his way through a half-dozen women before reaching our table. "How's my happy little tribe of egg heads tonight?" he asked. He orbited the table, as he always did, slapping the men on the back and pulling the women to their feet for a hug. He hugged Gwen and Effie and then danced to the side where I was sitting between Chick and David. He bent over me and cooed in his easy bebop way: "How 'bout a squeezaroo, Dolly?"

I didn't mind Sidney's attention at all. It was all in good fun. But David Delarosa for some reason did mind. He yanked Sidney's hand off my shoulder. "Save it for your horn, sonny boy," he said. There was beer foam on his upper lip.

Sidney figured David was just kidding. We all did. He laughed and put his hand back on my shoulder. But David wasn't kidding. He yanked Sidney's hand away again. "I said save it!"

Sidney kept smiling but his eyes narrowed with anger. I'm sure he wanted to knock David on his ass. And even though David was a wrestler, Sidney could have done it. But the fire in his eyes quickly dimmed to fear. Maybe he was Sidney Spikes, local bebop god, but he was also a black man playing in a white man's club. He held up his hands in surrender. "We've got no problem, man," he said.

David stood up. Sidney waved his hands. David threw a punch. It landed square on Sidney's mouth.

Sidney wobbled a little then stepped back. He checked his lips for blood. "We got no problem," he said again. David cocked his arm for another punch. But he didn't throw it. Sidney went back to the stage and played like a demon for two hours without taking another break.

When the detectives questioned me that day in my kitchen, I didn't say boo about the trouble between David and Sidney. The only thing I was thinking about that afternoon was that goddamned poppyseed kuchen. But somebody must have told them about it. Sidney Spikes spent two miserable nights in a holding cell.

"About this woman Sidney was ensconced with?" I asked Dale. "Did the police reports say who she was?"

Dale fed the last piece of Styrofoam into Big Bertha. He grinned devilishly. "It was an old friend of yours. Fredricka Fredmansky."

"Effie? Well heavens to Betsy! Of course it was Effie!"

While Dale and I were leaning on Big Bertha, yakking about David Delarosa's murder and a dozen other things, the police were slowly evacuating the people in the apartment building. Then inch by inch, a SWAT team moved down the fifth floor hallway toward Kurt Depew's door. They didn't exactly knock. A battering ram tore the door off its frame. Tear gas canisters were fired in. We heard their woosh. Then we heard three quick shots.

Dale would learn later that the first of those shots was fired by Kurt Depew. It struck Sargeant Brian Boyle's metal-plated Kevlar vest and caused no more damage that a doughnut-sized bruise on his spongy belly, which he proudly showed to everyone he could before it faded. The second and third shots were fired by the police. One shot made mincemeat out of Kurt Depew's hip. The other made mincemeat out of his heart.

10

Friday, March 30

It was Friday, a day I usually coast a little more than usual. But that Friday I couldn't wait to get to the paper. I took a quick shower. Left my hair damp. Made instant oatmeal.

You can understand why I was in such a hurry. Dale had dominated Page One most of the week. His Wednesday story had detailed Kurt Depew's fatal shootout with police. His Thursday story had dug deeper into the possible link between the Depew brothers and Congresswoman Zuduski-Lowell's brother. His story in today's paper was going to knock a lot of politically sensitive socks off. I wanted to be there to see them fly.

According to well-placed sources, after weeks of pressuring police to speed up their investigation into her brother's death, the congresswoman was now warning them to move slowly. I'd stayed around long enough Thursday night to see the story before it went to press. The headline was wordy but wonderful:

Zuduski-Lowell To Police:
"Don't you dare embarrass me"

I'd caught Dale just as he was getting into the elevator. "This well-placed source wouldn't happen to include a certain detective of Scottish heritage, would it?" I asked. He'd done his best to speak in a brogue: "Now lassie, behave," he croaked, poking the elevator button. "You know darn well that's something I've got to keep under me kilt."

So that morning I ate half of my oatmeal and left the rest to harden into cement. I threw on my coat and headed for the garage. And wouldn't you know it the damn phone rang. It was Eric Chen. "I think I lost my truck keys," he said.

"You *think* you lost them?"

"Well, I know I lost them. Just not how thoroughly."

So instead of zooming straight downtown, I had to zigzag north through the morning traffic to the old Cedar Hill apartments where Eric lived.

"You should have a second set," I snarled when

he got into my Shadow with his daily six-pack of Mountain Dew.

"That was my second set," he said.

I fought my way over to Cleveland Avenue and started south through an exasperating gauntlet of traffic lights.

Eric took my cursing at the red lights personally—which he was smart to do—and did his best to get my mind on something else. "Any of that toxic waste stuff I gave you panning out?" he asked.

"Too early to tell," I said. "But I have confirmed that eighteen drums of toluene are still out there somewhere. And I did learn that Gordon was involved with the original EPA investigation. And that the Wooster Pike landfill was one of the suspected sites. And that Kenneth Kingzette was paroled in November."

Eric added another *and*. "And you think he killed Sweet Gordon before he could find those other drums?"

The light ahead of us turned red. "I think it's a possibility," I said.

It was only eight-thirty on a very chilly day, but Eric couldn't resist the temptation. He twisted the cap off one of his Mountain Dews and took a long chug of the green goop. "How would Kingzette even know Gordon was digging out there?" he asked. "He's been in prison for several years, right?"

"In prison in Lucasville, not on the moon," I said.

"You ever been to Lucasville?"

I jabbed my finger at the canvas bag crowding his feet and told him to find the folder marked ROWE/DIG. "You remember that day at the bookstore when you called me a sweet potato?" I asked.

He pulled the bag onto his lap and dug through the thick stack of folders. "I think you called yourself a sweet potato, Maddy."

The light turned green, but not long enough for me to get through it. "I guess it was me," I admitted. "But only because you were already thinking it. I don't know why you think I'm incapable of doing a computer search on my own."

He found the folder and opened it. "Fifteen years of empirical experience—whoa!"

He was looking at the printout of a story written by Doris Rowe. Read the headline:

GORDON'S GOLD MINE

College garbology class is a blast from the past

"As you can see, it's hardly an in-depth story. It ran in that Our Crazy Town column that used to run in the back of the Sunday magazine. Four summers ago. When Gordon first started digging out there."

"So you think Kingzette may have seen this, held his breath hoping the professor wouldn't find the missing toluene, and then when he got out—*bang*—to make sure he never did?"

Not only did I get caught by another red right, I found myself in the left turn-only lane. I had to detour off Cleveland Avenue through a maze of one-way streets. "I checked with the prison library," I said. "They don't have a subscription for *The Herald-Union*. But Kingzette's son has one. And apparently he's pretty thick with his father. At least he brought him into his moving business as soon as he was paroled. Maybe they were in cahoots back then, too."

Eric finished his Mountain Dew. "Good work."

I found my way back to Cleveland Avenue and headed for the Memorial Bridge. "Maybe it's all just a bunch of rubbish. But it keeps Kingzette in the mix a while longer."

I still don't know why I had such a bug up my behind about Kenneth Kingzette and those missing drums of toluene.

It was such a silly probability. As silly as thinking Andrew J. Holloway III killed Gordon. As silly as thinking Gordon's murder had something to do with David Delarosa's murder. As silly as thinking Chick Glass killed Gordon over that alleged slice of cheese. There could be a million things buried out there that somebody didn't want found. And there could be a million other reasons somebody wanted Gordon dead.

But, good gravy, my dander was up. And so was my curiosity. As silly as those four possibilities were, and as silly as I knew I'd look when Scotty Grant arrested the real murderer, I knew I simply could not stop my silly investigation.

The worst thing about Eric losing his keys, which he manages to do three or four times a year, is that he attaches himself to me like a barnacle on a shrimp boat until he finds them. But that particular Friday I was glad he'd lost those damn keys again. Right after work I was going to see Effie. It would be good to have Eric with me. Not for physical protection, of course. And certainly not for moral support. He was absolutely worthless in both of those departments. But Eric's irritating presence would make it easier for me to make a quick exit if things didn't go well. "I'd love to stay and talk," I could say to Effie, "but I promised to get Eric home by six. Bye-bye!"

So at five o'clock I herded Eric into the elevator, and into my Dodge Shadow, and headed across town to Hemphill College.

Effie's used book store, Last Gasp Books she called it, was located in a ramshackle shopping plaza at the corner of White Pond and Parvin, just two blocks west of H.E. Hemphill's glorious statue. It was a narrow storefront sandwiched between rival Mexican restaurants.

I made Eric open the door for me. I protectively covered my elbows with my hands and went inside. "Maddy!" Effie sang out. She was wearing a sleeveless denim jumper and a pair of lace-up boots better suited for marching across the Gobi desert. Several turquoise necklaces were orbiting her wrinkly neck. And of course she was wearing those big yellow lollypop glasses.

Seeing that my elbows were covered, she drilled Eric's. "This your boy toy, Maddy?"

"I'm too old for boys or toys," I said. "This is Eric Chen, my assistant at the paper."

Effie tried to give him a welcoming hug. But

Eric, still rubbing the pain out of his elbow, kept backing away. Effie loved that. "I like skittish," she said.

She gave us the nickel tour. The front of the store was bright and airy. There were tables piled high with newer books. There was a rack of humorous greeting cards and a display of fancy pens and stationery. The middle section of the store was dark and cramped, a claustrophobic maze of ceiling-high shelves crammed with thousands and thousands of musty books. "These are my meat and potatoes," Effie said. "When you can't find it anywhere else, you find it here, and you pay dearly." At the back of the store was a narrow doorway. The sign above the arch said, in Old English, *Ye Dirty Stuff.* "My erotica collection," she said. "None of it later than the Kennedy administration."

We headed back toward the front of the store, to Effie's tiny office behind the counter. Eric immediately excused himself. "Think I'll browse a bit," he said. He headed straight for Ye Dirty Stuff.

Effie didn't have any tea bags, but she did have a coffee maker. She divided what was left of the sludge in the carafe. "I guess I'm having trouble with Gordon's death," I began.

"Aren't we all," she answered.

She offered me an ancient jar of artificial creamer. I waved it off. "I'm afraid the police may get the wrong idea, Effie," I said. "About some people."

"Some people like Andrew Holloway?" she wondered.

I nodded. "He seems like a nice boy. And a smart boy. But I gather he's pretty thin in the alibi department. And God knows what his relationship with Gordon was."

She put a lethal dose of the creamer in her mug and stirred it with her pinky. She took a bitter slurp. "I can't vouch for Andrew's predilections."

"How about Gordon's?"

She laughed like a flock of ducks. "If you didn't know me as well as you do, I think I'd have to be insulted."

More than likely I was blushing. "You know what I mean, Effie."

"Yes I do, Maddy. And I can swear on a stack of Masters & Johnson studies that Gordon was quite fond of the opposite sex." She paused and took a quick sip. "If he went the other way, too, well, I never saw any evidence of it."

"Which brings me to David Delarosa," I said.

The ducks were back. "I'll have to put on

another pot of coffee if you're going to bring up every man I've slept with."

I forced a smile. "I can't help but think Gordon's friendship with Andrew was a little like his friendship with David."

Effie spread her fingers across her necklaces, like she was Scarlett O'Hara or something. "My oh my! I don't think you're getting enough sleep, Maddy."

This time I made sure I was frowning. "As I recall, Gordon's friendship with David Delarosa was quite intense, and quite out of the blue. And then a few weeks later David was dead."

Effie now told me something I hadn't known. "The way I remember it, David hired Gordon to tutor him. In biology. And they just hit it off."

"Gordon did do a lot of tutoring," I said. "So I suppose you're right."

Effie backtracked a little. "But, to tell you the truth, I'm not sure David was as crazy about Gordon as Gordon was about him." Her voice shrank to a whisper now, as if we were surrounded by ghosts. "I think he latched onto Gordon to get laid. He was a horny boy from the boondocks. And Gordon was up to his armpits in female acquaintances majoring in liberal arts. So he figured he could put up with a little poetry and bebop jazz in exchange for a little beatnik—"

The store's heavy wooden door squealed open. The windows shook from the hurricane of cold air gushing inside. "That'll be Edward," she said.

A man hidden deep inside a fur-lined parka appeared at the counter. Effie excused herself. She handed him a stack of discreetly wrapped books from under the counter. He handed her a Ziploc bag filled with half dollars. "One of my regulars," she said when the man named Edward left. "He likes Victorian stories about bisexual pirates."

If I was going to get anything useful out of Effie, I knew I'd have to risk telling her my discreetly wrapped theories. "At the memorial service, you said maybe Gordon had been digging where he shouldn't have been digging."

"Ah—so you're the one who put that bug in Detective Grant's ear."

"He's already talked to you about all this?"

"Not the David Delarosa stuff," she said. "That's all yours."

If Eric had been there, I'm sure that's when I would have made my excuses and fled. But he was back in the erotica, immersed in stories about God knows what. I had no choice but to plow on.

"There are lots of other possibilities, of course," I said, "but I think maybe Gordon was looking for the weapon used to kill David Delarosa. And maybe somebody figured that out. And killed him."

Effie was sitting two feet away from me, but she might as well have pushed her chair across the street. "I don't know anything about that," she said.

The eyes inside Effie's lollypop glasses widened. "So you really have no idea what Gordon may have been digging for?"

"No, I do not."

I bent forward and grabbed her hands. "Oh, Effie, I don't want to see anybody put through the wringer if they don't deserve it," I said. "Not Andrew or Chick or anyone else."

I got exactly the reaction I wanted. "Chick?"

"That old argument over the cheeseburger," I explained. "They fought about it at the Kerouac Thing, two days before Gordon was killed. You saw them, didn't you?"

"Yes, but it was nothing."

"But the police might interpret it as something," I said. "You remember what happened to Sidney after that little incident at Jericho's. If you hadn't come forward the way you did who knows what would have happened."

Effie laughed. Not like a flock of ducks. Like a single, very nervous duck. "How in the world do you know about that?"

I pawed the air, to make her believe I'd known forever. "It took a lot of guts, Effie, times being what they were. I don't think I could have done it."

"Slept with Sidney or told the police about it?"

I stood and buttoned my coat, to make her think I was finished prying. "I promised to get Eric home by six," I said.

We put our arms around each other and headed for the back of the store to extricate Eric from his fantasies. "Why do you think Chick and Gordon fought about such a stupid thing all those years?" I asked her. "It's so absurd."

"Absurd but not absurd," Effie said. "Both Gordon and Chick considered themselves Kerouac's apostle at the college. They were the best of friends, but they also wanted their version of his legendary visit to prevail. To fortify their own legends. So if Chick was right, and Jack had a cheeseburger, then Chick would be the rock upon which Kerouac's Hemphillite church was built. But if Gordon was right, and Jack ordered a plain burger—well, they're hardly the first college professors to get caught up in some meaningless turf war."

"No, I guess not," I said. I got Eric's attention and impatiently motioned for him. He put the tiny green book he was reading back on the shelf and sheepishly trotted toward us. Effie drilled both of us in the elbow before we made it out of the store.

It was exactly six o'clock. The westbound lane was clogged with cars fleeing downtown. Our side of the road was nearly empty. We zoomed along at thirty-five, missing as many red lights as we hit. "You learn anything useful in there?" Eric asked.

"Not as much as you did, apparently," I said.

"It was erotica, Maddy. High art."

I groaned. "Unfortunately, so is reading Effie's mind." I turned onto Pershing Avenue and headed north toward Cedar Hill. "Either I learned a lot from her or nothing at all. Either intentionally or unintentionally."

"You think she's covering up for someone?"

"Protecting maybe."

"Protecting a murderer?"

"Good gravy, no! Protecting the right of people to be different. To be left the hell alone. Fredricka Fredmansky marched to a different drummer long before she ever read Thoreau. Her father was a rabbi and her mother danced in a burlycue, if that tells you anything. She's the most virtuous woman you'll ever meet, but for better or worse her personal morality is cherry picked from a rather large and varied orchard of truths."

"She sounds a lot like you," Eric said.

Eric opened the car door, swung his sneakers into the puddle along the curb, grinned at me over his shoulder. "You want to come in for a bite?"

I'd been in his apartment. It was not an invitation I welcomed. "That depends what's going to bite me? A spider? Cockroach? Rat?"

"I thought maybe we could call out for a pizza," he said.

"Something to nibble on while we're looking for your keys, I gather?"

So I followed him up the slippery, noisy iron stairs to his apartment. He'd lost his apartment keys too, of course, and so the door was not only unlocked, but wedged shut with a huge yellow bath towel. He took hold of the towel, and then the knob, and pushed the door open. He explained: "I was afraid if I closed the door I might accidentally lock it—you know how I am—and then I'd really be up shit creek."

We went inside. "Speaking of shit creek," I said.

Eric was genuinely surprised by my commentary on his housekeeping skills. "It's not that bad, is it?"

I stepped over a duffel bag of dirty clothes and crackled across the crumb-laden carpet to the kitchen. I hung my coat on the only chair that didn't already have a coat hanging on it. "Anything but onions or anchovies," I said.

And so Eric called the pizza shop and I got busy washing his sink full of dishes. "When you get some time, there's a couple people I want you to locate for me," I said.

Eric got a Mountain Dew from the refrigerator and then a paper towel and a ballpoint. "Shoot."

"The first is a man named Howard Shay," I said. "I know where he lives in Mallet Creek, but supposedly he's in Florida for the winter. See if he has a house or a trailer down there. He was an education major, so more than likely it's a trailer."

"One of your old beatnik friends?"

"David Delarosa's college roommate."

Eric was having trouble writing on the bumply towel. "You're thinking he wasn't really in Florida when Sweet Gordon was murdered?"

"Oh, I suspect he was," I said. "But he might remember something interesting about the hoopla surrounding Delarosa's murder."

I found a Brillo pad under the sink and attacked a sauce pan caked with the remains of something red. "I also want you to find my husband Lawrence's fourth and final wife. Her name is Dory. D.O.R.Y. But I suppose her real name is Dorothy, or maybe Doreen."

"And her last name is still Sprowls?" Eric asked.

"Lawrence died fifteen years ago. She could be remarried. But start with Sprowls. And start in Pittsburgh. That's where they were living when he died."

Eric folded the paper towel and put it in his shirt pocket. "Does this have something to do with the professor's murder? Or are you just taking advantage of my generosity to satisfy your jealous curiosities?"

"Jealous curiosities?" I hooted. "Believe me, jealousy does not describe my feelings for Lawrence's ex wives."

"More like empathy?"

I began searching his kitchen drawers for a clean dishtowel. "More like pity. But this isn't about ex wives, Eric. This is about a dead husband's old college clippings." I told him about my visit to the college newspaper office the week before, how I'd learned that the paper's old files were destroyed in a fire, how I'd hoped to search them for clues.

"Lawrence wrote for *The Harbinger* all through college," I said. "He kept every story he ever wrote. And I'm sure he never threw them out. Journalists just don't do that. They keep every word they've ever written. They lug them from house to house, and spouse to spouse, like they're ancient biblical texts, written by The Almighty himself."

Eric showed me where he kept his towels. The drawer was empty. "So Lawrence covered the Delarosa murder for the college paper?"

"Actually, he didn't," I said. "The editor wanted him to—he was the best reporter on the paper by far—but Lawrence told him he was a personal acquaintance of David's and couldn't possibly be objective. Lawrence just oozed integrity back then."

"What exactly do you hope to find in his clips?"

"Something I'm not looking for," I said.

Eric retrieved the same bath towel he'd used to keep his front door from locking. We finished the dishes and then started looking for his keys. We were still looking when the pizza came. And still looking when the pizza was gone.

"I heard a lot of what you and Effie were talking about," Eric admitted. We were in his living room now, digging into the cracks between his cushions.

"And?"

"She slept with a lot of guys."

"Apparently."

"You think she's still active in that department?"

"She does have sex on the brain, doesn't she?"

Eric was flat on his belly now, his left arm under the sofa up to his shoulder. "I don't pretend to understand the libidos of old people but—"

I didn't just pretend to be offended. I was offended. "Old people?"

He wisely ignored my outburst. "All that erotica. That boy-toy stuff. Every other word out of her mouth. It seems to me she may be a little obsessed."

"Effie is still Effie."

"That's exactly what I'm saying, Maddy. At one time or the other she's slept with just about every guy in your investigation."

I pawed at the seriousness of his suggestion. "Which means what? That's she's some kind of sexual psychopath?"

Eric rolled over and started flipping through

the comic books and newspapers piled under his coffee table. "Maybe she and the professor were involved in some kind of wacky lovers' triangle with somebody. Maybe she's aware of something so weird that even she can't talk about it."

I was furious. "Why does everybody think Gordon's murder is about sex?"

"Can you be sure it isn't?"

I struggled to my feet and headed for the mess that surely awaited me in his bathroom. "You've got to understand something," I growled. "In Effie's world, having sex with a lot of people is like me having lunch with a lot of people."

Before he could respond with one of his smart-ass remarks, I yelled, "Bingo!"

I'd found his keys. In his shower. In a soggy, half-eaten bag of microwave popcorn stuffed in the soap holder.

I didn't ask him for an explanation and he didn't volunteer one.

11

Monday, April 2

The coroner finally released the autopsy report on Gordon's death. Dale brought me a copy as soon as he got to the newsroom. "No surprises," he said, flopping it into my hands.

The coroner officially listed Gordon's death as a homicide. The cause of death was a single shot in the back of his head, right on that bump where the spine joins the skull. The barrel of the gun was less than a foot from his head when the fatal shot was fired. The coroner knew that because there were particles of gunpowder embedded in the skin around the wound. The bullet dug from Gordon's brain was a 9mm, jacketed in brass, in all probability fired from a semiautomatic pistol. "The cops found only one cartridge in the grass," Dale said.

"The round that hit him was almost certainly the only one fired."

"The killer knew what he was doing then," I said.

Dale nodded. "A well-planned assassination, apparently. Coolly carried out."

The coroner's report also supported the police department's belief that the murder occurred approximately 36 to 48 hours before the first officers responded to Andrew J. Holloway III's call from the landfill. "The rigor mortis that stiffens up a body had already faded," Dale said. "And there was very little decomposition. So they figure he was shot sometime Thursday."

"Sometime Thursday afternoon or evening," I said.

Dale squinted at me. "And how do you know that?"

"According to Andrew, he and Gordon had lunch at Wendy's at noon that Thursday, as they did every Thursday. So if Andrew is to be believed—"

"Andrew didn't happen to mention what the professor ordered, did he?" Dale asked.

"As a matter of fact, yes. Andrew said they always ate there because Gordon liked their chili."

Dale grinned and turned the page for me. "I

guess you can believe him on that point, at least," he said.

I read the paragraph he was snapping with his index finger and thumb. "Well, well," I whispered. According to the coroner, Gordon's stomach was filled with undigested chili.

I knew Dale had a story or two to write. I put the report in my top drawer for closer study later. "Any idea when they're releasing Gordon's body?"

Dale was ready for me. "Already been released. To Godfrey & Sons."

Godfrey & Sons was a small funeral home known for its no-frills burials and cremations. I immediately called them. According to the sleepy girl on the other end, Gordon's interment was scheduled for Wednesday, at 2 p.m., at the old Lutheran Hill Cemetery east of downtown.

Wednesday, April 4

I took half a vacation day to attend Gordon's burial. And it immediately raised suspicions. "What gives here, Maddy?" Suzie squeaked when I turned in my planned absence form. "Two weeks ago a sick day and now four full hours of vacation time?"

I knew she was joking but it still made me uneasy. "I'm not trying to ease myself into retirement, if that's what you're hoping," I snapped.

Well, you can see the predicament I was in, can't you? I couldn't exactly run around town on company time investigating Gordon's murder. It would give Bob Avery the ammunition he needed to give me the boot. But if I kept taking sick days and vacation days, that would raise eyebrows, too. Until two weeks ago, I hadn't taken a sick day in thirty years. And I probably hadn't used a tenth of the vacation time I had coming. And now if I wasn't careful, the pathetic life I'd lived was going to rear up and bite me.

So as silly as it seems, taking those four hours made me as anxious as an earthworm at a robin convention. But no way in hell was I going to miss Gordon's burial!

I left the morgue at noon. I had a bagel and tea at Ike's then drove to Lutheran Hill. It was one of those April days in Ohio when Mother Nature can't decide which would make people more miserable, freezing rain or slushy snow, so she decides to give them both, with a knock-you-on-your-keister wind thrown in just for fun.

Lutheran Hill is located just east of downtown. In the old days it was packed with German immigrants. Now it's a rich mix of Blacks, Pakistanis,

Koreans, Mexicans and Appalachian Whites. The cemetery sits right in the middle of this gumbo, like a big saltine cracker.

I drove through the wrought-iron arch and crackled slowly along the winding gravel drive, past a million forgotten tombstones. Just beyond the statue honoring the city's Civil War dead, I spotted a small caravan of vehicles parked half on the drive and half on the mushy brown grass. There was a hearse, a rusty pickup truck pulling a small yellow forklift, and one of those cute little Subaru station wagons with an empty antler-like rack on the roof. I kept my distance, parking a good hundred yards away. I rolled down my window and watched.

The doors of the three vehicles opened together, as if on cue. From the hearse emerged a man wearing a black topcoat and bright blue earmuffs. From the pickup emerged a bony man in a faded flannel shirt and tattered, insulated vest. From the Subaru with the antlers emerged a hairy young man wearing a buckskin coat with fringed sleeves, and a black cowboy hat with silver discs around the brim.

They gathered in the driveway and talked for a minute. Then the man in the flannel shirt went to his truck and unhitched the forklift. He maneuvered it to the back of the hearse, raised the tongs high and removed Gordon's casket. He drove to a freshly dug grave on a small knoll above the drive. While the other men dug their hands into their pockets and watched, Flannel Man guided the casket onto the metal frame erected over the grave. They watched, and I watched, as he lowered the casket to the bottom of the rectangular hole. Good gravy, was I the only one of Gordon's friends who knew he was being buried that day?

The young man stayed until Gordon's casket was covered. He knelt and patted the mound of dirt. Then he got in his Subaru and drove off. I followed him.

He wound through downtown—having the same trouble with the one-way streets that all strangers have—then sped out West Tuckman. At one traffic light I got close enough to see that the Subaru had West Virginia plates. We reached Meriwether Square and then the campus. He took a sudden wide turn onto Sunflower Court, a narrow brick street lined with wonderful old Arts and Crafts bungalows. I did not make the turn. I was afraid the man in the Subaru might rightfully think I was following him. Instead I zigzagged aimlessly through the campus for ten minutes or so. Finally I drove back to

Sunflower Court. I stopped one house away from the gray clabbered house Gordon Sweet bought the same year he returned to Hemphill College with his Ph.D. The Subaru was in the driveway. I mustered all the fortitude I could, which didn't feel like much, and shuffled up the walk to the door.

I only had to knock once.

The young man raked the hair out of his eyes and made sure he was smiling. "Ah," he said, "the mysterious woman in the Dodge Shadow."

I made sure there was a smile on my face, too. "You saw me, did you?"

He motioned me inside. "At the cemetery and in my rearview mirror."

I stuck out my hand. "I'm Maddy Sprowls. I'm an old friend of your—you are Gordon's nephew, aren't you? The one from Harper's Ferry?"

He grimaced. "Yup. Mickey Gitlin."

With all that hair in his face, and that stubble on his chin, it was hard to tell if Mickey shared many of Gordon's features. He did have brown eyes like Gordon. And I guess the same nose. But unlike Gordon, who was always a little on the pasty side, Mickey had outdoorsy pink skin.

He led me into the living room. We looked for a good place to sit and decided on the swayback,

1960s-style sofa under the picture window. "I didn't know the burial was going to be private," I said. "So I kept my distance. But I did want to express my sympathy to the family."

The need to explain tightened his face. "I couldn't make it to the memorial service. And my mother's not too mobile these days."

"The obituary said she lives in Florida."

"Captiva Island. She has MS."

I bobbed my chin sympathetically. "I knew your uncle since college, but I don't think I ever met any of his family."

"There never was much," he said. "And there's only Mom and me now."

I couldn't exactly ask him if he was Gordon's heir. But that's exactly what I wanted to know. "So I guess all the legal stuff has fallen on your shoulders."

He was surprisingly candid. "It's all a little weird. I really never knew the man. Saw him a few of times when I was a kid, funerals and things, but that's about it. Then I get a call that he's dead and I've inherited everything."

Boy, did I want to know what *everything* meant. "I guess you've got your hands full."

He chuckled wearily. "What I've got is an old house full of junk."

I found a way to ask him if he had a wife, or children.

"I guess that's the other thing I inherited from him," he said. He heard what he'd said and laughed. "I don't mean his gay gene. I mean his loner gene."

I assured him I knew what he meant. "So what exactly do you do in Harper's Ferry?"

"At the moment I'm going broke teaching people how to kayak."

"The funny little Eskimo boats?"

"Yup. The funny little Eskimo boats."

I maneuvered the conversation back to Gordon's estate. "I guess you'll have to sell the house."

"It's a great little house," he said. "I wished there was some way I could zap it down there—or zap the Potomac River up here."

"Well, I don't think you'll have trouble finding a buyer."

He nodded with his eyebrows arched high and happy. Clearly he figured to make a pretty penny on Gordon's house. "Getting rid of his stuff is the problem," he said. "He's got ten tons of rubble that could be worth a lot or nothing."

"I wouldn't give you a dime for this old couch," I said. "But some of this other stuff looks like it might be worth something."

"I'm not talking about his furniture. I'm talking about all that stuff from his archeological digs."

I finagled a tour of the house. It was indeed filled with, well, junk: old bottles and cans and boxes, tools and toys, kitchen gadgets, kitschy wall plaques and dime store paintings. "I suppose you could hold a tag sale."

"That's exactly what I'm going to do," Mickey said. "But not up here."

"You're hauling all this stuff down to Harper's Ferry?"

"Summer's coming fast. I've got a barn full of kayaks to get ready. And Harper's Ferry is pretty much the flea market capital of the world."

"I think the Hannawa Chamber of Commerce would challenge you on that," I said.

We squeezed into Gordon's small downstairs office. There were bookshelves on all four walls. "Boy, I bet our old friend Effie would love these for her shop," I said.

"She's been bugging me since the funeral," he said.

"Since the funeral? You were there?"

He shook his head, sourly. "She called me down in Harper's Ferry. About six times. A very persistent woman."

"Yes, she is—you're going to sell them to her?"

"At some point maybe," he said. "But I'm going to take them back to Harper's Ferry with everything else. I need to evaluate what I've got. Think things through."

"That's wise," I said.

Effie's eagerness to buy Gordon's books didn't surprise me at all. Effie had known Gordon forever. She'd undoubtedly rummaged through his library a thousand times. And she was a businesswoman. Collections like that didn't come on the market every day.

We snooped around the kitchen then headed down the basement steps. I spread my fingers across my face. "Oh, my!" The basement walls were lined with crudely constructed shelves, all stuffed with junkyard treasure.

"It'll be a bitch hauling this stuff out of here," he said. "But it'll make my creditors happy. One or two of them anyway."

I circled the basement like a visiting head of state reviewing the troops on the White House lawn. I stopped in front of the shelves next to the furnace. I studied the rows of cocoa cans. I struggled to remember my conversation with Andrew Holloway, and the catchy little question Gordon always asked his students at the dig: "Anything interesting today, boys and girls?" he'd ask. "Old soda pop bottles? Betsy Wetsy Dolls? Perhaps an old cocoa can or two?"

Without appearing too nosy, I scanned the other shelves in the basement for old bottles or dolls. There weren't any. I motioned for Mickey to join me. "You wouldn't want to sell me these old cocoa cans, would you?"

He did want to sell them to me. For five dollars a can. There were twenty-two of them.

So I wrote Mickey a check for $110.00 and felt like an absolute fool carrying them out to my car.

I drove away with more than a back seat full of cocoa cans. I also had a brain full of unanswered questions: Did Gordon save those cocoa cans for a reason? Did they have a story to tell?

Was Mickey really surprised to learn that he was Gordon's heir? And just how far in debt was his kayak business in Harper's Ferry? Why hadn't he come to Gordon's memorial service? Harper's Ferry isn't that far from Hannawa. And why did he sneak into town to bury him now? The minute the coroner released his body? Without a minister for a graveside prayer? Without inviting any of

Gordon's friends?

And what was that crack about his not inheriting Gordon's gay gene?

I drove home for what I planned to be the most boring evening of my life. I was going to eat popcorn and suck on peppermint swirls, and watch six or seven hours of old sitcoms on Nickelodeon, until Gordon's murder, and David Delarosa's murder, were no more a bother to me than the dust bunnies under my bed.

But when I pulled into my driveway, Jocelyn and James were waiting on my porch. Jocelyn's usual happy-as-an-apple face was puckered with anguish. I struggled toward her with my three shopping bags of old cocoa cans. The first words out of her mouth were not exactly promising: "Oh Maddy, I don't know how to ask you this."

I put down my cocoa cans and scratched James' ping-pong paddle ears. He reciprocated by slobbering on my elbows with his big pink tongue. "How long?" I asked.

Jocelyn pulled in her neck, as if I was about to pound her with a sledgehammer. "Five months?"

The last time she asked me to watch James it was for three days. "Five months?"

She started to cry—the kind of crying that includes a lot of shoulder shaking and throaty moans that sound like mating whales. She told me her daughter Deena's husband had been swept into the Pacific Ocean while collecting mussels for a paella, for their fifteenth wedding anniversary dinner, and now Deena was going to be a young working widow with three daughters at that awkward age. Jocelyn was going to spend the summer in Eureka, California, while the kids were out of school. "I don't know what's going to happen after that, Maddy," she said, "but if you could take in James until the end of August—I'll pay for all his food, of course."

I loved James. But I didn't want to love him that much. But heavens to Betsy, what could I do? "When do you have to leave?"

"The funeral's on Wednesday," she said. "I was hoping you could drive me to the airport tonight."

And so instead of watching old sitcoms on Nickelodeon, I was starring in a brand-new sitcom of my own: James & Me. My only hope was that it would merely be a summer replacement and not picked up for the fall.

12

Friday, April 6

I had a nice, peaceful lunch at Ike's and then took my good old time walking back to the paper. It was only fifty degrees outside but the sun was shining like it was the middle of July. I didn't dare do it, of course, but I felt like whistling that peppy theme song from *The Andy Griffith Show*.

On my way through the newsroom I wiggled my fingers at Louise and Margaret and even Ed Boyer in sports. Two out of three wiggled back. Then the second I lowered my happy behind into my chair, Suzie appeared out of the ether. "Mr. Averill wants to see you," she whispered. "Immediately."

I let the elevator take me to the fifth floor. I squeaked along the old hardwood floor to the sterile gray office at the end of the hall. I hate to admit it, but I was trembling like a just-hatched peep.

Bob Averill has been editor-in-chief for fifteen years. The owners of *The Herald-Union,* the Knudsen-Hartpence chain, sent him here to boost the paper's sagging circulation. They've pretty much given up on that impossible dream. Nobody reads newspapers anymore. So Bob's top priority now, or so it seems, is to coax me into retirement. But as you know, Dolly Madison Sprowls has no plans to hippity-hop into that briar patch any time soon.

I took half a minute outside Mr. Averill's office to get myself under control—and pick the dog hair off my sweater—then knocked on his door with as much vinegar as I could muster under the circumstances.

"No need to knock, Maddy!"

I was not only confronted by Bob Averill's sour frown. But also the sour frown of Managing Editor Alec Tinker, and even worse, the sour frown of Detective Scotty Grant. They were slumped in the leather swivel chairs that surrounded the glass-topped coffee table in the middle of the office, a star chamber of medieval inquisitors with a pinch of Larry, Curly and Moe. "My three favorite men," I said.

There were several empty chairs. Mr. Averill pointed to the one he wanted me to sit in.

I sat. I pressed my nervous knees together.

Tinker handed me a small folded newspaper. It was a copy of the Hemphill College student newspaper, *The Harbinger*. The story across the top was about a proposed tuition hike. The story across the bottom was about me.

It was not a hard news story, but one of those "notes" columns all newspapers run these days, where style and speculation take precedence over documented fact. The column was cleverly called "Campus Claptrap." The headline asked this question:

Is Maddy Sprowls At It Again?

As bad as that headline was, it was the byline under it that made me wilt:

By Gabriella Nash
Harbinger Editor

"Heavens to Betsy," I heard myself hiss, "that horrible girl with the green hair." I started to read:

Just eight months ago, Hemphill College alumna Dolly Madison "Maddy" Sprowls led police to the real killer of television evangelist Buddy Wing. Now it appears she is trying to beat baffled detectives to the person who murdered archaeology professor Gordon Sweet.

After graduating from HC in 1957, Sprowls went to work for *The Hannawa Herald-Union*. But not as a reporter. As a librarian. That's right, the diminutive, 68-year-old Sprowls is the deskbound gnome who watches over the newspaper's morgue, where the stories real reporters write are filed away for future reference.

And why is Sprowls so interested in Professor Sweet's murder? It seems that she and Sweet were old college friends. In fact, both were members of a quixotic band of campus bohemians called The Meriwether Baked...

"Did you get to the sentence about you not being a reporter?" Tinker asked.

"I sure did," I said. "It's right above the one that calls me a gnome."

Tinker was too agitated to let me read in peace. "We'd like to believe this *claptrap* is exactly that, Maddy."

Detective Grant seconded the motion. "And so would we baffled detectives."

I knew it would be hard to plead guilty and not guilty at the same time. But I knew I'd have to try. I finished reading, let out a long, Reaganesque *"Wellll"* and then launched into a breathless explanation that I hoped would save me from collecting my pension: "It's true enough that I've been asking a few people a few questions, about Gordon's murder, and other things that may or may not be related, or even important, but I sure as heck didn't tell that girl at the college what I was up to."

"Or us," Tinker pointed out.

"Or us," Scotty Grant added.

Now Mr. Averill took a turn at me. "So this Miss Nash didn't give you a heads-up about her story? Didn't give you a chance to respond?"

"I'm as surprised by this as you are, Bob."

I watched Mr. Averill's troubled eyes drift along his office walls. They were lined with a century's worth of important front pages, in thick black frames, from the Wright Brothers' flight at Kitty Hawk, to the Japanese attack on Pearl Harbor, to the most recent addition, the one revealing Buddy Wing's real killer. "I suppose you've earned the right to explain yourself," he said. "If you think that's possible."

So that was the start of my visit to the woodshed. It was the longest damn hour of my life. I apologized for my secretiveness. I apologized for my carelessness. I apologized for my impulsiveness and my *loose-cannonness*. I agonized out loud over my incurable curiosity, like some bad actor in a Shakespearean play. I also told them everything I knew about Gordon's murder, who I suspected and why. By the time I finished, they were as exhausted as I was.

Mr. Averill made a motorboat sound with his lips. He drummed his fingers on the armrests. He stood up and buttoned his suit coat over his middle-aged belly. "I don't think we need to take any disciplinary action here, do you Alec?"

Tinker gave him a terse, "No, sir."

"How about you, Detective Grant? Mrs. Sprowls hasn't broken any laws, has she?"

"Not yet," Grant said.

Mr. Averill walked me to the door. "Now you keep yourself out of trouble, Maddy," he said. "And if you can't, I hope you'll at least keep us in the loop. We do like to sell newspapers around here."

"And we like to solve crimes," Detective Grant said.

I squinted at them until their cat-like grins withered. "You bastards," I said.

I got off the elevator and went straight for the ladies room. Not to pee. To seethe. That hadn't been Shakespeare up there. That had been a goddamned puppet show. And I'd been the puppet. Detective Grant wanted Gordon's murderer. Tinker and Mr. Averill wanted a good story. They knew I just might deliver both. I sized myself up in the mirror, my silly hair and my wrinkled face, my gravity-ravaged boobs and shoulders. I took a deep breath and stood as tall as I could. "We'll just see who's gonna pull whose strings," I said.

I went back to my desk. I got my tea mug and headed for the cafeteria. It was empty, except for one rumpled man slumped over a bottle of tomato juice. Detective Grant.

I filled my mug with hot water and dunked my teabag. I walked toward him, not like the frightened puppy I'd been upstairs. Like a full-grown Doberman pinscher. "If you're staking out the cafeteria to see who's been stealing the cheese and crackers from the vending machine, I confess. A totally justifiable act of mercy."

He gave me a culpable smile. "Sorry about that little kabuki dance in Averill's office."

I sat across from him. "Did they call you or did you call them?"

He toasted my pugnacity. Took a painful sip of tomato juice. "If I hadn't called them, I'm sure they would have called me."

"I'm sure they would have, too."

He turned sideways, propped his feet on the chair next to him. Started retying his shoes. "You promised me you weren't going to get involved, you know."

"I guess I just couldn't stop myself."

"And I guess I'm glad you couldn't."

"So we're even-steven then?"

"Oh no, Mrs. Sprowls. We are not even-steven. I'm still the big bad police detective and you are still the private citizen who's going to mind her p's and q's."

"And it will forever be thus?" I asked.

"Sayeth the Lord," he said.

Our verbal duel was put on hold for a few minutes, while Dusty Eiffel, *The Herald-Union*'s talented young political cartoonist, shaking a double handful of quarters like a rattlesnake's tail, planted himself in front of the candy machine. He bought a bag of M&Ms, a Baby Ruth, a Butterfinger, and a package of Strawberry Twizzlers. He grinned at us. "Drawing funny pictures is hell," he said.

After Dusty went off for his afternoon sugar buzz, Detective Grant got serious. "The fact is, Mrs. Sprowls, I'm running in place with this investigation. In a big pair of muddy clown shoes. As far as physical evidence is concerned, I've got zilch. No fingerprints, no footprints, no tire tracks, no nothing. As far as—"

I stopped him. "What about Andrew Holloway's vomit?"

His Golden Arches eyebrows shot up. "Oh, I've got a whole bag of that. But no proof he didn't throw up when he said he did."

"So his alibi is pretty tight?"

"That's my other problem," he said. "Nobody's alibi is tight. I've talked to everybody you have, and obviously a few more. None of them can prove where they were or weren't that Thursday. Not Andrew Holloway, not Professor Glass, not Fredricka Fredmansky, not the Moffitt-Stumpfs, not the infamous nephew."

Now I looked at him with surprise. "Infamous? What makes Gordon's nephew infamous?"

"A nickel bag of drug convictions for one thing. Possession. Cultivating. Dealing. Selling pipes and bongs out of the trunk of his car. Thirty-seven months of accumulated prison time. The sheriff down there has good reason to believe he's still active in that area, growing marijuana up in the mountains."

I'd found Mickey Gitlin a little spooky, too. Still I felt he deserved the benefit of the doubt. "He wouldn't exactly be the only person in West Virginia doing that, would he?"

"True enough. It's the new moonshine. But his dealing—past and maybe present—does suggest a predilection for making money in less than legal ways."

"It's a big leap from marijuana to murder," I said.

"A leap occasionally made. You are aware of the big monthly nut he has on his kayak business?"

I nodded. "He did say he was having money trouble. And he's sure eager to sell Gordon's house and belongings."

Detective Grant ran his pinky around the inside rim of his empty bottle, collecting the last stubborn drops of tomato juice. He thoughtfully licked his finger like it was a miniature Popsicle. "Eager or desperate?"

I suppose that would have been a good time for me to tell Detective Grant about all those cocoa cans I bought from Mickey. But for some reason he was taking me seriously and I wanted to keep it that way. "Is it really that suspicious?" I asked. I presented him with a plausible scenario: "He hardly knew his uncle. He finds out he's his heir. He quietly goes about his business collecting what's legally his."

"I can buy all that," said Grant. "I can also buy it the other way." He gave me his scenario: "He doesn't know his uncle very well, just as you say. But somehow he does know that he's his heir. Maybe his uncle actually told him. 'Don't worry Mickey, I've taken care of you.' Maybe he snooped around and saw a copy of the will. And maybe he's a greedy, cold-hearted bastard. The world's full of them. And he says, 'Hey, man, I need that inheritance now.'"

"If you can buy my theory, I guess I can buy yours," I said. "But Gordon was hardly a rich man. He taught at a tiny college. He lived in a tiny house full of junk. I'm sure he must have had some insurance and some savings maybe, but heavens to Betsy, I bet I'm worth more than he was. I doubt any of my relatives are plotting to kill me."

Detective Grant folded his arms. Puckered his lips. Let his eyes smile. "Well, I can't offer an opinion on that. I don't know your family. But I would guess you've probably inherited a few bucks here and there yourself, haven't you?"

Boy, did that infuriate me. "You mean an old bag like me must have a lot of dead relatives?" Then I realized what he was saying. "Oh, I see—maybe Gordon had inherited some money himself?"

"More than maybe," he said. "Two years ago Gordon and his sister inherited three hundred thousand each from their well-heeled, 92-year-old father."

"So Mickey would know his uncle at least had that much," I said.

"You've got to figure he did," he said. "Add that

three hundred grand to the value of the house and other assets, and I'd say Mountain Man Mickey will soon be worth a half-million more than he was before dear Uncle Gordon was murdered."

"Oh my."

He reached across the table and tapped my knuckles. "That's why I want you to steer clear of him, Mrs. Sprowls. More than likely he's just a lucky sonofabitch. But there's also a chance he's the kind of lucky sonofabitch who makes his own luck. Which brings us to Kenneth Kingzette."

"You want me to steer clear of him, too, I gather?"

Detective Grant's eyes narrowed, darted uneasily. "Don't you think that theory of yours about the missing toluene is a little—how can I put this without you clunking my noggin with that tea cup of yours—far-fetched?"

I raised my mug playfully. He flinched playfully. I rattled off a string of questions: "Those eighteen drums of toluene are still missing, aren't they? And the Wooster Pike landfill was one of the sites they checked, wasn't it? And Gordon was on the EPA team, wasn't he?"

"All true," he said. "But there are things about that case you don't know."

I bristled. "I know that the president of Madrid Chemical is still missing."

"Which is a good reason for you to stay away from Kingzette—yes?"

"But not the real reason?"

He smiled wearily. "Just do us both a favor, Mrs. Sprowls. Scratch Mr. Kingzette off your list of human curiosities."

"Along with Mickey Gitlin?"

"If you can manage it."

"Anybody else while I'm scratching?"

"That'll do it for now."

Detective Grant put on his overcoat. I rinsed out my mug. He walked me back to the newsroom. "I don't know why you're letting me talk to anybody at all," I grumbled, "if I'm such a royal pain in the bum."

"In a word, desperation," he said. "That's why I asked Tinker and Averill not to be too hard on you. It's come down to either calling in a psychic or letting you dig around. And I must admit, you do have some good instincts for this kind of thing."

"You think so?"

"Yes, I do."

It was an opportunity I couldn't let slip by. "Then let me ask you this—Do you think there might be a link between Gordon's murder and the 1957 murder of David Delarosa?"

He chuckled deep in his throat, like a man who'd just been swindled out of his life savings. "So that's why Marabout wanted that cold case file. You're a real piece of work, Mrs. Sprowls."

I admitted that I was. Then I told him about David's murder. That David and Gordon had been friends. That the musician named Sidney Spikes who was questioned about that murder was the same Shaka Bop who'd played at Gordon's funeral. "So, Detective Grant, do you think it's possible?"

He answered with a sly smile and an indecipherable shrug.

My tête-à-tête with Detective Grant had been a boatload of fun. But it had left me exhausted. And frightened. And embarrassed. And confused about what to do next. If anything at all. And then there was that green-haired girl. I didn't know how to feel about her. Should I cause a stink? Call her professors? Scream at her on the phone until she was reduced to tears? Destroy her skyrocketing journalism career while it was still on the launch pad? Or should I call her and thank her for the story? Yes, she'd broken one of the cardinal rules of journalism by not giving me a chance to respond. But everything she wrote was true. And it had forced me to fess up to Mr. Averill and Tinker. Something I should have done from the get-go.

While I was looking up the college paper in the phone book my own phone rang.

"That you, Maddy?"

It took me a few seconds to place the voice. "Gwen?"

"I'm not keeping you from your work, am I?"

"Other people have already accomplished that," I said.

"Anyhoo—I just wanted you to know how impressed I am. I didn't hear it myself. But Rollie did."

"I don't have the slightest idea what you're talking about, Gwen."

"Your trying to find Sweet Gordon's killer. Charlie Chimera has been talking about you all afternoon. Rollie called me from the office."

Charlie Chimera has that awful talk show on WFLO. He's got quite a racket. He reads the morning headlines in *The Herald-Union*, decides which stories will get his readers' juices flowing, throws in his own two cents, if that much, then yaps and yaps all afternoon like he's a goddamned expert on the subject. Apparently he'd seen *The Harbinger*. "Good gravy! Exactly what is he saying?"

"Oh, you know—how sad it is that the police have to leave solving crimes to little old—"

"Don't you dare finish the sentence."

"Anyhoo—I think it's just terrific that you're taking an interest."

The pythons were back in my stomach. "He's not saying bad things about *The Herald-Union*, is he?"

She artfully evaded the question. "I've told Rollie a million times he'd be more productive if he listened to NPR."

"That bad, is it?"

"I was thinking, Maddy. Why don't you come over for lunch one of these days? You haven't been to the house since we added the lap pool, have you?"

I'd never been to her house at all. Or any of the increasingly bigger houses she and Rollie had occupied over the years. I wasn't exactly on their A list. Or their B, C, D or E lists. "No, I haven't," I said. "And I'd love to come for lunch. You just say when."

To my surprise she did say when. "How about Tuesday?"

I asked Eric to find everything the paper had ever run on Gwendolyn Moffitt-Stumpf.

13

Tuesday, April 10

Eric found a ton of clips on Gwen. There was the huge society page story on her June 1957 wedding to Rollie. There was that horrible Page One story on the plane crash that killed her only child, her 19-year-old son, Rolland Jr. And there was story after story about her good works.

Over the years Gwen had raised her public profile—and the profitability of her husband's insurance agency—by raising money for good causes. She'd raised money for every hospital in the city. She'd raised money for the art museum. For the symphony. The zoo. For Hemphill College. Over the years *The Herald-Union* must have run two or three dozen photos of Gwen handing one of those phony tablecloth-sized checks to some thrilled-to-death recipient.

But it wasn't all hoity-toity, high profile stuff. Gwen also raised money for women's shelters, for food banks, for inner city scholarships, for poor families whose houses burned down around them. After a spate of rapes downtown in the early eighties, she'd even organized self-defense classes for women through the city's Adult Enrichment Program. We'd run a number of stories on that, including a photo of her throwing former Mayor Jerry Hazel for a loop in a jujitsu class.

Gwen was also a big supporter of the democratic process. Her fundraising parties for Republican presidential candidates over the years had won her five invitations to the White House. Her parties for Democratic mayoral and council candidates won Rollie's insurance agency a wheelbarrow full of city contracts.

All in all, Gwen was a real mover and shaker. And even though I'd known her since she was a silly college girl, I was shaking in my boots all the way to her house.

Maybe I'd never been to her house. But I sure knew where it was. It was on Hardihood Avenue, Hannawa's ritziest quarter-mile. And she and Rollie not only lived on Hardihood, they lived within squinting distance of Trawsfyndd Castle, the grand

Tudor-style mansion built in 1911 by Richard Pembrook Hooley, an impoverished Welsh immigrant whose life took a turn for the better when he invented a faster way to bottle beer. Trawsfyndd today is owned by the Hooley family trust. They offer tours seven days a week, at $9.50 a pop. They make you wear those embarrassing elastic booties that look like shower caps.

Gwen and Rollie's house wasn't as big as Trawsfyndd, but it was still a castle, a monstrous gray-bricked Georgian with way too many windows and dozens of shrubs trimmed into perfect circles. I parked under the portico.

I was half expecting to be greeted at the door by a stuffy butler. But it was Gwen herself. And a pair of tap-dancing dachshunds.

Gwen made eye contact with my Dodge Shadow before she made eye contact with me. "Maddy—isn't it good to see you?"

She was wearing a bright yellow cashmere turtleneck and matching silk slacks. She looked like a fancy banana. "And isn't it good to see you?" I said.

She hugged me. She let me hug her back. She threw back her arm like one of those prize girls on *The Price Is Right* and welcomed me inside. The floor in the foyer was covered with alternating black and white tiles. I felt like the last remaining pawn on a giant chessboard, cornered by a crafty queen. "This is just beautiful, Gwen."

She started telling me about the trouble her designer had finding wall sconces that matched the urns she bought on her Aegean cruise, but the dachshunds were begging for attention. I bent as low as I could go and scratched the tops of their flat heads. "And what are your names?"

Gwen introduced them: "This sweet old girl is Queen Strudelschmidt and this handsome fellow is her son and heir, Prince Elmo IV." They dutifully sat back on their long hind-ends and lifted their stubby right paws, which I dutifully shook.

"You a dog person, Maddy?"

"Sort of." I told her about my temporary acquisition of James. About my total ineptitude in canine care.

My misery made her laugh. "All you've got to do is love them," she said.

"Apparently wiener dogs don't have digestive systems," I said.

Dog talk out of the way, Gwen gave me the nickel tour of her million-dollar house. There was one white-walled room after another, every one of them filled with white rugs and white furniture.

The only room that even came close to feeling comfortable was Rollie's den. But even that looked more like a display in a fancy furniture store than a real room. The walls were covered with expensive paneling. The drapes and rugs were hunter green. The pillows on the leather sofa bore the embroidered heads of horses. There was a pair of battered duck decoys on the coffee table. It was a *man's room*, no doubt painstakingly put together by Gwen to give poor Rollie a bit of self-confidence. The wall behind the enormous oak desk was filled with his many awards for selling insurance. The mantel above the fireplace was lined with Rollie's college debate trophies. They were as shiny as the day he won them. I went to admire them. "With Rollie's gift of gab I always figured he'd go into politics," I said.

Gwen scowled. "Thank God he got that dream out of his system."

She led me through the solarium—a tad bit more opulent than the one in Chick Glass' house—to the *natatorium* and the new lap pool she'd bragged about on the phone. "It was hugely expensive, as you can imagine," she said. "But Rollie simply had to have it."

Well, I knew who simply had to have it. Gwen simply had to have it. To keep her husband healthy, wealthy and by all means alive. I crept across the fancy green tiles and peered into the clear, blue-tinged water. I could imagine poor Rollie churning through the water, back and forth and back and forth, while Gwen sat in a lounge chair timing his laps with a stopwatch.

Finally we made it to the kitchen. It was as big as my entire house. Newly remodeled, too, like one of those gourmet pleasure palaces they create right before your eyes on HGTV. She sat me at a tiny bistro table by the bay window overlooking their outdoor pool. She bustled to the kitchen, returning with two crystal bowls filled with unappetizing brown balls. To my relief, she put them on the floor for the dogs. Her second trip to the kitchen produced two steamy black plates, which, to my joy, she put on the table. She introduced me to my lunch: "Poached salmon with basil mayonnaise, saffron rice, and a medley of snow peas, yellow bell pepper and Portobello mushrooms."

"Beats the vending machines at the paper," I said, wishing I hadn't.

She trotted to the serving island for a bottle of blush wine and two slender goblets. "I admire your decision to be a career woman, Maddy. And stay in that same job all those years. It's all I can do to get Rollie out the door in the morning."

The lunch was delicious. The conversation was sometimes hard to digest.

"Are you really investigating Gordon's murder?" she asked as soon as our forks were clinking. "Or is that all just a bunch of media hooey?"

"I wouldn't exactly call it an investigation," I said, trying to spear a wedge of the flaky salmon. "I'm just curious about a few things."

She was having no trouble at all with the salmon. "Aren't we all."

My goal that afternoon, of course, was to get more out of Gwen than she got out of me. To do that I'd have to watch what I said. And listen carefully to what she said. "To tell you the truth," I said, "I'm worried that the police will start barking up the wrong tree."

"Barking up Chick's tree, you mean?"

She was taking me in the direction I wanted to go. I proceeded gingerly. "Up any number of wrong trees. Though Chick could find himself out on a rather flimsy limb, couldn't he? That fight with Gordon at the Kerouac Thing, I mean. Over that damn cheeseburger."

Gwen snapped a snow pea in half with her big white expensive teeth. "They got into that same fight every year."

"This was the first year Gordon ended up dead," I pointed out.

Gwen grew a little testy. "You weren't there, Maddy. This year or any of the others."

I retreated. "You're right. I wasn't. But neither were the police. I want to make sure they see that little annual brouhaha in the right light."

She retreated, too. "Their argument was a little more intense than other years, I guess."

"Really got into it, did they?"

She put down her fork. Folded her hands in her lap. "More than they should have, let's say that."

"They didn't actually slug each other, did they?"

"No, but Chick did throw a bowl of baked beans into the fireplace."

"That's not too bad," I said.

"It was Gordon's bowl of beans," she said.

"I see. Were they drinking?"

"We were all drinking. But no one was intoxicated. Not especially."

"When exactly did the argument start?" I asked her. "Was it right away? Later in the evening?"

"It was a week night. So the party started early. Six-thirty. I suppose they started arguing about nine. After the poems and storytelling."

"What time did the beans go into the fire?"

"Maybe nine-thirty."

Maybe I hadn't been to a Kerouac Thing in thirty years, but I'd attended any number of retirement parties at the Blue Tangerine. The party room there was very fancy and very small. It would have been impossible for Chick and Gordon to keep their argument to themselves. "It sure must have put the kibosh on the fun, huh?"

"At first it was amusing—you know, Chick and Sweet Gordon at it again—but it got uncomfortable after awhile. Embarrassing."

I asked her what happened after the baked bean incident.

She tried not to giggle. "They tried to throw each other into the fireplace. I know it's not funny, but they looked like a couple of bulimic sumo wrestlers."

I had no trouble picturing those two old skinny men pushing at each other. "Did anybody try to stop them?"

"Effie herded Chick into one corner and I herded Gordon into the other."

"You were able to cool them off then?"

Gwen squinted at her rice, as if she'd discovered one of those famous kernels inscribed with the Lord's Prayer. "We tried," she said, "but they were so worked up, Maddy."

"Don't tell me they started wrestling again?"

"No. But they kept sputtering at each other. Chick finally left without him."

I wasn't expecting that little nugget. "Left without him? They came together?"

"They always went to things together, Maddy. To parties. To movies. Even their vacations, I guess."

"They were friends for a lot of years," I said.

Gwen pressed her lips together, as if she were going to cry. "Effie used to say they were like an old married couple. God. I hope Chick didn't lose his head."

"You mean you hope he didn't murder Gordon?"

She dabbed at her eyes with the heel of her hand. Reached for her wine goblet. "You don't think it's possible, do you?"

"Of course not. So who took Gordon home that night?"

Gwen peeked at me over the top of her goblet. "I did."

We talked for another half hour, a little about my life and a lot about hers. We agreed it was a crying shame that it took a tragedy to bring us together again. Then it was time for me to beg off the cherry-almond clafouti she'd baked and head back to the morgue.

I went back to work with a lot of questions. Not the least among them how they got a snazzy place like the Blue Tangerine to serve baked beans.

Saturday, April 14

I'd learned the hard way to James-proof the house before leaving. I made sure the toilet seat was down. I put my slippers in the closet. I went to the kitchen and filled his food and water bowls to the brim. I left a mountain of assorted dog snacks and rawhide chewies on the throw rug in front of the sink. I turned on the TV and flipped the channels to CSPAN, in the hope the boring political talk would put him in a coma. I turned down the ring on my telephone. For some reason when he hears it he goes bananas and starts gnawing on the legs of my dining room table. Finally I gave him a good ear-digging and told him a dozen times what a good boy he was. I headed for the garage, serenaded by his anguished howls.

I drove to Chick's house. This time he didn't know I was coming. I ran through the icy rain to his porch. I rang the bell. I straightened my vertebrae and waited.

He came to the door in a baggy pair of walking shorts, inside-out sweatshirt, messy hair and bare feet. He was not exactly happy to see me. "Miss Marple, I presume?"

I smiled weakly. "I guess you saw the college paper."

"Pretty hard to miss."

"That's why I came. I figured I should explain myself."

He led me to the living room. He motioned for me to sit on the sofa. He sat in a wing-backed chair, on the other side of the room. "I didn't want you to think I suspected you of anything," I began. "Because you know I don't."

"Do I know that, Maddy?"

If he was going to be snippy with me, well, then I was going to be snippy right back. "If you don't, you should."

He softened a smidge. "Why didn't you tell me you were looking into Gordon's murder? I would have helped you any way I could."

"That still goes?"

He leaned back in his chair and wrapped his arms around his skinny torso. Between his big pointy nose, scowling eyes and long bony legs, he looked like the freeze-dried cadaver of a whooping crane. "Of course it still goes," he said.

It would have been a nice time for him to offer me a cup of tea, or even a glass of ice water. But he offered me nothing and I started into the speech I'd been rehearsing all morning and still didn't know how to end: "I don't suspect you of anything. But I'm not so sure the police don't. I know you're a private man, Chick, but unless you're totally forthright about things, you might find yourself in a lot more trouble than you deserve."

He hinged his knees and leaned forward, as if he was going to spring at me, and peck out my eyes. "And just what do you think I should be forthright about?"

"About anything you need to be forthright about," I said. "Like your fight with Gordon at the Kerouac Thing. You told me it didn't amount to anything. And you probably told the police it was nothing, too. But it did amount to something. And from what I hear, you can't account for your time that Thursday."

Chick unfolded from the chair and stalked to the fireplace. "I taught my morning class. Came home. Had lunch. Worked all afternoon grading papers. Had a sandwich. Curled up with Carl

Sandburg and went to bed."

I chose my words carefully. "It's just that some people are questioning your relationship with Gordon."

He swung around. His walking shorts fluttered. He knew what I was getting at. "Do I look like a homosexual to you?"

"Heavens to Betsy, Chick. At my age I don't even remember what a heterosexual man looks like. But people are wondering."

"You mean you're wondering."

He was right, of course, but I stuck to my guns. "People are wondering."

He started to boil. "If Gordon and I were that—wouldn't that make it less likely that I killed him?"

"People who are just friends rarely kill each other," I said. "Lovers, all the time."

He flopped next to me on the sofa. Rested his head on the Indian blanket across the back. "I did not kill him, Maddy."

"And you've got Carl Sandburg to vouch for your evening?"

He threw up his hands, like an Italian waiter carrying giant bowls of pasta. "People can believe what they want to believe. You included."

I stood up and fidgeted with the bottom of

my sweater. "Would it be okay if I used your bathroom?"

My luck was with me. He told me the bathroom was upstairs. Which is exactly where I wanted to go.

I climbed the hollow steps. I leaned on the bathroom sink and took off my shoes. I remembered the day I'd visited how I could hear the floor squeaking above me. I slid carefully into the hallway and shuffled in my stocking feet to his office. I quietly orbited his big messy desk. I searched the row of photographs on his bookshelves, until I found the one I wanted—the one he'd shown me the day I came to lunch, the one of Gordon and him at Jack Kerouac's grave.

I studied their young faces. Were those the faces of friends or lovers? I studied the easy, intimate way they were leaning against each other. Had I missed something all those years ago? Was I missing something now? Then I heard the floor squeak and saw Chick's frozen silhouette in the doorway. He came toward me. He lifted his arm. He took the photograph. He studied it the way I'd been studying it.

I took a shaky breath. If he intended to kill me, it apparently was not going to be immediately. "I'm sorry. I just wanted to see it again," I said. "It's such a wonderful picture of you two."

He looked at my feet. He smiled sadly. He wasn't buying my explanation but he didn't seem to care. "That was a long time ago, Maddy. A million years."

I hadn't come to wheedle a confession out of Chick. Or to convince myself that he was innocent. I'd come to see that photograph again and somehow get an answer to the question I was now going to ask: "Who took it, anyway?"

He glared at me over his beak.

I played down my curiosity. "It's just something I always wonder when I see an old photo like that. Who was there but couldn't be in the picture because they had to take it. My father took us all over the place on vacations—to Niagara Falls and Maine and Atlantic City and one year in the middle of summer to Florida—and it was like he never went along, because he was never in any of the pictures. Of course, maybe you had one of those cameras with a timer."

He put the photo back on the shelf. "Penelope Yarrow took it," he said.

"I don't think I ever met her."

"She was Gordon's old girlfriend."

"Oh."

14

Saturday, April 28

The Easter Bunny didn't bring me anything but a long, cold, rainy, boring-as-hell weekend with James. But Eric Chen had a nice present for me on Monday—the address and phone number of my Lawrence's fourth and final wife. I immediately picked up my phone and punched her number, before I could chicken out. I caught her at home, right as she was leaving for work. I apologized for bothering her. She apologized for not having time to talk. "Let me get right to the point then," I said. "Do you have any of Lawrence's old clippings from his college newspaper days?"

"Oh my, yes," she said. She invited me to lunch.

And so the next Saturday Eric and I headed for Sharon, Pennsylvania. Eric agreed to drive his pickup. I agreed to buy his gas, his breakfast, and his six-pack of 20-ounce Mountain Dews.

We left Hannawa at nine-thirty in the morning, heading north on I-491 under a blanket of dirty spring clouds. We shivered at a McDonald's for a half hour—my egg-and-sausage sandwich making a better hand warmer than an appetizing breakfast—and then we headed east on State Route 82, across Ohio's half-empty northeast corner. We went through Mantua Corners and Hiram, Garrettsville and Levittsburg, Warren and Brookfield. At eleven-thirty we slipped across the Pennsylvania line and headed for Sharon.

Sharon is only one-tenth the size of Hannawa—sixteen or seventeen thousand people—but it has the same big problems. The steel mills and factories have closed, robbing thousands of local families of the good, steady wages they once depended on. Most of the stores downtown have either gone out of business or moved to the suburbs. The old residential neighborhoods in the hills above the Shenango River are slip-sliding into despair.

Ironically, Sharon in recent years has become something of a tourist destination, drawing a steady trickle of daytrippers from Pittsburgh, Cleveland,

Erie, Buffalo and Hannawa. They don't exactly come to suck up the scenery. They come to shop. Sharon boasts the world's largest candy store, the world's largest outlet for off-price women's clothing, and the world's largest shoe store.

It was at this shoe store—Reyers is the name of it—that I was to meet Lawrence's widow. She was an assistant manager there.

I'd never been to Reyers before. But I'd sure heard about it. It was located in an old supermarket right downtown. It had over 150,000 pairs of shoes to sort through, in every size, style and color imaginable.

There was a NO FOOD OR BEVERAGES sign on the door. I folded my arms and waited while Eric guzzled the last two inches of his Mountain Dew.

Inside, Eric and I went our separate ways. He headed for the men's shoes. I headed for the women's. I hurried through the high heels and pumps, lingered in the flats, finally gravitating toward a sale table piled high with Indian moccasin slippers. They were only six dollars and James, as you remember, had gnawed my old fluffy ones. I started looking for a size seven.

I was spotted by a dowdy saleswoman in a beige pantsuit. She had short gray hair, fake pearls the size of turtle eggs, a smile poured from quick drying cement. "Is someone helping you?" she asked.

"Actually, I'm here to see Dory Sprowls."

"Actually, I am Dory Sprowls," she said. "Which probably makes you Maddy Sprowls."

"It does."

We shook hands like a couple of bankers. Gave each other the once over. I don't know what she was expecting, but I know what I was expecting. I was expecting a much younger woman. A much more attractive woman. A tootsie-type with big bazooms, like Lawrence's second and third wives. But looking at Dory Sprowls was like looking at my reflection in an old storm door. In size, shape, age and general lack of attractiveness, we were two old peas in a pod. "I'm sorry I'm early," I said. "You never know how long it's going to take you to drive anywhere this time of year. Especially when you're not exactly sure where you're going."

She pawed the air, just the way I do. "Don't I know it," she said.

We found Eric in the boot department. We headed for his truck. I sat in the middle. We drove to her house on the bluffs east of downtown. It was a modest Cape Cod surrounded by unruly shrubs.

She gave us the nickel tour and then sat us down at the kitchen table. Before leaving for work, she'd put on a crock pot of beef stew. She ladled out three big bowls, tore apart a loaf of rye bread, and put on a kettle of water for our tea. She gave Eric a fancy goblet for his fresh bottle of Mountain Dew.

I'd promised myself that I wasn't going to compare notes with her about Lawrence. But that's exactly what we both started to do, before we could swallow our first spoonfuls of stew.

I told her how I'd met Lawrence at Hemphill College, in a freshman English class. How it wasn't exactly love at first sight, but a long friendship that eventually *soured* into romance. She loved that.

She told me how she'd met him, in Pittsburgh, in a community college cooking class for singles. How their mutual difficulty mincing garlic evolved into something more.

We discovered that we'd both been married to Lawrence the same number of years—six. We discovered that neither of us had taken the time to find another man.

For a long while we howled about the quirky little things we couldn't stand about our mutual husband—his annoying habit of singing at the breakfast table, the way he clipped his toenails in the living room, how he'd leave his ashtrays on the floor in front of the toilet. It was finally Dory who got down to brass tacks: "He told me he'd been a skunk with you," she said. "And the two wives after you."

"You knew about all that and you married him anyway?"

She laughed at her stupidity. "Yes, I did. And he was a skunk with me, too. Until his angina got so bad he couldn't climb our bedroom stairs let alone somebody else's."

I could see in her eyes that she'd loved him. And I suppose she saw that same weakness in mine. "He did have his good points," I said.

"Yes, he did," she agreed.

When neither of us could think of any, we turned to the reason I'd come. "Like I said on the phone, Dory, there's been a murder at the college. A very popular professor. And there's a chance—a very small chance—that his murder is related to another murder. Back in the fifties. When Lawrence and I were seniors. I thought there might be something helpful in his old college clippings."

She pointed to a big blue Rubbermaid storage tub on the kitchen counter. "Help yourself."

My stew was already getting cold but I went

straight for the tub. I peeled off the lid and ran my fingers across the tops of the folders stuffed inside. The air around me was immediately thick with the beautiful stench of old newsprint. "This is so good of you. Eric and I can get them copied and back to you in a couple of hours, I'm sure."

She pointed at me and then my bowl. "Finish your stew. You can take Lawrence's folders with you. And keep them."

"Keep them? You sure?"

Again she jabbed her finger at my bowl. I obediently tiptoed back to the table. "Those years belong to you," she said. "I've got lots of other tubs that belong to me."

We finished our stew. Eric put the Rubbermaid tub in the back of his truck. We drove Dory back to the shoe store. I went inside with her and bought two pairs of those darling six-dollar moccasins.

Then Eric made me go with him to Daffin's, supposedly, as I said before, the world's largest candy store. We ogled the chocolate animals on display—the 400-pound turtle, the quarter-ton rhinoceros—and then stocked up on leftover Easter candy. We headed for home.

Eric had one hand on the steering wheel and the

other around the neck of a huge milk-chocolate rabbit. He'd already eaten one ear and was making quick work of the other. "She was nice, wasn't she?" he said.

I was nibbling on a marshmallow peep. "Yes, she was." I just love those marshmallow peeps, especially when they're stale and chewy. This one, unfortunately, was still fresh. But I knew that wasn't going to stop me from eating ten or twelve of the damn things before we got back to Hannawa.

Eric finished the other ear. "No offense, but she reminded me of you."

I had to agree. "Spooky wasn't it—almost like Lawrence came back to me after all those years of flopping around."

The rabbit's entire head now disappeared into his mouth. "Feel vindicated, do you?"

"Vindicated? It made me feel like shit."

And it did make me feel like shit. Lawrence, I'm sure, had loved me well enough. But he threw it away for better sex. For twenty-five years he hopped from one anatomically advantaged woman to another, marrying some of them, not marrying most. Then in middle age—older and wiser, his body parts apparently starting to wear out—he married me again. Or at least he married a woman exactly like me. And then the bastard cheated on me all over again! By proxy!

Meanwhile, I'd holed myself up in that damn little convent of mine on Brambriar Court. Pitying myself for the way I was. Pitying Lawrence for the way he was. Romanticizing that nano second of a marriage we had until it was right up there with Romeo and Juliet. In all those years the only man I'd been intimate with was Dale Marabout. He was just an awkward horny kid at the time, twenty years my junior. As nice as it was—and it was nice—it was only a brief sexual vacation. Dale moved on to a woman his own age. I slinked back into my emotional exile, into my martyrdom, into my Morgue Mama-ness.

And now, thanks to the beast who put that bullet in Sweet Gordon's head, I was being forced to fall in love with Lawrence Sprowls all over again. To dream about a future with him all over again. To have my soul shattered by his infidelities all over again. One thing was clear—I was going to get the sonofabitch who killed Gordon if it killed me.

I made Eric stop his truck, right in the middle of the road. I slid out and went to the back. I pulled out the plastic tub and lugged it back to the cab. I squeezed in next to it. I ordered Eric to "Drive!"

I put an entire marshmallow chick in my mouth. I pulled out a folder full of Lawrence's clippings and started to dig.

Every clipping I read dislodged a memory. Every memory stirred an emotion:

There was Lawrence's story on Adlai Stevenson's suffocating speech at the college in the fall of 1955. I remember Effie leading us in a hilarious fake prayer afterward at Mopey's. "Good and merciful God," she implored, "please do not let the Democrats nominate Adlai again in fifty-six. Eisenhower will surely humiliate him again, and we beats are already as beat as our beatness can bear."

There was Lawrence's story on the controversial decision by the college to put television sets in the dormitory lounges. I showed it to Eric. "Believe it or not," I said, "I was one of the forty-seven snobs who signed the petition to have them removed."

"You'd still sign it today, wouldn't you?" he said.

"In a heartbeat," I said.

There were oodles of sports stories—Lawrence absolutely hated writing sports—and oodles of stories on the useless projects undertaken by the college's fraternities and sororities. There were also lots of those inane "man on the street" stories asking students what they thought of the latest world events. I found one where he'd actually quoted me. It was about the Montgomery, Alabama, bus boycott: "Negroes should be able to sit wherever they darn well please," opines sophomore library science major Dolly Madison. I remembered how upset I was that he'd quoted me saying *darn well* instead of *damn well.* I remembered how I'd ranted on and on about censorship and the need for journalistic courage at such a crucial time in history. I remembered refusing to kiss him for a week.

There was a story on the debate team winning the state championship. DEBATERS TALK THEIR WAY TO THE TOP, the headline read. Above the story was a photograph showing Rollie and his three equally nerdy debating partners—Don Rodino, Herbert Giffels and Elgin "Bud" Wetzel—standing stiffly in front of the Ohio State capitol with their big first-place trophies. Lawrence had taken the photo, too. I recalled how angry Lawrence had been when the editor sent him to Columbus to cover the debate tournament. It was Easter vacation, after all, and the Baked Bean Society had planned a week's worth of sleepless celebrating. I remembered seeing him off at the bus stop. He had his ugly plaid suitcase, his portable typewriter and *The Harbinger*'s big clunky camera around his neck. I could still see the long neck of the flashbulb attachment banging him in the chin every time he turned his face. "They better win the fucker," he growled as I hugged him good-bye.

They did win, of course, and Lawrence dutifully took the photo and wrote the story. According to the date scribbled in the margin, the story ran one week after Easter.

Winning a state title in anything is a big story for a college paper, even in debate. But I doubt too many students read Lawrence's story. They would have been more interested in another story that ran in that same edition—the one about David Delarosa's murder.

I flipped through the files, forward and backward. I knew Lawrence hadn't written any stories himself on David's murder, of course, but I thought maybe he'd saved some of the stories written by others. If he had saved them, they weren't in that tub.

But I did find one very small story on Jack Kerouac's visit to the college the previous November that tickled me. I read it aloud to Eric. "Listen to this: 'Nationally known avant-garde poet Jack Kerouac will appear at The E Pluribus Unum Coffee House, 2748 West Tuckman St., on Friday,

November 23, at 8 p.m.' Paragraph. 'Kerouac's novel, *The Town and the City*, was published in 1949. A new novel, *On the Road*, will be published some time next year.' Paragraph. 'The appearance is sponsored by The Meriwether Square Baked Bean Existentialist Society. Admission is free.'"

Eric was not exactly impressed with Lawrence's story. "That's it? The great Jack Kerouac was coming to your puny backwater college and that's all the ink they gave it?"

I put the little clipping back in the folder. I put the folder back in the Rubbermaid tub. "Kerouac was a nobody then," I said. I rested my head on the back of the seat, closed my eyes and chewed the head off another marshmallow peep. "We were all nobodies then," I said.

Eric was thoughtful enough to carry the tub inside for me. But he wouldn't stay for dinner no matter how many times I asked him. He was anxious to get to Borders, to play chess with his worthless friends. "Go on," I said, "leave an old woman all alone on a Saturday night."

I laughed along with him. I wished he'd realized I wasn't joking.

I watched him back out of my driveway. I

watched his truck disappear up my street. I'd lived by myself in that house for forty years, but I couldn't remember ever feeling more alone than I did that afternoon. Not even James' silly face could cheer me. I put on my old gardening clothes. It was only four o'clock. I could spend a couple hours in my flower beds before the sun went down. But I made it no farther than the glider on my back porch. I pulled my legs up to my chin. I wrapped my arms around my shins. I rocked myself like a baby in a cradle. I watched the squirrels. I watched the rabbits. I watched the sparrows hop about on my trumpet vines. I watched the daylight fade. I wiped my nose and my eyes on my sweatshirt and went inside.

I dumped a can of tomato soup into a saucepan and put the burner on low. I pulled out my plastic cutting board and assembled my favorite sandwich—two thick pieces of Texas toast, two pieces of provolone cheese, a layer of thinly sliced tomato, a sprinkling of oregano. I sprayed my big iron griddle with Pam. I grilled my sandwich until the provolone was gooey, until the sad scent of oregano filled every inch of my little house. I clicked on the living room TV. I watched the news and then an old Lawrence Welk rerun on PBS. I put on my pajamas and moved my exciting night of television viewing to my bedroom.

Luckily for my mental health there was nothing worth a damn on television that Saturday night. The more I clicked my remote, the angrier I got—at the cable company, at the culture that produced such drivel, at God and the wicked world he created, finally at myself. "Get a grip, Dolly!" I heard myself growl.

I rarely call myself by my real first name like that. So when I do, I know I'd better obey.

I got out of bed and made a mug of Darjeeling tea. I gathered up my portable phone, my address book, some stationery, and a big flat book to write on. I crawled back into bed. I had work to do.

First I called Eric. It was only ten o'clock but he was already home. Knowing Eric, I did not have to ask if he was alone. "I've got another person for you to find," I said. I waited for him to find something to write on. I waited for him to find something to write *with*. "Her name is Penelope Yarrow. Y.A.R.R.O.W. She's an old girlfriend of Gordon's apparently. From the sixties."

Next I called Andrew J. Holloway III. I expected to get his answering machine, but he, too, was home, and from the silence on the other end, apparently just as alone as Eric and me. I got right to my question: "Exactly how long could a little slip of paper survive in a dump? Before rotting away or whatever paper does?"

"That depends on a lot of things," he said. "Was it buried? Was it exposed to the air? To moisture? Was it sealed in something? If so, in what?"

"So theoretically, a piece of paper could survive for fifty years or more out there?"

"Under the right conditions—sure."

I got down to the nitty-gritty. "Did Professor Sweet ever tell his students to be on the lookout for a restaurant receipt? Bags or wrappers with the word Mopey's on it?"

"Uh—no."

I put a chuckle in my voice. "Just the Betsy Wetsy dolls, old soda pop bottles and cocoa cans?"

He put a chuckle in his, too. "That's right."

Now I made sure my voice sounded deadly serious. "Did you know he actually saved all the cocoa cans—in his personal collection?"

"No, I didn't," Andrew said.

15

Monday, April 30

I woke up in a surprisingly good mood for a Monday. I hadn't caught up on any of my yard work over the weekend. And I wasn't one inch closer to finding Gordon's murderer. But I had managed to exorcise a demon or two, my what-if-Lawrence-hadn't-strayed demon in particular, and good gravy, I was just feeling better about things. I took James on a longer walk than usual and doubled up on his treats. I put on a spring blouse and a pair of lightweight khakis. I dug around in the jewelry basket on my dresser for my bluebird brooch.

I got to the morgue right at nine. I made my tea and got to work marking up the weekend papers. At noon I headed down the hill to Ike's.

"Morgue Mama!" he sang out. "I didn't know

you were rewarding us with your presence today."

"I didn't know myself until five minutes ago."

"Well, it's good to see your face," he said. "I just hope you're in the mood for chicken salad."

"Sounds delightful." I sat at a table by the window. It gave me a beautiful, unimpeded view of the empty storefronts across the street.

Ike brought me my tea then got busy making my sandwich. "What kind of bagel you want that on?" he bellowed over the top of his espresso machine.

"Surprise me," I bellowed back.

He chose pumpernickel. He piled the chicken salad high. He went crazy with the cream cheese.

Ike's lunchtime rush only lasts about twenty minutes. As soon as things quieted down he joined me, bringing me a free bag of potato chips. "You getting anywhere with that murder?" he asked.

It tumbled out of my mouth before I could stop myself. "You're pretty well plugged into the black community—right?"

He laughed and helped himself to a potato chip. "I'm black, if that's what you mean by plugged in."

I knew I was blushing. "Let me try that again—What's the general opinion of Shaka Bop?"

He laughed harder. "Good Lord, Maddy, that was even worse than before. There are eighty thousand black people in this city. We don't exactly get together every Saturday night in some big hall and vote on general opinions."

If he could tease, I could tease. "No? We white people do."

"Oh, I know you do!" he answered. "Oh, I know you do!"

We laughed and ate potato chips and then we got down to a serious appraisal of Shaka Bop.

Shaka, of course, was still going by his real name when David Delarosa was murdered. One night at Jericho's, during his last set of the night, he announced his plans to leave town. It came just two weeks after the police tried to pin David's murder on him. He hooked the neck of his saxophone over his shoulder and pulled the microphone to his lips. "If Hannawa don't love Sidney Spikes no more," he said in an affected sharecropper's voice, "then ol' Sidney's through with Hannawa." It was an angry good-bye. We begged him to stay but we understood when he didn't.

I remember Effie and Chick being especially upset that the city's racist police had driven Sidney away from the people he loved. But to tell you the truth, I had the feeling that he was ready to move on anyway. He was a very talented musician. His reputation was spreading. It was time for him to move on to a bigger city and a bigger life.

The bigger city Sidney chose was San Francisco. As the years went by, word got to us that he was playing up and down the west coast, from Vancouver to L.A., that he was making occasional forays into New York to record. Sidney seemed to be on the cusp of fame. But the 1960s were not good to jazz musicians. Clubs closed by the bucketful. Record labels switched to rock and roll and soul. I remember Gordon reading us a letter from Sidney at one of our parties. It was a sad letter. Sidney said he'd been forced to "hang up my horn for a while" and take a job as a mechanic at a garage in Oakland.

In 1968 we learned that Sidney had joined the Black Panther Party. We also learned that he'd changed his name—legally changed it—to Shaka Bop. I was divorced from Lawrence by then. And I'd pretty much stopped running with the old Hemphill College crowd. But I do remember Gordon and Effie dragging me to Hannawa's first McDonald's about that time, to see what all the fuss was about. I remember Gordon explaining to us over those miserable little hamburgers that Shaka was the name of a great Zulu king during the early nineteenth century, famous both for his brilliance and his brutality.

Anyway, Shaka moved back to Hannawa in 1973. He formed a band and played at weddings and block parties. He helped organize a food bank for the poor. He ran for City Council and lost. He opened a small auto repair shop in Thistle Hill, a gritty inner city neighborhood just south of downtown.

A few days after Gordon's funeral, I'd gone to my files in the basement and dug up a feature we'd run on Shaka back in 1978. It was one of the last stories Cynthia Buckland wrote for *The Herald-Union* before moving up to *The Columbus Dispatch*:

> HANNAWA—Shaka Bop says he isn't just fixing cars, he's fixing lives.
>
> Since moving back to Hannawa five years ago, the popular jazz musician and one-time member of the radical Black Panther Party has been making sure that the city's working poor can

get to their jobs.

"Being poor isn't easy," said Bop, who was born on the city's south side as Sidney Thomas Spikes in 1933. "You get a job that doesn't pay anything and it's nowhere near where they let you live. Maybe you can get there by bus but maybe you need a car."

And those cars, he pointed out, are hardly brand new.

"You scrape together a few hundred bucks and buy an old beater," he said. "You pray every morning it's going to get you to work and you pray all day long it'll get you home at night."

That's where Shaka

> Bop's Auto Run Right shop in Thistle Hill comes in. Bop and his team of talented young mechanics work with missionary zeal to keep the city's old cars on the road, whether customers can afford to pay for the repair work or not.
>
> "Half the time we charge only half of what other garages would charge," Bop said. "And half the time we charge nothing but a smile."

"You're not saying Shaka Bop had something to do with that professor's murder, are you?" Ike asked. His voice was uncharacteristically defensive.

I pawed the air. "No more than I'm saying he had anything to do with David Delarosa's murder. But he was a part of the crowd Gordon ran with. On the periphery of it anyway. Back then and now.

Maybe he has some helpful impressions."

Ike squinted at me. "And that's why you came to see me today, is it, Maddy? To see if Ike the Black Man had some helpful impressions of him? Before you ask him for helpful impressions of others?"

"Something like that," I admitted.

Ike softened. Pretended to pout. "And I thought it was my chicken salad."

"I've offended you."

He didn't move in his chair. But I could feel his soul reach across the little table and give me an enormous hug. "Oh, Maddy," he whispered, "why does this world have to be the way it is? Everybody categorized by this and that? What was God thinking?" He took the last potato chip from the bag and broke it in half. He didn't hand my half to me. He slipped it straight into my mouth. "We black people have a very high opinion of Shaka Bop. Including this black man. It pissed us off when they hauled him in fifty years ago and it would piss us off again if he got unnecessarily dragged into this."

I sucked on the chip like it was a communion wafer. My knees were quivering from the intimacy Ike had allowed to flower between us, as innocent as it was. "I hope I haven't unnecessarily pissed you off, Ike."

"You know, Maddy," he said. "I have always wanted to meet the great Mr. Bop in person. When you gonna go see him, anyway?"

I walked back up the hill to the paper. My bluebird brooch felt like it weighed five hundred pounds. Which was a good thing. After that half hour with Ike both my brain and my heart felt like they were pumped full of helium.

Anyway, the second the elevator door opened I knew a big story was breaking. People in the newsroom were talking louder. Walking faster. Huddling for impromptu meetings. Using other people's phones. Mindlessly gulping from other people's coffee mugs. "What gives?" I asked Margaret Newman, who was wiggling into her raincoat as she ran by.

"They got the other brother," she said.

I raced to Dale Marabout's desk. His phone was cradled under his chin. His feet were propped on the corner of his desk. From the way he was rhythmically tapping his toes together I gathered he was on hold, listening to some peppy tune. "Randy Depew?" I asked him.

He Grouchoed his eyebrows. "They got him in Las Vegas. Some hot sheets motel. Pizza delivery guy recognized him from *America's Most Wanted*."

Before I could ask another question, Dale twisted toward his computer screen and started spitting questions into his phone. I headed for my desk.

I just love it when a big story breaks like that. Oh yes, big stories are usually tragic stories. But just the way the newsroom comes alive to cover them, it's better than—well it's better than almost anything.

And so I settled in at my desk and watched everybody else work. Dale had the lead story to write, about how Randy Depew was apprehended and what was likely to happen to him when police got him back to Hannawa. Bob Beyer and Nan Ritchey put a sidebar together chronicling events from Paul Zuduski's murder to the shootout in Hannawa Falls. Margaret was pulled off her feature on the county's disappearing frog population and sent to police headquarters to catch any crumbs that came out of there. Burl Chancellor was given the politics sidebar, how a future trial would affect Congresswoman Zuduski-Lowell's re-election. Our TV writer, Roxanne Kindig, was assigned the *America's Most Wanted* angle, how that show was making it impossible for criminals to evade justice. Other reporters were pulled in to the coverage as needed. All afternoon Managing Editor Alec Tinker trotted from desk to desk, like one of those damn plate spinners you used to see on *The Ed Sullivan Show*, to make sure it all came together by deadline.

There was one angle of the story that we weren't covering. The angle that affected me. With Richard Depew safely locked away, Scotty Grant just might find a little more time for Sweet Gordon's murder. To tell you the truth, I wasn't sure if I liked that prospect or not.

I stayed in the morgue until six-thirty and drove down to pick up Ike. The lights in his shop were already turned off. He flipped the CLOSED sign. Locked the door behind him. Trotted to my car. "If I'm going to close early for you, the least you can do is get here when you say," he complained.

Downtown Hannawa doesn't have much rush hour traffic anymore, and what little it does have was over long ago. I made a wide U-turn and headed south. "I'm a woman with responsibilities," I said.

He laughed until I laughed.

And I needed to laugh. I was so nervous about seeing Shaka Bop I could barely breathe.

"He knows you're coming?" Ike asked.

"What fun would that be?" I asked back.

We were in Thistle Hill in two minutes. The streets there were narrow, mostly brick, mostly one-way. The houses were a hundred years old and looked it. Many yards were surrounded with chain-link fences. Many of those fences featured BEWARE OF THE DOG signs.

We passed Garfield High School and a half-dozen abandoned factories. We crossed Sixth Street and pulled into the bumpy, gravel-covered parking lot that surrounded Shaka Bop's garage. We wound through the uneven rows of old cars until we found a place to park.

The garage was modest but it was big. It was constructed of cement blocks. It had five bays. A hand-painted sign ran the full length of the building. SHAKA BOP'S AUTO RUN RIGHT it said.

A tall, wide-shouldered man appeared out of nowhere at my car door. He bent low and smiled at me through the window. It was Shaka Bop himself. He wasn't wearing his signature dashiki or porkpie hat that day. He was wearing a crisp white shirt and a blood-red necktie, a navy blue spring jacket zipped tight around his ample belly.

I rolled down the window. "You remember me?" I asked.

He squinted at me and then smiled. "Pop your hood for me, Dolly."

"I didn't come for my car, though God knows the old thing needs plenty of work," I said. "I came to see you about Gordon."

Shaka's smile faded. Then recovered. "Pop it!" he said.

So I popped my hood and he strolled slowly to the front of my car. He lifted the hood and hooked it open. Ike and I joined him.

Shaka rested his hands on the grill and leaned over the engine. He studied all the dirty old parts, scatting some wonderful jazz under his breath. I introduced him to Ike. "This is my friend, Ike," I said. "Ike's Coffee Shop downtown."

Shaka didn't take his eyes off my engine. "Oh yes. Ike's Coffee Shop. Good to see you making a stand down there, Ike."

Ike put out his hand, but when no hand came back at him, withdrew it into his coat pocket. He remained cordial nonetheless. "Maddy's told me all about those years in Meriwether Square."

Shaka looked up now. "Too bad you couldn't have been there," he said.

I'm sure Ike knew what he meant. I know I did. Meriwether Square was as segregated as every other neighborhood in Hannawa in those years. Unless a black man had a saxophone or a trumpet or a pair of drumsticks, he was not welcome in any of those clubs.

Shaka checked my oil and antifreeze. He carefully lowered the hood, as if it might disintegrate if he let it drop. "You've got some catastrophically cracked belts and hoses, Dolly. God knows you need a tune-up. But other than that, everything appears surprisingly copacetic for an old honey wagon like this."

Shaka wrapped his arm around me and walked me to the garage. Ike followed. By the time we reached his office, Shaka had my car keys and my agreement to let a couple of his *miracle men* give my Dodge Shadow a *good going over* while we talked.

Shaka had a huge wooden desk, piled high with car parts, diet Coke cans, old newspapers and magazines. He sat behind the clutter. He folded his hands across his belly. Ike and I sat across from him, on an old car seat propped against the wall.

"The love sure flowed back then, didn't it, Dolly?" Shaka said. He was swiveling back and forth in his chair, like the confident king he was. "Though I don't recall any of your love ever flowing my way." His eyes studied my reaction, then shifted to Ike, to study his.

I wanted to see Ike's reaction, too. But I didn't dare look at Ike. Instead I watched as my car disappeared into one of the bays at the other end of the garage. "I guess by now you know I'm looking into Gordon's murder," I said.

Shaka sifted through the newspapers on his desk, pulling out a copy of *The Harbinger*. He snapped the story about me with his thumb and forefinger and grinned. "Soon as I saw this little nugget of journalistic joy, I knew it would just be a matter of time before I saw you, too."

I stretched my neck toward his desk like an ostrich, as if I'd never seen the story before. "You did?"

He handed me the paper. "Murder ain't a big thing in Thistle Hill. I've been to more premature funerals over the years than I care to think about. But over on your side of town, Dolly? Around that happy little college? Those happy little neighborhoods filled with all those happy, happy people? There've been just two murders in fifty years and both involving Sweet Gordon. Next stop Coincidence City and don't forget your luggage. First his libidinous chum. Then the professor himself. Oh, yes! Soon as I saw that little write-up, I knew the sagacious Dolly Madison Sprowls must've put two and two together. Knew sooner or later she'd squeeze the saxophone man into her math."

Shaka always had a way with words. They were musical notes to him, to be arranged in surprising ways, to agitate and enlighten. So while I was prepared for all sorts of interesting things to come out of his mouth that evening, I hadn't expected anything quite as poetic as *libidinous chum.* "Why'd you call David Delarosa that?"

"Because that young beagle was always sniffing for a snuggle bunny. You remember that night at Jericho's, don't you, Dolly? That sucker punch I took for you?"

A squeaky self-conscious giggle spilled out of me. "I don't think many men ever took me for a snuggle bunny, no matter how drunk they were."

Shaka laughed like a horse. "That had more to do with your attitude than your attributes, Dolly. And you stuck to that boyfriend of yours like wallpaper on a convent wall."

"Lawrence and I were engaged by then," I said.

"Indeed, you were," said Shaka. "But that night, as I recall, you were quite alone."

I told him that Lawrence was in Columbus,

covering the state debate tournament.

"Doesn't matter where he was," he said. "You were alone. And David Beaglerosa was on the hunt."

I didn't much like it that Shaka was questioning me—after all I'd come to question him—but I did want his impression of David Delarosa. "He never hit on me," I said.

Shaka horse-laughed again. "But he sure hit on me."

"But that was a racial thing, wasn't it?"

Shaka was studying Ike again. "The fact that I was of the Negro persuasion didn't help matters, I'll give you that. And to tell you the truth, I don't know if he specifically had designs on you or not. Chances are you were just a handy feminine foil. A way to keep me from digging any and all the white birds perched around the table that night."

"Chances are," I agreed.

He playfully patted his stomach. "I'm a fat old man now. Can't get a bird of any feather to look at me twice. But in my prime I rarely had the pillows to myself."

"Including that night I understand."

Memories of a different time drained the confidence from Shaka's eyes. "Thank God I didn't."

"And thank God it was Effie sharing the pillows?"

He nodded. "Imagine if I'd gone home with some other white girl that night? It took some real cojones for her to tell the police she'd been with me, I'll tell you that."

Ike hadn't said a word since we'd lowered ourselves onto that old car seat. He said something now: "They would have strapped you in the electric chair fast as they could."

Shaka's answer was little more than a whisper. "That they would have, my brother."

"Let's hope they don't get any ideas now," I said.

Shaka leaned back in his chair. He put his hands behind his head and rocked. "That your way of asking me if I have an alibi for the day Sweet Gordon was killed?"

"She's not the most subtle woman," Ike said.

Shaka winked at him. "No, she's not. But as long as I've got her old Dodge hostage in there, I'm going to operate on the assumption she's on my side."

"I'm on Gordon's side," I said.

Shaka took off an imaginary hat and tipped it to me. "So am I. He was a fine man."

"And you're a fine man," I said.

Shaka didn't quite know what to do with that. First he smiled and then he frowned. "I was here until ten-thirty that Thursday. Seeing if I couldn't coax another hundred-thousand miles out of the Apple Street Baptist Church's old Sunday school bus."

"Have the police talked to you?" I asked.

"I've told them that, yes. But I was here alone. From five on, anyway." He hesitated. "I don't know if that gets me off the hook or not."

The coroner's report, of course, had put Gordon's death sometime between noon and midnight that Thursday, anywhere between 36 and 48 hours before Andrew J. Holloway called from the landfill. "Neither do I," I said.

Shaka rubbed the twitch out of his nostrils. "Well, they haven't hauled me downtown yet."

I struggled off the car seat and peered through the glass office door. My car was high on a rack. Two young mechanics were standing underneath it, heads tipped back like a pair of bewildered turkeys trying to figure out where the rain was coming from. "Did the police ask you why you weren't at this year's Kerouac Thing?"

"No, they didn't ask me that."

"And what would you have told them?"

"The brutal truth, Dolly. That sometimes those stuffy old poops are more than I can take. Every damn year reading those same old cob-webby poems. Telling those same old hyperventilated stories. Living in the past like they're already dead."

"One of them is," I said.

"Another premature funeral," Shaka said.

I asked him what he knew about Gordon's argument with Chick over Jack Kerouac's hamburger. "Another reason why I didn't go," he said. "Who wants to listen to two old white men argue about cheese?"

"They really got into it this year," I said.

"That's what I hear," he said.

I asked him what he knew about Gordon's relationship with Chick.

"Sometimes I got one vibe, sometimes I got another," he said.

I asked him if he thought Chick could have murdered Gordon.

"No more than I could've," he said.

Then I asked him if he thought Gordon could have murdered David Delarosa.

"I'd like to give you the same answer," he said. "But the truth is, after those unrequited fisticuffs at

Jericho's, I was neither surprised nor dismayed to learn of that boy's fatal fall. There was something infinitely unlikable about Mr. Delarosa."

Finally I asked him if he knew what Gordon might have been looking for at the landfill. "The young cat he used to be," he said. "That's what I always figured."

"So, you were aware of his digging out there—long before he was murdered?"

"Long, long before," he said. "Like all the beans in the jar."

I was following Shaka's jive just fine, but Ike's Republican mind was having trouble with it. "Beans in the jar?" he asked.

I explained: "Members of the Baked Bean Society," I said. "And by virtue of that membership, the sizable number of suspects in Gordon's murder."

"Right-o-roonie," said Shaka. "One big black bean and a whole bunch of little white ones."

My Dodge Shadow had new belts and hoses, a tune-up, five quarts of fresh oil, the proper amount of air in the tires. It was scooting through Thistle Hill like a rocket ship on its way to the moon. The ancient streetlights were as dim as stars. "I'm glad you came along, Ike," I said.

I was expecting him to say something supportive, something like *I wouldn't have missed it for the world.* Instead he said this: "Wish I hadn't."

"Wish you hadn't? You begged to come along."

"I know I did. He just seemed so life size."

"Heavens to Betsy, he's big as a bear."

"It was just tough watching him squirm, I guess."

I wasn't smart enough to let up. "Squirm? Were you and I looking at the same man?"

"No, I don't think we were."

"Good gravy, Ike."

"Don't good gravy me, Maddy. He's an important man in the black community."

"I know that."

"Not the way I know it, you don't."

It was my turn to be the bear. "This is not a black and white thing. A friend of mine has been murdered."

"Oh yes, and you just wanted some impressions."

"That's right. I would never do anything to get Shaka in trouble. Not if he didn't deserve it."

"And you think there's a chance he does?"

"I think we better talk about something else."

"I think we better talk about this."

I'd known Ike for twenty years. And he'd never spoken to me like that. Like a man that mattered. And, to tell you the truth, I rather liked it. "I don't know what to think," I whispered. "Not now."

He softened, too. "You pick up on something, did you?"

"You remember when he shuffled through all those papers on his desk and pulled out that copy of *The Harbinger*?"

Ike bristled. "You were surprised somebody from Thistle Hill reads the college newspaper?"

"Don't go there again, Ike. The only thing that surprised me was the address on the mailing label. Last Gasp Books. Effie's store."

Ike pondered the implications of that. "I think I understand—no, I don't think I do."

I explained: "Effie, as I'm sure you've already gathered, was a lot closer to Shaka than the rest of us. She provided police with his alibi for the night David Delarosa was murdered. Now when she sees in the college paper that I'm looking into Gordon's death, she goes straight to Shaka."

Now Ike did understand. "Gave him a heads up?"

We were back downtown, where the streetlights were bright enough to illuminate the inside of the car. "When that story in *The Harbinger* came out, I'd already been to see Effie at her book shop. I'd asked her oodles of questions about David Delarosa. So she knew where my mind was going on this. And then she gets her copy of *The Harbinger* and sees that Maddy Sprowls isn't just concerned about Gordon's murder—she's investigating it. "

"It could be innocent enough," Ike said.

I turned onto South Main and floated past the empty storefronts toward the Longacre Building. "You remember that *libidinous chum* stuff about David Delarosa? That beagle sniffing for a snuggle bunny stuff? Effie didn't put it quite so colorfully, but she pretty much told me the same thing."

"So you think she's trying to get you to look under the wrong rock?"

I pulled up in front of Ike's coffee shop. "I think maybe the rocks are in my head."

He reached across the seat and gently patted my shoulder. I reached across the seat and gently patted his. He got out. Closed the door with a gentle *kloomp*. He bent low and waved good-bye through the window. I gently waved back.

16

Saturday, May 5

My washing machine was whirring through the spin cycle. My Reeboks were bumping in the dryer. My radio was turned to the smart-alecky quiz show guy on NPR. Somehow I heard the phone ringing. I clicked off my iron and hurried upstairs to the kitchen. It was Gwen. "How's your dog-watching going?" she asked.

I looked out my window at James. I had him tied to my pin oak in the backyard. He was howling at Jocelyn's house like a lovesick wolf. "Just fine."

"You seemed a little frazzled by it the other day."

"Frazzled? I've never been frazzled in my life."

We both laughed at my lie. And then she got to the point of her call. "Anyhoo," she said, "I was telling Rollie about your unexpected house guest and he suggested we take you with us to Pettibones."

I knew what Pettibones was. It was the new pet supermarket in West Hannawa. According to a story we ran in the business section a few weeks ago, the store lets you bring your dogs with you—to bark, sniff and sample the snacks, and even pee on the floor if they're so inclined. I'd been thinking of taking James there myself.

So an hour later Gwen and Rollie were sitting in my driveway and I was loading James into the backseat of their enormous Mercedes-Benz SUV. Gwen was behind the wheel. Rollie was riding shotgun with two squiggly dachshunds on his lap. "Your house is just darling," Gwen said after I'd squeezed in alongside James. "It reminds me of that cubby hole we rented when Rollie was getting his insurance agency off the ground. Remember that awful little place, Rollie?"

Rollie was fighting a losing battle with Queen Strudelschmidt's affectionate tongue. His face was shiny with dog saliva. "That was eleven houses ago, Gwendolyn."

Gwen talked dogs and houses all the way to Pettibones. Rollie and I listened all the way.

The dachshunds were eager to get inside. They pulled Rollie across the parking lot like a couple of huskies in the Iditarod. I had to drag James to the door. "You look like a prospector pulling a pack-mule," Gwen happily observed.

"James' personality skews toward the cautious side," I said.

James balked completely when we reached the automatic door. Unfortunately so did my brain. While I was trying to drag him inside, I let go with that biblical verse about it being easier for a camel to go through the eye of a needle than for a rich man to enter heaven. Oh, the look Gwen gave me.

"Present company excepted," I said, trying to make light of my *faux pas.*

Gwen pulled a Ziploc bag from her purse and with her thumb and forefinger extracted a cube of pink steak. James followed her inside. I followed James.

Pettibones was everything I'd read about. It was a big as a people supermarket, with long, wide aisles and five busy checkouts. There was one aisle for cats, one for fish, one for birds, one for rodents, reptiles, spiders and the like, and five for dogs.

While Rollie headed for the squeak toys with Queen Strudelschmidt and Prince Elmo, Gwen and I got shopping carts. I tethered James to the handle of mine and away we went.

Gwen let the dachshunds pick out their own toys. They passed up the rubber hotdogs and hamburgers—too working class apparently—and chose T-bone steaks. James chose a rubber skunk. We headed for the aisle marked "Yummies!"

As James was sniffing the biscuit bins, debating between red fire hydrants and green mailmen, Prince Elmo turned up his stubby hind leg on the wheel of my shopping cart. James' territorial instinct ignited. He swung around angrily, growled his way to my cart and showed the little prince what peeing was all about. When Rollie tried to pull the dachshunds out of the path of the spreading puddle, he backed into a pyramid of Milkbone boxes. The boxes went down, Rollie went down, and their royal highnesses, frightened out of their wits, wound around Gwen's legs, who, wouldn't you know it, twirled right into James' pee. She joined Rollie on the floor.

Were this still the 1950s, and Gwen, Rollie and I still beatniks, this unfortunate chain reaction would have been accompanied with as much laughing as barking. But it was not the fifties anymore. And we were anything but beatniks. Now there was only the barking and my breathless apologizing.

"I was afraid something like this would happen,"

Gwen snarled at me, dabbing at her white slacks with Rollie's handkerchief.

My attempt at a joke landed with a thud. "And yet you went right ahead and invited us along. How courageous."

Gwen answered with a string of blue words. But it was a short string. Her good breeding kicked in. Her grace and good humor quickly restored. She sent Rollie and the dachshunds back to the SUV to wait, and then led James and me to the book section. "'I hope you've got your credit cards, Maddy dear," she said. "Because you and Bladder Boy here have a lot of reading to do."

I was leafing through a book called *I'm OK, My Dog's OK*, when Gwen suddenly brought up Gordon's murder. "You remember the other day at lunch how we talked about Chick maybe losing his head?"

I figured when Gwen invited me along there was more on her mind than my struggles with James. I put the book back on the shelf. "Yes, but I don't think it's worth worrying about. The odds of Chick shooting Gordon over a questionable piece of cheese are right up there with me being crowned Miss Universe."

"It's not just the cheeseburger. It's that other stuff."

I knew where she was going. I played dumb. "Other stuff, Gwen?"

"Their relationship."

"I've had a few uneasy thoughts about that myself," I said. "But I can't believe there's anything there."

"I hope you're right, Maddy."

"But you don't think I'm right?"

"I've heard some things. About Gordon and his graduate assistant."

I'd wondered about Gordon's relationship with Andrew J. Holloway III, too, of course. But I figured it best to keep my lip buttoned—and do my best to unbutton hers. "That nice young man, Andrew? Wherever did you hear that?"

Gwen knelt in front of James and started scratching his ears. So she didn't have to look me in the eyes, I think. "Let's just say through the proverbial grapevine."

"Do you think it's true?" I asked, certain the busybody on the other end of that grapevine was Effie.

Gwen gently kissed James on the top of the head. Went back to scratching his ears. "I think it's possible that Gordon and Chick were something more than friends. And maybe Gordon and that kid—"

She didn't finish the sentence. She didn't need to. "And their argument at the Kerouac Thing was about more than cheese? And the next day Chick killed him in a fit of jealousy? That's what you think, Gwen?"

Now she lifted her eyes. "No, Maddy. That's not what I think at all." She stood up. Put that book I was looking at in my cart. "If Chick was going to shoot anybody," she said, "wouldn't he shoot Andrew?"

17

Sunday, May 6

I had a couple of those awful frozen toaster waffles for breakfast and then headed for Mallet Creek. By myself. To see David Delarosa's old college roommate and wrestling buddy, Howard Shay.

Eric had never been able to find him in Florida, but I'd kept calling his house and just that past Wednesday I'd finally connected with him. He'd been back in Ohio just three days. "The house is still a mess," Howard said, "but if you want to come out, that's fine with me."

"I don't mind a mess," I said.

Mallet Creek is in neighboring Wyssock County, a tiny crossroads community surrounded by miles of cornfields. If you ignore the 35 mph limit on those empty county roads you can get there in an hour. I easily spotted all the landmarks he'd told me to look for: the fire station, the Methodist church, the meat packing plant with the huge plastic bull on the roof. The bull was sitting back on his haunches, joyfully eating a hamburger made out of the same plastic he was. Just two houses west of that monument to bad taste stood Howard Shay's house, a brick, sixties-style ranch at the end of long driveway. The lawn was choking with a half-foot of unmowed grass.

Howard was waiting for me on his front steps. If he hadn't spent the winter in Florida, he'd sure gone to great efforts to make it look like he had. His skin was as orange as a flower pot. He was wearing a Hawaiian shirt and Bermuda shorts. His only concession to the chilly Ohio climate was the white socks under his sandals.

He waited until I got to the steps before he stood up. He was a huge man, well over six feet, with wide shoulders and a barrel chest. "No problem finding me?" he asked.

Up close his tan looked real enough. His perfect white teeth did not. "Mallet Creek isn't exactly New York City," I said.

"Thank God for that," he said. He led me inside. When he'd told me on the phone that his house was a mess, he wasn't kidding. It was a pigsty.

I quickly found out why.

"I suppose you know my wife died," he said, steering me to his dining room table where amongst the clutter he had a pitcher of lemonade waiting. He poured me a glass. I took a sip. It was sour as hell.

"No, I didn't know that."

He poured himself a glass. "Two years in August. She had a heart attack driving back from my grandson's tenth birthday party. Who ever heard of a woman having a heart attack?"

"I guess it happens."

He nodded. Changed the subject. But didn't really. "As you can see, I'm not the housekeeper she was."

"So you went to Florida by yourself?" I asked.

"We always went together. Every winter for eight years, Nanzie and me. Since we retired from the school system here. We were both teachers."

A man losing his wife is a sad thing. But I was there to talk about Gordon's murder, not his loneliness or inability to plug in a vacuum cleaner. "I guess you didn't hear about Gordon's murder while you were down there."

"It wouldn't have meant much to me if I had."

"But in college you knew David hung around

with him, didn't you?"

Howard took his first sip of the lemonade. "Wooooo!" He trotted to the kitchen for the sugar bowl. "Christ, why didn't you say anything?"

One of my famous nervous giggles leaked out. "I figured that was the way you liked it."

He emptied the entire bowl in the pitcher. Swirled it until it was dissolved. "I don't think there's much I can tell you—about David or your friend."

Howard was a man in pain. A man trying to maneuver through the complexities of life without the woman who'd obviously done all the heavy lifting for him. I wasn't about to point out that our glasses were still filled with the old sugarless lemonade. I took another sip and tried not to pucker. "Were you at the college the night David was murdered?"

"Home for Easter like everybody else," he said. "At our family's farm on York Road. Just a quarter mile north of my place here. My brother Don has it now. It's a wonderful old place, Maddy, you should see—"

I interrupted him. He was getting nostalgic, and much too familiar. I had no interest in him doing either. "Being David's roommate, I suppose the police gave you a thorough going over when you got back to school the next week."

"Hell—they came out to the farm that same day."

"The Friday his body was found?"

Howard now was smiling at me like we were on a first date. "They were disappointed to hear I wasn't anywhere near the college the night before."

"So the police suspected you?"

"Yessirreebob, they did. I could tell by their hungry eyes they wanted to wrap it up right there. They figured I'd gone nuts and killed him because he hadn't put the cap on the toothpaste or something."

Howard was one to talk about hungry eyes. His were all over me, trying to find something to like. "But you were here in Mallet Creek?" I asked.

"Snug as a bug in my old twin bed. Donny in the other one. My mama and daddy right across the hall. I hope you believe me."

I pawed the air. "I didn't drive out here for your alibi. I'm just trying to see if there's a connection between David's death and Gordon's."

His eyes were studying my ringless fingers now. "You a divorced lady or a widow?"

"Happily divorced."

The hint went over his head—as high as a

damn weather satellite. "Divorce is easier than death, I suppose," he said.

"Everything's easier than death," I said.

Howard finally took another sip of his lemonade. His lips twitched and his eyes quivered. Like all men, he was too proud for his own good. He kept sipping. "This Gordon wasn't your boyfriend, was he?" he asked.

"Just an old friend, Mr. Shay. Now about David—did you have any suspicions at the time, about who might have killed him?"

It finally dawned on him that Dolly Madison Sprowls was not going to be the next Mrs. Howard Shay. Not his girlfriend. Not his housekeeper. Not anything. He settled back in his chair. "Not many people liked David Delarosa. Including me. He was a real so-and-so. Nasty off the mat as on it."

"That's right—you were on the wrestling team together."

"That's how we ended up as roomies," he said. "A lot of athletes shared apartments over there."

He was referring, of course, to the row of brick apartment buildings on Hester Street, on the eastern edge of the campus. They were privately owned apartments but approved by the college for upperclassmen and, as he said, athletes. "Girls seemed to like him," I pointed out.

Howard grinned at some old memory or the other. "David was a very handsome boy, wasn't he? And he knew it, too."

"Some people I've talked to think that's why he hung around with Gordon—to get girls."

Howard stuck out his bottom lip and nodded. "I can believe that."

"Believe, Mr. Shay? But not know for certain?"

"We didn't exactly have a lot of heart-to-hearts," he said. "But he sure didn't think much of those stupid beatniks, I can tell you that."

I confessed. "I was one of them."

"Whoops."

Now I got a chance to grin. "No need for a *whoops*. It was a long time ago, and besides, *stupid* would have pretty much summed up my opinion of the boys on the wrestling team."

He held up his lemonade glass. "Touché."

"No need for a *touché*, either." I let him squirm a bit then asked my big question: "Do you think there was any chance that David Delarosa was gay?"

"Hoo! He sure hid it well if he was. From himself especially."

"He definitely liked girls then?"

"He definitely liked what they had to offer—if

you get my drift."

"I get it."

Howard now leaned forward on his elbows and whispered, as if he were in a crowded restaurant. "The truth is I've always wondered if it wasn't a girl who killed him."

I took both our lemonade glasses to the sink and emptied them. I filled them with the sweet lemonade from the pitcher. I had the feeling I was finally getting somewhere and I wanted him to feel he was getting somewhere, too. "And just what makes you think it was a girl, Howard? He was overpowered and beaten to death."

He took a long, happy sip. I'd finally loosened up and called him by his first name. "I know it's hard to imagine how a girl could get the best of a guy like David," he said. "He was one of the best wrestlers in the state of Ohio. In the whole fudgin' country. But it's just as hard to see how another guy could've gotten the best of him, isn't it?"

"Another athlete might've."

He shook his head, resolutely. "He was a real alpha male, Maddy. He would have been on his toes for another athlete. Even for a guy who wasn't a jock."

I tried not to show my disappointment. "So

that's what leads you to believe it was a girl?"

His dentures lit up. "That and the upside-down seven."

"The upside-down seven?"

He explained: "David and I lived in 207. Those numbers were on the door, held with little brass screws. And David took the bottom screw out of the seven. So he could swing it up. Into an L. He used that as his signal that he had a girl in the room."

I made my thumb and index finger into a seven and then twisted my wrist to make an L. "So if you came in at night and saw that upside-down seven, that L, then you were supposed to go somewhere else?"

"That's right. 'That L means *later,* Howie,' he used to say. 'It means I'm getting *laid.*'"

I knew exactly where Howard was going with this. But I figured I'd let him tell it in his own words. I topped off his lemonade. "And?"

"And that next week when I got back to my room to pick up my things—the police wouldn't let me stay there while they were still investigating—the seven was upside-down."

"But you were back here in Mallet Creek that week, weren't you? Why would he bother turning the seven upside-down?"

"The upside-down seven was for everybody. You remember how it was in college, Maddy. Somebody was always banging on your door."

I did remember. And David was hardly the only college student—boy or girl—to have some kind of discreet "do not disturb" sign for their doors. "Were there any signs that he'd had a girl in there?"

He knew what I meant. "None that I saw."

"Did you share this suspicion of yours with the police?"

"I did. With the officer who let me in to get my things. God only knows if he passed it along."

In the all the weeks I'd been picturing David Delarosa's murder in my head, I'd never seen a girl taking that fateful swing at him, or beating the life out of him on the floor below. It had always been a male. A faceless male. Now I pictured a faceless female. "Why would a girl who willingly came back to David's room suddenly turn on him?" I asked. "And so viciously? Even the dumb clucks in my day knew what going back to a boy's room meant."

Howard shrugged. Frowned like a frog. "Who knows? Maybe the girl changed her mind. Before they even got in the room. Maybe she went in but didn't like the way she was treated."

"That ever happen before? To your knowledge?"

He jiggled his head no.

"So all you've got is that upside-down seven? That L?"

"That and my knowing the way David was," he said.

18

Tuesday, May 8

I gave the leash another hard yank. "You've got to go to the mountain, James. The mountain won't come to you."

James was not in the mood for proverbs. Nor for his morning walk. I'd gotten him as far as my front lawn and now he was planted like a petrified woolly mammoth in my pachysandra. I wrapped the leash around my knuckles and pulled harder. I was leaning backward like the damn Tower of Pisa. "For Pete's sake, James, get off your big curly duff and walk!"

James sank onto his front elbows. He laughed silently at me, the way dogs do. I dug a biscuit out of my raincoat and waved it in front of his nose. I showed him that it was in the shape of a mailman. I told him how "yummy wummy" it was. He sprang up on all fours and snapped it from my fingers.

While he chewed I pulled. Soon we were making our way along the sidewalk. So far, so good.

"You're one of the smarter dogs in the neighborhood," I said as we headed up Brambriar Court. "Who do you think shot Sweet Gordon?"

James didn't answer. He was preoccupied with a chipmunk hole on June Cardwell's tree lawn.

"I don't have a clue either," I admitted. I went over my list of suspects: "First, there's Andrew Holloway III, his graduate assistant. Andrew had lunch with Gordon only a few hours before he was killed. And he can't account for his time the rest of that Thursday. He not only found Gordon's body, he found his car, fifteen miles away. A tad fishy, I think. And I think Detective Grant thinks so, too. But Andrew had been tickled pink to get his assistantship with Gordon. He clearly admired him. From the time Gordon gave him every week, I'd say Gordon admired him right back. The question, of course, is whether that mutual admiration went beyond student and professor. Whether it led to a jealous pique that left Gordon dead."

James had given up on the chipmunk hole. He was waddling along at my side again. "Of course, if it was a jealousy thing, a gay thing, then maybe it wasn't Andrew who killed Gordon, but somebody upset about their relationship. Which, as you might imagine, James, leads us right to Chick Glass. I've known Gordon and Chick forever, but I can't for the life of me figure their relationship out. And that goofy argument over Jack Kerouac's cheeseburger! Good gravy! Were they really that vexed over *Ti-Jean*'s lunch? Or was it something deeper? All I know is that they had one helluva brouhaha at the Kerouac Thing, just a day before Gordon was killed."

James lifted his leg on Mindy Craddock's prized pink azalea. Then we turned north on Teeple and headed for the park. I continued: "Chick originally played down their argument at the Blue Tangerine. And so did Effie. But then Gwen told me how serious it was, the bean throwing and the wrestling match. And Chick was forced to admit it when I went to see him again. Maybe it was over the cheeseburger. Over which one of those two old fools would be, as Effie put it, 'the rock upon which Kerouac's Hemphillite Church was built.' Or maybe it was over something else. Which now brings us to David Delarosa."

I explained to James how Gordon was David's tutor. That they'd gotten very close in a very short time. "Then David was murdered. Brutally murdered. The same night he'd had a very public confrontation with Sidney Spikes at Jericho's. I don't know if you're a jazz fan or not, James, but today he calls himself Shaka Bop. Anyway, you can see where I'm going, can't you? Maybe Chick didn't like it when Gordon got too close to other men. David in 1957. Andrew now."

We were at the corner of White Pond Drive now, waiting for a break in the traffic to cross. "Yet there are a couple of big differences that make that particular theory unlikely, aren't there? In that first murder, it was Gordon's young friend who was killed. In the second it was Gordon himself. That was Gwen's point the other day at Pettibones. Remember what she said, James? If Chick was going to shoot somebody, why didn't he shoot Andrew? A very good point, don't you think?"

The last car passed. I gave James a yank and we trotted across the street. "Which brings us right back to Jack Kerouac's cheeseburger. Which is such a silly idea I don't even want to think about it."

We reached the park, a tiny wedge of grass at the intersection of White Pond and West Tuckman, Hannawa's main east-west artery. I sat on the park's only bench. It gave me a wonderful view of the gas station across the street. James made a couple of quick, territory-marking pees and then plopped down at my feet. I gave him another biscuit and continued my evaluation of Gordon's murder: "We also have to consider the possibility that Effie and Sidney are in cahoots. What if Sidney killed David Delarosa just as the police back then suspected? And what if Effie lied to protect him? And now all these years later, they learn that Gordon is looking for the murder weapon in that old dump? Or maybe they just suspect he's looking for it? Or fear he'll stumble across it? Because that's where they threw it? It's no coincidence that Effie's copy of *The Harbinger* showed up on Sidney's desk—that's for damn sure."

The bench was even more uncomfortable than it looked. I lowered myself to my knees and crawled over to James. I used his broad curly belly as a pillow. I didn't give a rip what people in passing cars thought. "If this is boggling your brain, James, wait until you hear my other Effie theory. David's old college roommate told me he'd always figured that David was murdered by a girl. Because David was too good an athlete to let another boy get the best of him. And because David was always luring girls back to their apartment. The seven was upside-down the night David was killed. So maybe

David's murder wasn't about Gordon's sex life. Or Sidney's sex life. But Effie's! Let's say she went back to David's room that night. And something went wrong. And she beat the bejesus out of David with something hard. Her alibi for Sidney was really an alibi for herself. And Sidney understood that. And protected her. Maybe out of gratitude. Maybe out of fear. The times being what they were, she easily could have let him take the fall for her. Plenty of other white girls would have. Which brings us back to the present. They're afraid Gordon will find the murder weapon out there. Effie goes nuts and kills David Delarosa. Sidney coolly puts a bullet in Gordon's head."

I could hear James snoring. I gave him a gentle poke in the ribs. "Not yet, Mr. Coopersmith. I've still got more. Effie has known Gordon and Chick since they were in college. She knows their history. Their predilections. Their passions. She knows Chick won't have an alibi. That he spends his evenings curled up with dead poets. And she knows they'll get into it at the Kerouac Thing. Maybe she orchestrates a bigger fight than usual." I turned over and buried my face in James' soft neck. "There is one little problem with all this—which I'm sure you've already seen. Sidney doesn't have much of an alibi. He told me he was at his garage that Thursday working on some old Sunday school bus. That after five he was working alone. According to the coroner, the murder occurred either Thursday afternoon or evening. If the police really pressed him, it would be hard for him to prove he was at the garage after his mechanics went home for the day. But maybe he and Effie figured half an alibi was enough. That there wasn't a chance in hell the police would link two murders fifty years apart anyway. And they didn't link them, James. I linked them. At least I'm trying to."

I dug out another biscuit for James. I was so lost in my thoughts that I actually took a nibble out of it myself. I gagged and wiped my tongue on my sleeve. James snapped the biscuit from my hand before I could take another bite. "Bon appetite," I said.

James swallowed the biscuit whole and then struggled to his feet. I'd been walking him enough mornings now to know what exactly was coming next. I reached into my coat for my wad of plastic bread bags. I waited patiently while he performed his ritual poop dance. He meandered across the park in ever-tighter circles until he found just the right spot. It was like cleaning up after a circus elephant. I tied a knot in the end of the bag, deposited it in the trash barrel and we headed for home.

"If you don't mind, James," I said, "there are two other people I'd like to run by you."

He accepted another biscuit as a bribe and I continued: "First, there's Mickey Gitlin and the greedy nephew theory. True enough, Mickey is a little shaggy around the edges. And a little secretive. And he's had some trouble with the law. And he's got financial problems. And he's Gordon's sole heir. But all in all, he seems like a good kid. Detective Grant wants me to stay clear of him. I suppose there's a chance he knows something I don't. But more than likely, he just doesn't want me mucking things up in case there is something there. Which is fair enough either way.

"Then there's Kenneth Kingzette. The toxic waste dumper. At best he's an amoral, money grubbing creep. Detective Grant told me to scratch him from my list. And I'd be happy to—if there weren't so many annoying coincidences. Gordon was not only involved in looking for the missing toluene, he started asking for permission to dig at the Wooster Pike dump just six months after the EPA called off its own search. And when does Gordon get killed? While Kingzette is safely behind bars? No. He gets killed four months after Kingzette is paroled. So why couldn't the toluene be buried out there? Why couldn't Kingzette's old boss Donald Madrid be buried out there, too? And why is Grant so adamant about me staying away from Kingzette? Could it be he suspects him even more than I do? And the only reason he wants me to keep snooping around my crazy old beatnik friends is to keep me out of his precious little hair? I sure have my suspicions, James. I sure have my suspicions."

We crossed back over White Pond Drive and headed down Teeple toward my bungalow. "So there you have it, James: Andrew Holloway, Chick Glass, Effie and/or Sidney, Mickey Gitlin or Kenneth Kingzette. Now what do you think?"

He looked up me at with sad, apologetic eyes. I stopped and scratched his big ears. "Don't feel bad," I whispered, "this is too much for my little brain, too."

19

Friday, May 11

The first thing I had to do was get Kenneth Kingzette out of my system. Take my measure of him. The way I'd taken my measure of Mickey Gitlin.

The question was how. I didn't want to foul up Detective Grant's investigation. And I sure didn't want to end up missing like Donald Madrid.

The answer didn't come to me until that Friday night, when I was curled up on my back porch, watching James watch me. I was also reading the *East Side Leader.*

Hannawa has only one daily newspaper, *The Herald-Union*. But like any big city, there are also a number of neighborhood weeklies: *The South End Trader, The Greenlawn News, The Brinkley Bee,* there are just oodles of them. Once a month or so I go through them to make sure I haven't missed anything important. So I was making my way through *The East Side Leader* when I saw a promising solution to my Kingzette problem. It was in the classifieds, under FOR SALE, MISCELLANEOUS:

> Charming 6 pc. patio set, glider, two chairs, coffee table, end table & serving wagon, wrought iron with floral cushions, $250.

I'd been thinking about buying new furniture for my porch for years. The wicker set I had out there now was wobbly and musty smelling, real bird's nest material. Lawrence and I bought it the same year we bought the house. Now here was a way to feed two fish with the same worm, as my Uncle Wally used to say, assuming that patio set was as charming as the classified promised.

Saturday, May 12

Saturday morning I called the number listed with the ad, to make sure the patio furniture was still available. The eager woman on the other end told me it was. I made sure James' food bowl was full and headed toward Union City.

Union City is anything but a city. It's a little nub of a community on the eastern edge of Hannawa's suburban sprawl. There are some impressive houses out there these days. And some pretty modest ones. The woman with the patio furniture lived in one of the modest ones. She led me through her house to the patio. It was a ten-foot square of red brick overlooking the back alley of a strip mall. "When we moved here it was a beautiful woods," she lamented. She was in her late fifties, overweight, overwrought and newly widowed. She was selling her house and moving into a condo.

Well, the patio set was not exactly charming. But it wasn't horrible either. The iron frames on the chairs and tables were painted a pale yellow. There were a few speckles of rust here and there. The cushions were faded from years in the sun, making the crazy red and orange floral pattern a tad bit easier on my eyes. "This is exactly what I've been looking for," I said. I wrote a check for the full $250.

When I got home I bolstered my nerve with a strong cup of tea and then called the Kingzette Moving Co. "I just bought this patio set on the other side of town," I told the unfriendly man on the other end, "and I was hoping you could help me out."

"That's why we're in business," he said. From the pitch of his voice I gathered he was a younger man, presumably Kingzette's son.

And so I made arrangements for them to deliver my patio set the following Thursday afternoon. It would cost me another $150.

Thursday, May 17

Right after lunch I told Eric I was starting to "feel a little woozy." Which was a lie. I was actually feeling a lot woozy. My wooziness had been growing all week, since I'd made those arrangements to have Kingzette Moving deliver that awful patio set.

Eric dislodged the Mountain Dew bottle from his mouth long enough to speak. "I suppose that means you're going home early."

"You think I should?"

He rolled his Chinese-American eyes. "Maddy, you've been preparing to go home since you got here."

So I drove home and camped in front of my picture window, getting woozier and woozier waiting for that truck to pull up.

It pulled up at three. There was a big gold crown

painted on the side, along with these words:

KINGZETTE MOVING
Expect The Royal Treatment

I looked over my shoulder at James, who was sprawled on the floor in front of my sofa, gnawing on a log of rawhide. "I don't expect you to turn into Lassie—dial 911 with your snoot or anything—but if things start going wrong I do hope you'll reach down deep in that wolfen soul of yours and maybe growl a little."

James gnawed away, promising nothing.

Two men slipped out of the truck. The driver was young and tall, and had way too many muscles for his tee shirt. The other man was a foot shorter, but just as burly. He had the thin gray hair of a man pushing sixty. He leaned against the fender and lit a cigarette while the younger man headed for my door. I opened it before he could knock. "You're Mr. Kingzette, I gather?"

"One of them," the young man said. His face was as sour as Howard Shay's lemonade.

I nodded toward the older man. "And that's your father?"

"Where you want the furniture?"

I ignored his impatience. "It must be nice to

work together like that—I remember how I used to help my father milk the cows."

"Patio in the back, ma'am?"

"Screened porch," I said.

I followed him back to the truck. There were only six lousy pieces of furniture in there. If I was going to make an adequate appraisal of the older Kingzette, I'd have to get in their way as much as I could.

I greeted Leonard Kingzette with a wiggle of my fingers. He nodded at me. Took a long, painful drag on his cigarette and then flicked it into the street. I joined them at the back of the truck.

They unloaded the furniture onto my front lawn. It took about thirty seconds. The son picked up the two chairs and headed for my backyard. I helped his father with the coffee table. "I have a confession, Mr. Kingzette," I said, as we waddled sideways with the table. "When I told my neighbor who I'd hired, he got a little nervous. Because you'd been in prison."

The word *prison* hit Kingzette like one of those poison darts Indians in the Amazon use to shoot monkeys out of treetops. His chest caved in. His eyes sagged against the bridge of his nose. The coffee table between us quivered. I moved quickly to reassure him. "But I said, 'Good gravy, James, if the man has done his time, then the man has done his time. He has the right to make a living.'"

He recovered. Gave me a quick, uneasy smile. "Not everybody's so charitable."

"James is a real worrywart. He's probably peeking out the window right now. Anyway, you checked out just fine."

A second dart struck him.

"With the Better Business Bureau," I said quickly. "They didn't have a single complaint." That part of my lie was true. I had checked with the BBB.

Kingzette managed another smile. "Well, Mrs. Sprowls, I appreciate your going the extra mile."

We reached the back of my house. Kingzette's son trotted past us, heading back to the truck for more. "Your son's all business, isn't he?" I said.

Kingzette pushed the porch door open with his backend. "He sees to it I don't get into any more trouble—that's for sure."

And that was pretty much it. By a quarter after three, the patio set was on my porch, the old wicker crap was on my tree lawn, the Kingzettes were on their merry way. And I was regretting the whole miserable affair.

Oh yes, I'd had a few minutes to take my measure of Kenneth Kingzette. But like the damned fool I am, I'd also given Kenneth Kingzette a few minutes to take his measure of me. So instead of enjoying my new patio set that evening—sliding back and forth in my glider with a mug of tea, sleeve of Fig Newtons and that new Dana Stabenow mystery I'd been dying to read—I was perched by my living room picture window, in that uncomfortable wingback chair I just hate, watching the street like a nervous parakeet. I had my phone on one armrest and my butcher's knife on the other. I just knew that any minute I was going to spot Kenneth Kingzette sneaking through my hostas.

There were so many things about my encounter with Kingzette that bothered me. For one thing, he'd called me Mrs. Sprowls. "Well, Mrs. Sprowls," he'd said, "I appreciate your going the extra mile." Fair enough. It was my name. It was written on the bill. But he'd said it in such a familiar way. As if he were sending a subtle message that he knew who I was.

And why wouldn't he recognize my name? I was no longer the anonymous newspaper librarian I used to be, was I? My name was all over the news during that Buddy Wing business. And just a few weeks ago that awful girl with the green hair told the whole world I was looking into Gordon's murder.

And even if he hadn't recognized my name at first—even if he'd arrived at my house thinking I was just some sweet old penny-pinching broad—I'd sure given him a lot to worry about. I told him I knew he'd been in prison. I told him I'd checked him out. What if I'd made him as nervous as I'd made myself? Nervous enough to check *me* out?

I sat by that picture window all evening. The darker it got outside the madder I got inside. Mad at myself for concocting such a damned-fool idea. Mad at myself for not realizing it was a damned-fool idea until it was too late.

What exactly had I expected Kingzette to do? Confess his sins to me? Somehow convince me with his body language, or some soulful Bambi-like look in his eyes, that while he'd once been callous enough to dump those drums of toluene, he wasn't the kind of man who shot people in the back of the head?

The thing that was bothering me most, of course, was that little quip he'd made about his son. The one when he went rushing by us, and I commented about him being all business. And he said: "He sees to it I don't get into any more trouble—that's for sure." Good gravy! What did he mean by that? Was I worried about the wrong Kingzette?

I kept my vigil by the window until midnight. Then I Kingzette-proofed my bungalow. I put spoons and forks in empty water glasses and put two glasses on every window ledge, so there'd be plenty of clanging and crashing if somebody tried to crawl in that way. I slid my dining room table against my front door and my kitchen table against the back. I turned on every light. I mined the hallway floor with James' squeak toys. I tethered James to my dresser. I got into bed, fully dressed, with my phone and my butcher's knife. I even put a paring knife under my pillow as a backup.

The one thing I didn't do was call Detective Grant and confess my stupidity. Pride trumps fear every time.

Tuesday, May 22

After five sleepless nights in that booby-trapped bungalow of mine I called Detective Grant to confess. Even a proud woman needs her eight hours.

I caught him just as he was leaving for the day. We traded hellos and our thoughts about the rainy weather and then I got right to the heart of the matter. "I may have done something a little on the stupid side," I began.

"A little on the stupid side?" he asked. "I hope

you're not just being modest."

"You and me both," I said. I swallowed the last half-inch of cold tea in my mug, motioned for Eric to turn around and mind his own business, and then told Grant about my encounter with the Kingzettes.

"What's done is done," he said.

I wasn't expecting sympathy, but I was surprised by the indifference in his voice. "That's it? What's done is done?"

"What do you want me to do? Put a moat filled with alligators around your house?"

I didn't like that smart-ass question of his one bit. "I just want you to tell me if I'm in any danger, Detective Grant, that's all."

He snapped right back at me. "You've inserted yourself into a murder investigation, Mrs. Sprowls. Of course you're in danger. But probably not from the Kingzettes."

"Probably not? I was hoping for a little more reassurance than that."

He rattled my eardrum with a long, late-afternoon yawn. Then he said this: "Just hang in there for a few more days, Mrs. Sprowls. Okie-dokie?"

Thursday, May 24

And so I hung in there—not that I had any choice—lights on, squeak toys in the hallway, knives under the pillow, water glasses on the window sills, wondering exactly what Detective Grant was hinting at. The answer came at three-thirty Thursday afternoon. It was in the budget for the next day's paper. I was so angry I screeched like a 500-pound piece of chalk.

Eric was bent over his new issue of *Spider Man*, feeding miniature doughnuts into his mouth. "And just who's ruffling your feathers today?" he asked.

I tossed the budget at him. "Grant!"

I should explain that the budget has nothing to do with money. Not directly, anyway. The budget is the list of the stories the paper will be covering for the following day's edition. It includes local stories as well as the big national and international stories. Among the dozens of stories listed was this one:

Story name: DUMPERDEAL
Reporter: Margaret Newman
Length: 14 inches
Photo: File headshot

Description: The Ohio EPA has entered into a consent agreement with convicted toxic waste dumper Kenneth Kingzette. In exchange for immunity from future prosecution in the O.E. Madrid case, Kingzette has revealed the location of still-missing toluene.

I took two minutes to decide how nasty I should be, then called Detective Grant. He was not surprised that I'd called. Nor was he surprised that I began our conversation with the salutation, "You sneaky son-of-a-bee!"

"Now, now, Mrs. Sprowls—you know darn well I couldn't tell you until it was a sure thing."

All I knew about Kingzette's deal with the Ohio EPA, of course, was what I'd just read in the Friday budget. "And just where was the missing toluene?"

"Buried in an abandoned chicken house, over in Hinckley Township."

"They dig up anything else out there?"

He knew what I was getting at. "There is no evidence that Donald Madrid is dead. Or that Leonard Kingzette killed him if he is."

"How about evidence that he's still alive?"

He chose his words carefully. "Suffice it to say, there are strong indications that Mr. Madrid's disappearance was of his own doing."

"Other than the wrinkle-free chinos and

Indiana Jones hat?"

I couldn't see him, of course, but I could tell from his noisy nostrils that he wasn't pleased with my knowledge of those things. "You conveniently left out the luggage," he said.

"Well, placing an order with Lands' End does suggest some planning," I admitted. "But if he was going to run away, why did he first tell the EPA he'd hired Kingzette to do the dumping? Why didn't he just keep his lip zipped and vanish into the good night?"

"Because he wanted to make it look like he was being cooperative," Grant said.

I offered an alternative because. "Or because it wasn't the EPA he was running from, but Kenneth Kingzette."

Grant countered with a string of other *becauses*: "Because his company's finances were in shambles. Because his beloved Woolybears were in last place. Because his wife was already seeking half of everything in divorce court. Because the last thing he needed on top of all his other problems was three or four years in federal prison."

Being an obnoxious old nag wasn't getting me anywhere. I tried a mix of contrition and vulnerability. "Well, I suppose you know more about the case than I do," I said.

"Infinitely more," he said.

"And I suppose there's no chance that Kingzette got to Madrid before Madrid got to the airport, or the bus station, or whatever mode of transportation I'm sure you've already checked out."

Grant cackled at me like a hen on helium. "Mrs. Sprowls—I am not going to dig up that entire landfill out there just because you've got some crazy-ass idea rattling around in your coconut."

20

Saturday, June 2

I bribed James into a quick walk up and down Brambriar Court. Then I headed for Speckley's. Not to have lunch with Dale or Detective Grant. To have breakfast with Gordon's old girlfriend, Penelope Yarrow.

It had taken Eric a month to find her. Her name was Penelope Oakar now. She was living three hours away, in Ottawa Hills, a suburb of Toledo. She was married to a Lebanese dentist. She was the mother of twin girls, both now in medical school.

When I'd told her on the phone that Gordon had been murdered, there was a deep rattle in her throat, as if she were taking her dying breath. When I asked if I could drive up to Toledo to see her, she said, "No—I'll come to see you." She said she wanted to visit Gordon's grave. See the college again. When I suggested that we meet at Speckley's for lunch, she laughed in that same sad way people laugh at funerals, and said, "Don't tell me that old place is still open."

I pulled in right at ten. Looking for a place to park. Speckley's is always a zoo on Saturday mornings. I spotted a car that just had to be hers. It was a freshly washed and waxed silver Volvo with Lucas County license plates.

Penelope was waiting for me inside, at an elf-sized table-for-two by the men's room door. I weaved through the crowded tables. We smiled at each other. Took inventory of each other. We both ordered the Spam and eggs, a Speckley's specialty nearly as famous as its meatloaf sandwiches, au gratin potatoes on the side.

Penelope was in her mid fifties but looked as good in her Ann Taylor jeans as any woman in her thirties. She folded her hands under her chin and listened patiently while I gave her a breathless account of my investigation into Gordon's death. "How is it you even know I exist?" she asked as soon as she could get a word in edgewise.

"I saw the photo you took at Jack Kerouac's grave," I said.

She squinted quizzically. "And just where did

you see that?"

"At Chick's house," I said. "He told me you were Gordon's old girlfriend."

"He told you I was Gordon's girlfriend?"

"You weren't Gordon's girlfriend?"

"Later on I was. When that photo was taken I was still Chick's girlfriend."

"Oh my."

She poured the silverware out of her white linen napkin and spread the napkin across her lap. "What can I say? It was the Age of Aquarius."

"And it was a long time ago," I said. "Why wouldn't Chick want me to know you were his girlfriend?"

"Maybe because he was still married to his first wife at the time," she offered.

Penelope was a good fifteen years younger than me. By the time she was in the picture—with Gordon and Chick and others at the college—I was long out of it. "Exactly what years are we talking about here?" I asked.

"I started seeing Chick my junior year," she said. "The fall of 1968."

I did the math in my head while the waitress brought our little blue teapots in for a landing. Gordon and Chick were both just a year older than me. In 1968 they would have been thirty-four. Penelope would have been just twenty or twenty-one. "And you were still with Chick in the summer of 1970?" I asked. "When the three of you went to Massachusetts to visit Kerouac's grave?"

There was a residue of bitterness behind her smile. "He gave me the heave-ho a couple weeks after we got back," she said. "Cleared the deck for the fall semester."

"And you started seeing Gordon?"

"Not right away," she said. "I went home to Mount Gilead for a few months, but missed the big wicked city." We both laughed, as anyone who'd spent time in Hannawa would do. "Then I came back, got a crappy job, and eventually bumped into Gordon."

I asked the obvious question: "It didn't bother Chick that Gordon was dating his old girlfriend? Age of Aquarius notwithstanding?"

"It was a little weird—for all three of us. But by then Chick had another gullible undergraduate on the side. And Gordon and I were in *love*."

Our Spam and eggs arrived. We started shoveling the fluffy eggs and little cubes of fried pork like a couple of lumberjacks. "Actually in love?" I asked. It came out a little more sarcastic than I wanted. But she was not offended.

"As much above the neck as below it, surprisingly," she said.

Well, I sure wondered what she meant by that! As you know, my head was filled with all those suspicions about Gordon and Chick's sexuality, and how their relationship, whatever it had been, might have something to do with Gordon's murder. "Surprisingly, you say?"

I got the exact opposite answer I expected. "Naturally, I'd always found Gordon physically attractive," she said. "But you know what an egghead he was. All those philosophical soliloquies that used to bore me to tears when I was with Chick were suddenly loosening me up better than a rum and Coke."

That was enough sex talk for me. For the moment at least. "So what eventually happened between you and Gordon?"

"I moved in with him—that's what happened. For three less-than-wonderful weeks."

"Not the love nest you expected?"

"Not the pig sty I expected."

"Let me guess," I said. "You committed the cardinal sin of a new relationship. You cleaned his apartment."

She nodded like a fisherman's bobber. "And I threw out his damn pine cones."

"You threw out his pine cones?"

"The ones Jack Kerouac gave him. It all seems so silly now."

"Jack Kerouac gave Gordon pine cones?" I squeaked. We'd both finished our Spam and eggs and were down to nibbling on the decorative orange slices.

"Little baby pine cones. No bigger than the tip of your little finger. A cocoa can full of them."

I almost jumped up on the table and tap danced. I was learning more during that breakfast with Penelope Yarrow than I'd learned all spring talking to my old beatnik friends. And while lots of intriguing little pieces were coming together in my mind, I had the good sense to play dumb. "So when you threw out his pine cones, Gordon popped his cork and threw you out?"

"Not right away. But when we couldn't find them at the dump—"

"What dump was that, dear?" I asked.

"That one on Wooster Pike," she said. "We crawled around in the snow for a week looking for those blessed pine cones."

I wasn't just puzzled. I was flat out thrown for

a loop. I'd known Sweet Gordon for fifty years. I'd been one of the founding members of the Baked Bean Society. I'd been there when Jack Kerouac came to town. And I'd been there through a thousand wine-inspired reminiscences of that famous visit. But I never knew about those pine cones! The question for me now, of course, was why I never knew about them. And maybe more importantly, did any of my other old beatnik friends know about them? I talked Penelope into sharing a piece of carrot cake with me.

"Did you know they were Jack Kerouac's pine cones when you threw them out?" I asked.

"Good Lord, no," she said. "That cocoa can was just one more piece of junk gathering dust on his window sill. Along with the empty beer bottles and dried up violets."

I'd only been married to Lawrence for six years. But it was long enough to know that when it comes to the perceptions of men and women, you're dealing with two distinct species. Where a woman sees a window full of junk, a man sees a well-ordered shrine. "And just how did Gordon react to your overzealous housekeeping?"

Penelope had the little frosting carrot on the end of her fork, deciding if she should surrender to temptation and eat it, as if that tiny half-inch of green and orange sugar was a time bomb packed with ten thousand calories. "A lot of yelling and screaming at first," she said. "Then he sort of went catatonic. He curled up on his couch and put a pillow on top of his head. 'Do you have any idea what you've done?' he kept asking. In a low whisper. Like a Hindu mantra. 'Do you have any idea what you've done? Do you have any idea what you've done?'"

If she wasn't going to eat that damn carrot, I was. I scraped it off her fork with mine, and popped it in my mouth. She thanked me with a wide smile. I pressed on. "Do you remember much about the cocoa can?"

"It was a cocoa can."

Since buying all those cans from Mickey Gitlin, I'd had Eric do a little research for me. "Was it a Hershey's can? There were lots of different brands in those days. But Hershey's is what most people bought."

Penelope grinned with embarrassment. "In my mind I see it as a Hershey's can—those silver letters on the brown background—but that was a long time ago."

I nodded sympathetically. "Wait until you're

my age. You won't be able to trust half your memories. But for the sake of discussion we'll have to assume your mind is telling you the truth. Now, was it a real old can? An antique?"

Her eyes went back and forth like one of those Krazy Kat clocks. "I think it was just a regular cocoa can. I doubt I would've thrown it out if it looked real old or valuable."

"That's a good point," I said. "Can you remember if it was made out of tin or cardboard?"

"Tin I guess. Why?"

"For a couple reasons," I said. "First, it would help date the can. The real old cocoa cans were made out of tin. Then during World War II when metal was scarce the sides of the can were made out of cardboard, with a tin top and bottom. And it easily could have been one of those World War II cans. According to what Gordon told you, Kerouac found it in 1956. Just eleven years after the war ended. That's not a long time for a can to be in a kitchen cupboard, let alone in a fire tower in the middle of nowhere. So if it was cardboard, it could have rotted in the dump along with the pine cones inside." Now I contradicted myself. "Of course from what Gordon's graduate assistant tells me, under the right conditions things made out of paper can survive underground for years and years."

Surprisingly, Penelope was following me. "So even if it was a cardboard can, Gordon still might have hoped to find it intact thirty years after I threw it out?"

"Yes, I think so," I said. "Anyway, Hershey went back to the all-tin cans in 1947. Other companies about that time, too. Everything's made out of plastic now, of course."

Penelope suppressed a yawn. "So it was probably an all-tin can, but it could have been part cardboard? But either way Gordon must have figured he had a good chance of finding it?"

"That's right. Now, did it have one of those oval snap-in lids?"

She answered quickly. "I'm sure it did."

I asked my next question slowly. "Did you bother looking inside the can before you threw it out?"

Now she suppressed a flash of anger. "That's exactly what Gordon asked me. Only he was screaming at the time. And the truth is, yes, I did look inside. If there was cocoa inside I was going to put it back in the kitchen."

"So you saw the pine cones?"

"I saw them."

"Didn't it occur to you that maybe he wanted them?" I asked.

The anger on her face was now directed toward herself. "I know I should have—but I was in a cleaning frenzy. Gordon had junk everywhere and I was going to get rid of it. To make him love me more. Consider me for a wife I suppose. God, I don't know how many bags I carried out to the trash."

The story Penelope told me that morning at Speckley's—as bizarre as it sounded—nevertheless jelled with my own research into Jack Kerouac's life. Or should I say Eric's research. Earlier that spring he'd Googled up all sorts of interesting stuff for me. Anyway, it boiled down to this:

In June of 1956, Jack Kerouac hitchhiked from San Francisco to the Mt. Baker National Forest in Washington State. He worked as a fire lookout for 63 days, perched alone in a tower, atop a mountain, watching the horizon for wisps of smoke, bored to near insanity by the desolation of the place. Each night, to mark the passing of another interminable shift, he placed a tiny pine cone in an old cocoa can he found amongst the tower's clutter. When he began working his way east at the end of the summer, he took that can of pine cones with him, as a souvenir of his foolishly spent summer. In November he dropped in on Gordon and Chick here in Hannawa. And before leaving for New York, he gave his pine cones to Gordon.

According to what Gordon told Penelope fifteen years later, the gift had been "purely a materialistic one." Gordon had given Kerouac several bottles of cold Schlitz beer for the bus trip and he simply had to make room in his duffel bag. "Why don't you hold onto these for me, good daddy?" he said to Gordon.

I'm sure Gordon fantasized about Kerouac coming back for his can of pine cones some day. I'm sure he fantasized how Kerouac, overcome with gratitude, would invite him to join his inner circle. To wander America's back roads with him, hobnobbing with the likes of Allen Ginsberg, William S. Burroughs, Neal Cassady, Larry Ferlinghetti and Lucien Carr. I bet he even fantasized how Kerouac would make him a character in one of his novels.

Jack Kerouac never came back for his pine cones. But that apparently did not diminish their value to Gordon. I can only imagine how precious they became when Kerouac published *Desolation Angels* in 1965. In that novel, Kerouac described his 63 days on Desolation Peak as a fire watcher.

He described how his alter ego, Jack Dulouz, each night dropped a new little pine cone into an old cocoa can, to mark the end of another excruciating day. When Gordon read that, I'd venture to say he pretty much figured he had the beatnik version of the Holy Grail in his possession.

When Penelope told me about the pine cones that morning at Speckley's, I simply could not believe that Gordon could have had such a treasure in his possession and not told anyone. Only after a long afternoon at Ike's, rattling his patient eardrums with my cockamamie theories, did Gordon's secretiveness begin to make sense to me: Jack Kerouac had given those pine cones to *him*. And the fact he didn't tell anybody underscored just how deeply it had touched his young bohemian soul. So much that he created a secret shrine to Kerouac's gift on his window sill—a shrine that included beer bottles that just maybe touched Kerouac's lips, and pots of violets that, despite his good intentions, he forgot to water.

"Now wait a minute," Ike objected when I explained all this to him. "I can understand why the professor didn't tell you about those pine cones. And maybe some of those other crazy folks. But I can't believe he wouldn't have been tempted to rub Chick Glass' nose in them. Considering how those two carried on over that cheeseburger all those years."

I was nodding, watching the dribble of traffic outside his coffee shop. "I think maybe it just comes down to the kind of guy Gordon was," I said. "He knew those pine cones would trump what the great Jack Kerouac had or didn't have for lunch. He knew it would make him Kerouac's undisputed apostle at Hemphill College, and not Chick. He also knew it would destroy their friendship." It was six o'clock. Ike got up with a long, Saturday afternoon groan. He flipped the sign on the door over to CLOSED. I kept talking. "And so for fifteen years Sweet Gordon kept that cocoa can of pine cones to himself. A literary artifact of immeasurable value. Until his new girlfriend in a fit of love-induced tidiness threw them out."

Ike returned to the table with a handful of Ghirardelli chocolates from the counter. "So how does all that help you find Gordon's murderer?"

I popped one of the balls of chocolate into my mouth and attempted to answer. "Who the hell knows? But I am certain about one thing, Ike. Gordon was not out there digging for drums of toluene, or the weapon used to kill David Delarosa, or even a restaurant receipt from Mopey's. He was digging for that cocoa can of pine cones."

Ike had a ball of chocolate in his mouth, too. "Sounds reasonable. Crazy as shit—but reasonable."

Ike was right on both counts.

According to Penelope, she and Gordon spent several nights in a row out at the Wooster Pike dump, on their hands and knees, looking for that cocoa can in a week's worth of God's snow and Hannawa's garbage. Only when the city bulldozed a fresh layer of trash over the top did Gordon give up. Penelope, of course, was quickly out of the picture. When Gordon tossed her out, she traded her crappy job in Hannawa for a good one in Toledo. She eventually met her Lebanese dentist and put her bohemian years behind her. Until one Dolly Madison Sprowls gave her a jingle.

Ike and I said goodnight on the sidewalk and I drove home to James. I knew I had nothing more to fear from Kenneth Kingzette, but I left my booby traps in place. I curled up in bed with a notepad and my television remote. Hannawa's local PBS station was doing a fund drive featuring the pop songs of the fifties. Patty Paige. Mel Torme. Perry Como. The McGuire Sisters. Half of the singers they were remembering were dead. The other half were older than Methuselah's mother.

I didn't make a lot of notes that night, but what I did write guided me through the rest of my investigation, inspiration-wise at least:

You can be almost certain that Gordon was only digging for his can of pine cones out there. For years he'd given up any hope of ever recovering them. Every week they were somewhere under another week's worth of trash. And then when the city built the new adjoining landfill, they covered the entire old dump with three feet of dirt. But those pine cones certainly stayed in Gordon's brain, and in his heart, and years later when Dr. William Rathje of the University of Arizona started the whole garbology movement, Gordon saw an opportunity to reclaim his secret treasure.

Gordon's dig wasn't completely selfish. Above all, Gordon was a teacher. A dedicated teacher. Yes, he was looking for a can of pine cones. But he was also doing important academic work. His students were learning how to be good archeologists. How to patiently pursue the truth.

Gordon also subliminally instructed his students to be on the lookout for cocoa cans: "Anything interesting today, boys and girls?" he'd regularly ask. "Old soda pop bottles? Betsy Wetsy dolls? Perhaps an old cocoa can or two?" Over the years he'd collected a whole shelf full of cocoa cans. But apparently not the one he was looking for. All of the cans I'd bought from his nephew were as empty as the feeling I'm sure Gordon felt when he opened them.

So, if Gordon was murdered because of what he was looking for, then what he was looking for was not what the murderer thought he was looking for! And Gordon was murdered for nothing!

21

Tuesday, June 5

Effie called me. Bright and early Tuesday morning while I was reading the obits. She told me she'd bought all of Gordon's old books from his nephew. She was driving down to Harper's Ferry to pick them up. On Thursday. In a U-Haul van she'd rented. She begged me to come along. "It'll be like old times," she said. "Two old beatnik broads killing the road."

Killing the road. Now there was a phrase I hadn't heard in a while. When we Baked Beaners were flitting around in Gwen's pink Buick, we didn't take the road, or travel the road, or even hit the road. We killed the road. We gave the road, and ourselves, all we had.

I hemmed and hawed. I was way too old to kill the road. Especially with someone who may have had something to do with killing Sweet Gordon.

On the other hand, who knows what I might wheedle out of Effie on that long drive to the eastern tip of West Virginia? Or from Mickey Gitlin when we got there? "I'm not a wealthy tycoon who can come and go as she pleases, like you can, Effie," I joked. "I'll have to see if I can get a couple days off."

As soon as Effie hung up I called Detective Grant, while the receiver was still tucked under my chin. I told him about Effie's offer. My fingers were crossed that he'd say no. But he said, "Sure—knock your socks off."

"But didn't you tell me to stay away from Gordon's nephew?" I protested.

"Two months ago I did."

"And what's changed in two months?"

"Unfortunately not that much," he admitted.

"In other words, nothing at all?"

"Now, now," he growled. "Would I be giving you the green light if I thought you were in any real danger?"

I growled right back. "So you're saying I'll be in *un-real* danger?"

I expected him to backtrack a bit. But he didn't. "We've talked to both Mickey Gitlin and Miss Fredmansky several times now," he said. "There is nothing to believe that either is involved in Professor Sweet's murder."

"Then why should I bother going?"

"You tell me," he said.

So I told him. About the pine cones. About Effie's copy of *The Harbinger* ending up on Shaka Bop's desk. About Howard Shay and Penelope Yarrow. About Gordon's ambiguous relationship with Chick, Andrew J. Holloway III and David Delarosa.

"Then by all means go," he said.

"You're sure you're not just dangling me out there as bait?" I asked.

"The Hannawa police don't dangle," he said. "As much as we'd sometimes like to."

Then I called Suzie and made an appointment to see Managing Editor Alec Tinker. He was so happy that I'd kept them in the loop that he gave me Thursday and Friday off without counting it against my vacation time.

Finally, I called Effie back. I told her I'd love to kill the road with her. "But there is just one small complication," I said.

I could hear the suspicion in her voice. "How small?"

"Actually, not so small," I said. "A rather rotund water spaniel named James."

Thursday, June 7

Effie pulled into my driveway at five o'clock—in the morning. It was still dark. Very dark. And drizzly. I dragged James across the slippery grass to the van. Effie helped me lift him inside.

To be honest with you, I could have pawned James off on Eric for a couple of days. Or even put him in a kennel. But I just felt more comfortable bringing James along. I knew he'd be worthless if I got into trouble. But Effie wouldn't know that. And neither would Mickey Gitlin. So James was just a big, happy, tail-wagging St. Christopher's statue.

We took Route 21 south. Right past the entrance ramp for the interstate. "Did we miss that on purpose?" I asked Effie as we flew by in the dark.

"You bet we did," she said. "As Sweet Gordon used to say, 'If it ain't a back road, it ain't a road worth taking.'"

"He said that, did he?"

Effie laughed. "Well, somebody said it."

I poured Effie a cup of coffee from her Thermos. I poured a cup of Darjeeling tea from mine. I gave James a big shrimp-flavored fire hydrant from the Ziploc bag of doggie treats I'd brought. Effie started singing that awful Willie Nelson song:

"On the road again, da-da-da-da, I'm on the road again...."

"Is it necessary to be cheery this early in the morning?" I snarled.

"I can't help it," she said. "I'm a morning person."

"I thought you were a night person?"

She knew I was alluding to the romantic excesses of her youth. "I'm that, too," she said. She kept on singing.

A few miles south of Massillon we picked up U.S. 250 and headed east. At six-thirty we stopped at a roadside park so James could pee. And frankly, so we could pee, too. I've never understood it, but there's something about a long drive that puts a woman's bladder in a tizzy. Men can bounce along all day and not have to pee once. Which wouldn't be fair if it wasn't the only biological advantage their gender has. Anyway, the sun was coming up now and I could finally see how Effie's traveling outfit stacked up against mine. She was wearing a baggy pair of khakis and a bright blue denim shirt with a big Tweetie Bird embroidered on the back. Her shirttails were down to her knees. She was also wearing a pink baseball hat and those big yellow glasses. Suffice it to say, I didn't look much better.

We took U.S. 250 all the way to the Ohio River. We crossed into Wheeling. We looked for a cozy mom and pop diner for breakfast. We settled for a Burger King. Disappointed, but full, we continued our journey southward through West Virginia's knobby hills. In the bustling metropolis of Pruntytown, we picked up U.S. 50. It would take us all the way to Harper's Ferry.

We'd been on the road for four hours already and neither of us had said boo about Gordon's murder. We just rattled on about our families, the television shows we watched, or refused to watch, and of course the beautiful green mountains. Which was fine with me. Even though I had my suspicions, Effie was an old friend. Someone whose company I'd always enjoyed. There would be plenty of time for me to wheedle.

Harper's Ferry! Of all places, why did Mickey Gitlin have to live in Harper's Ferry? Harper's Ferry was that historic old town on the Potomac where the abolitionist John Brown tried to start a slave revolt by raiding the union arsenal there. You all know what happened. The revolt fizzled and John Brown was hanged. So chugging along U.S. 50 in that U-Haul with Effie, I couldn't help but wonder whether my visit to Harper's Ferry would go as badly as his.

U.S. 50 is one of America's great old highways. It runs from Ocean City, Maryland, to Sacramento, California, some 3,000 miles, straight across the middle of the country. Except that here in West Virginia U.S. 50 isn't quite so straight. It's as wiggly as a worm. Between the harrowing mountain curves, and the pee breaks, and lunch at a roadside drive-in in the ominously named town of Mount Storm, it took us five more hours to reach Harper's Ferry. Another hour after that to find Mickey Gitlin's kayak livery.

Mickey's place was actually located two miles north of Harper's Ferry, in a thick woods right on the banks of the Potomac. I'd been expecting some dark, seedy looking place, with rusty pickups and pot-smoking mountain men. Instead we found a freshly paved parking lot filled with expensive SUVs. On the hillside to the left stood a modern two-story cabin, made of beautiful butterscotch-colored logs. On the right stood a long, sturdy barn, painted a happy green. The mural above the barn door featured a toothsome black bear skillfully paddling his tiny kayak through the rapids. Below the paddling bear it read:

MICKEY'S KAYAKS
Rentals, Lessons, Sales

Effie and I slid out of the van and stomped some life back into our wobbly legs. There was no one around, but in the distance we could hear splashing water and people having way too much fun. We helped James out. I snapped on his leash. We headed off to find Mickey.

First we went to the cabin. Then to the barn. We finally found him on the riverbank, scrunched down in an huge Adirondack chair, bare-chested, in baggy shorts and sneakers, hair in a ponytail, clipboard in his lap, cell phone pushed into his ear, can of beer balancing atop his raised naked knee. A serious businessman at work. In the fast water just below him were a half-dozen frolicking kayakers.

Mickey spotted us right away but he made us wait for ten minutes while he finished his call. "Sorry about that," he said. He was not the sourpuss I'd encountered the day of Gordon's burial. A wide, friendly smile was hooked over his sunburned ears.

Mickey took a minute to scratch James' ears then walked back to the van with us. He carried our suitcases to the cabin. Showed us our rooms. They were spotless. The beds were covered with colorful country quilts. Effie's room was decorated with the head of a huge buck deer. Mine with a stuffed owl. When we came downstairs Mickey was waiting with two tall tumblers of iced tea. "There's enough daylight left for a quick kayak lesson," he said. "If you ladies are game."

Effie was. I wasn't. But she skillfully teased me into it anyway. "Oh, come on, Maddy," she said, squeezing Mickey's elbow. "Do you think this beautiful specimen of a man is going to let anything happen to us?" Ten minutes later Effie and I were outfitted in baggy men's swimming trunks and tee shirts that said "Capsizing Is Fun."

Well, you can imagine all the crazy thoughts going through my head as we walked back down the trail toward the river: Effie and Mickey were in cahoots, and they planned to drown me in the Potomac. My death would look like an accident. Mickey and Effie would get away with another murder. They'd divide Gordon's estate. Carry on some sick May-December romance. Or maybe it was just Mickey who wanted me dead. Maybe it was his idea that Effie bring me along. Effie never said it wasn't. Maybe Mickey said, "Say, why don't you bring Maddy Sprowls along with you?" Or maybe it was just Effie. Or Effie and some other cohort. Somebody hiding in the trees. Chick or

Shaka or God knows who. With a rifle. Or a crossbow. Or a big feather pillow to smother me in my sleep. Oh, my synapses were snapping with all sorts of crazy scenarios.

When we reached the river I froze, wrapping the end of James' leash around my hands like it was the ripcord on an inflatable lifeboat. I'd seen the river before, of course, but now I had a stake in its ferocity. Good gravy! The slate-blue water was flying past us at a million miles an hour, exploding over sharp half-submerged rocks, swirling into whirlpools. The kayakers dumb enough to be out were all young and muscular. "We're going to get lifejackets and helmets like those guys, aren't we?" I asked Mickey.

"If I've got any left," he said. I was too preoccupied with my impending death to know if he was kidding or not.

Mickey led us along the bank through a thicket of wild rhododendrons. We emerged on the rim of a small, square pond. Kayaks were stacked on the bank, along with a pile of helmets and lifejackets. "The practice pool," he said.

I was embarrassed. But not enough to keep me from asking how deep it was.

"Three feet," he said. "And all the alligators

and piranha are vegetarians."

I tied James to a tree. Gave him an hour's worth of biscuits to gnaw on. Effie and I fought over the pile of lifejackets and helmets like it was a sale table at Wal-Mart.

Mickey dragged two small kayaks to the edge of the water. He helped us squeeze into the cockpits, those little round holes in the middle where the Eskimos stick out. He showed us where to put our feet and our knees. How to hold the paddles. How to use our hips to stay balanced.

He towed me into the water first. When we got to the center of the pond, he gently pulled his hands away. "Feeling steady?" he asked.

"Like an oyster cracker in a big bowl of soup," I said.

He backed away from me and pulled Effie into the water. The second he let go of her kayak, she flopped over like a porpoise at Sea World. Mickey quickly uprighted her. She came up spitting and coughing and swearing a blue streak. "Just remember what your tee shirt says," he said. My giggling made me wobble, but my ample post-menopausal bottom kept me stable.

Mickey showed us how to paddle forward. How to paddle in reverse. How to stop and how to turn. Soon Effie and I were scooting around the little pond like a couple of water bugs.

It was right in the middle of all that mindless, childlike glee that my fears came back to me like an iceberg full of hungry polar bears. I heard a low, long growl. I twisted my head toward James. A few feet behind him, in the shadows of the rhododendrons, stood a man. A tall, bulky man. Even at that distance I recognized his eyebrows. It was Detective Grant.

The rational front part of my brain told me to be happy. That he'd followed me, and now revealed himself to me, just so I wouldn't worry. But the old reptilian stalk at the back of my head told me to be afraid. That Detective Grant wouldn't be hiding in those rhododendrons if he didn't think I was in danger. I instinctively threw up my left hand. I'm not sure if I intended to wriggle my fingers hello or just flash one particular finger. But the next thing I knew, the top of my head was scraping the bottom of the pond, wrapped in a swirl of air bubbles. I felt a pair of strong hands on my shoulders. I saw a flash of sunlight and heard Effie's hyena laugh.

Mickey was laughing, too. He started to give that same line about my "Capsizing Is Fun" tee shirt he'd used on Effie: "Just remember what your—"

"Finish that sentence and this paddle will be sticking from your ass like a beaver's tail," I said.

I said nothing to Effie or Mickey about seeing Detective Grant in the rhododendrons. By the time Mickey pulled me out of the water he was gone. And maybe while the two halves of my brain couldn't agree on what his presence in Harper's Ferry meant, they did agree on one thing: Grant had wanted to keep his presence a secret. Good gravy! If James hadn't growled, I wouldn't have known he was there either. What a good dog.

Mickey chased the last two kayakers away. He lit the propane grill on his porch. He put on an entire package of chicken legs, slathered with thick brown sauce, and a wire basket of fresh vegetables—green peppers, zucchini, fat rings of sweet onion, pea pods and mushrooms. We ate like pigs.

At ten o'clock or so, Mickey led us to the barn. Gordon's belongings, what he hadn't sold already, were stacked in an orderly mound. I bet there were two dozen boxes of books.

Mickey had refused to sell Effie the books while they were still in Gordon's house in Hannawa. Now

Effie was paying him back. She wanted to look at every book. If it wasn't sellable, she wasn't going to buy it. "Nothing sinks a bookstore faster than books nobody wants to read," she told us. Mickey and I sat in aluminum lawn chairs and watched in awe as she evaluated the books.

She not only judged the books by their subject and the author, but also by their condition, whether they were first editions or not. And she flipped carefully through the pages to see what might be tucked inside.

"I've already looked for hundred dollar bills," Mickey said with a laugh.

"I hope you found plenty," Effie said. "Because that's not what I'm looking for. I'm looking for old letters, clippings, that sort of thing. What we in the antiquarian book biz call *ephemera*. Sometimes it's more valuable than the book itself."

"For you or for Mickey?" I teased.

"For both of us," she said. "To be honest with you, I normally wouldn't tell anyone about that. But Sweet Gordon was like a brother to me. Which sort of makes Mickey my nephew, too. And I would never screw a relative." She threw back her head and ha-ha'd like Bette Davis. "Although he is kind of cute."

It was two in the morning before Effie was finished evaluating the books. She offered Mickey a rather impressive sum and he quickly accepted it. We headed for the cabin and our beds.

When I got to my room I put on my travel pajamas, a baggy blue-flannel pair that covers every inch of me. I bought them during the Nixon presidency when I was still foolishly filled with the notion of being a world traveler. I figured if I ever had to flee a motel because of a fire or hurricane, I could run out into a crowd of people without worrying about hypothermia or embarrassment.

I locked the door. I pulled a small braided rug in front of the door for James to sleep on. I positioned my new Indian moccasin slippers on the floor. I peeked out the window hoping to spot Detective Grant leaning against a tree. If he was out there I didn't see him. I turned the stuffed owl around so I wouldn't have its bulging glass eyes staring at me all night. I knelt by James and gave him a final good-night ear-scratch. "Just in case you haven't read your watch dog manual lately," I whispered to him, "you're supposed to sleep with one ear cocked." I bent his ear to show him. When I let go it flopped like a dish rag. I clicked off the light and felt my way to the bed.

There is nothing more comforting in the world than sinking your head into a big, cool, fluffy pillow. And there's nothing more disconcerting than a loud crackle. I popped up like a slice of toast. There was a note on the pillow. I fumbled for the lamp. I read:

Mrs. Sprowls,
I need to see you without Effie.
Meet me on the back porch when you think she's asleep.
Mickey.

Good gravy! What possibly did Mickey want? Did he want to threaten me? Strangle me? Did he have some important information about Effie? And how did I know that the note was really from Mickey? I considered my meager options: I could stay put. "I didn't see your note until this morning," I could whisper to Mickey, when Effie was taking her turn in the bathroom. I could open the window and scream at the top of my lungs for Detective Grant. Or I could stop being such a melodramatic old fool and meet Mickey on the back porch.

As usual, my curiosity outweighed my better judgment. I swung out of bed and put on my slippers. I folded the note into a small square and wedged it under my left heel. Detective Grant would need it for evidence if I ended up dead. I started to snap the leash on James' collar but thought better of dragging him along. His obstinacy would surely wake up Effie. I gave him a rawhide instead.

I unlocked the door and slipped into the hallway. I padded down the stairs. Crossed the dark kitchen. Opened the screen door. Peeked outside. Mickey was comfortably wedged in a wicker chair. His bare feet were propped on the porch post. His hands were cradled around a beer bottle, standing straight up in his lap. I heard myself say what only someone with Effie's deviant mind would say. "That is a beer bottle, isn't it?"

He grinned. Toasted me with it.

I sat in the chair next to his.

"I hope the note didn't scare you," he began.

"I'm here," I answered.

He offered me a swig from his beer. To my surprise, I took him up on it. "I know you've got your suspicions about me," he said.

"Don't take it personally," I said, handing the bottle back. "These days I've got suspicions about everybody."

"That's why I wanted to see you without Effie."

He pulled an envelope from his shirt pocket.

"That stuff Effie said about ephemera tonight? About it sometimes being more valuable than the book? I already knew that." He watched me open the envelope. "I found it in an old archeology book, by Heinrich Schliemann, on his excavation of the lost city of Troy. It's from David Delarosa. To my uncle. It's dated December 26, 1956."

I unfolded the letter but I didn't read it. "Who told you I'm interested in David Delarosa?"

"Effie," he said. "During one of her calls I told her I'd met you. I may have said something about you being nice but nosy."

"You were half right," I said.

Mickey took a swig of his own. Handed the bottle back to me. "She said you were running all over Hannawa investigating my uncle's murder. Suspecting everybody. Even trying to link it to a murder fifty years ago. A young wrestler named David Delarosa. I'd already gone through his books looking for money and personal stuff. So the name rang a bell."

I was not surprised that Effie knew I was investigating Gordon's murder. My visit to her bookstore in March made that fairly obvious. "So it was your idea that I come down here with Effie? So you could give the letter to me?"

Mickey pushed himself out of the chair and

pressed his face against the kitchen window, to make sure Effie hadn't tip-toed after me. He sat on the edge of the porch in front of me, six inches from my moccasins. "I want to know who killed my uncle, too," he said. "I thought maybe you could tell me something."

I handed him the beer bottle. It was time for me to read the letter:

Gordon,

Christmas was just as wretched as I expected. My mother insisted on having her asshole boyfriend here. Christmas Eve right though this morning. This isn't that truck driver I told you about before. This new goof works at the washing machine plant down the road in Clyde. Given all the ugly sounds at night, this one looks like true love. It might even last until Easter.

I'll be glad to get back to the college. Thanks to your most-excellent tutoring, my grades were just good enough to keep the scholarship jack jingling in.

I know you don't exactly dig the idea, but be warned my friend! I fully intend to resume my biological quest for Miss Forty Below. A little wine and Charlie Parker mixed and shaken with my ample animal charm, and that tiny chip of ice will just be a nightlight showing me the way.

See you after the ball drops!

David

I put the letter back in the envelope. I flashed an apologetic smile at Mickey. "There's a lot to decipher here," I said.

"Just tell me what you can when you can," he said.

I promised I would. I went upstairs to bed. James was happily gnawing away. I took the rawhide from him. I clicked on the lamp by the bed. I crawled in with my moccasins on and started deciphering.

The first thing that struck me was the letter's style. It was written in Beatnik. Or at least in what passed for Beatnik to a kid from Sandusky on a wrestling scholarship. Clearly he was trying to impress Gordon.

The next thing was David's obvious hatred for his mother. Or more accurately, his hatred for the way his mother behaved with men. I know Sigmund Freud isn't as popular as he was when I was taking college psychology, but I think that *ugly sounds at night* comment spoke volumes about his own sexual aggression.

David also made sure to show his appreciation for Gordon's help with his grades. *Thanks to your most-excellent tutoring*, he wrote. I had no reason to doubt he was sincere about that.

But the real point of the letter, or so it seemed to me, was that last part about his intention to pursue Miss Forty Below. *I know you don't exactly dig the idea*, David began. Now what exactly did that mean? Did it imply some kind of jealousy on Gordon's part? Or was Gordon merely concerned about David's pursuit of a particular woman? A woman he shouldn't be pursuing? Whichever is was, it was clearly an issue between them. And David was telling him in no uncertain terms that he was going after Miss Forty Below whether Gordon approved or not.

And just who was this Miss Forty Below?

I'd overheard enough man-talk in the newsroom over the years to know that women unwilling to jump into bed after the first howdy-do are quickly labeled as frigid. I'd never heard the phrase before, but *forty below* was clearly shorthand for forty below zero. Based on everything I'd heard from Effie and Shaka, and especially from Howard Shay, the handsome David Delarosa was accustomed to bedding young women without much effort. Apparently Miss Forty Below was not thawing out as quickly as he wished.

The other intriguing line in that paragraph was the last one: *A little wine and Charlie Parker mixed and shaken with my ample animal charm, and that tiny chip of ice will just be a nightlight showing me the way.* David intended to loosen up the mystery woman with the help of alcohol and bebop and then close in for the kill with his enormous ego—not a particularly new strategy. What really made me squint, however, was the *tiny chip of ice* reference. That just had to mean a diamond ring. Apparently Miss Forty Below was engaged.

The final thing for me to ponder that night was why Gordon had kept David Delarosa's letter all those years. One possibility was that Gordon didn't even know he'd saved the letter. Maybe he'd stuck it in that old book and forgotten about it. But in a book by the famous Heinrich Schliemann? On his historic excavation of Troy? No, I think Gordon would have gone back to that book again and again.

So my guess was that Gordon not only knew he had the letter, but kept it in that safe, secret place for a reason. Was it simply because David had meant so much to him? Was it another very personal treasure? Like that can of Jack Kerouac's pine cones? Or was it something else?

David's murder hit Gordon hard. He sulked for days then took the bus to Sandusky for the funeral. He returned to Hannawa full of anger. He wanted David's killer found. But he never believed it was Shaka. Maybe the letter held a clue to David's real murderer.

I refolded the letter and put it in the envelope. I folded the envelope and wedged it under my other heel. I turned off the lamp. "Does it, Gordon?" I whispered. "Does that letter say who killed David? Who killed you?"

22

Friday, June 8

We had a good country breakfast—scrambled eggs and onions—and then headed out to load the books into the van. Effie saw to it that Mickey did most of the work. "Save your back, Maddy," she said. "It's just going to be me and you when we get to the bookstore."

We wedged James into the small space we'd left for him behind the front seat. Then we crawled in ourselves, Effie behind the wheel, me shotgun. Our freshly filled Thermoses were lying between us on the seat like a couple of unexploded artillery shells. I cranked down my window to say good-bye to Mickey. "When you get back to Hannawa tell Detective Grant I said hello," he said, grinning like a raccoon. "Assuming he didn't fall in the river and drown yesterday."

I didn't say anything.

Effie did. "We can only hope he did." She backed the van around and headed down the long drive, blowing a big, theatrical kiss at Mickey in her rearview mirror.

I felt foolish. Like this whole trip was a badly staged junior class play and I was the only one who thought it was real. But I was also relieved. Mickey and Effie were taking Detective Grant's not-so-secret presence in good humor. The way people with nothing to hide would. I gave James a cat-shaped biscuit and nestled back in the seat for the long drive home.

We crossed the Potomac into Maryland and headed north on Route 65 toward Sharpsburg, where one of the Civil War's most inconclusive bloodbaths took place, the Battle of Antietam Creek. I suggested we take a quick drive through the battlefield but Effie was in a hurry to get home. She had her books and most likely her fill of James and me. She planned to connect with the Pennsylvania Turnpike and shoot straight west into Ohio. No more of that, "If it ain't a back road, it ain't a road worth taking" stuff for her.

"I've been doing an awful lot of thinking about the old days," I said after an hour of silence. "Who we were back then and what we meant to each other."

"Those were special times," Effie said.

"Yes," I said. "Even the crappy times seem special now."

Effie motioned for me to pour a cup of coffee for her. "There were plenty of those, too, weren't there."

I'd been maneuvering toward a particular crappy time, of course, and figured now was as good a time as any to bring it up. "None crappier than the night David Delarosa was killed."

"That does win the Oscar," she said.

"I didn't know him as well as you, of course."

Effie cackled. "I've already admitted to sleeping with him, if that's what you're getting at."

"He was quite the ladies' man, I guess."

Said Effie, "That's putting it mildly. It was easier to keep track of who he didn't sleep with than who he did."

I handed her a sloshing cup of coffee and then screwed the lid off my Thermos of tea. "So—who didn't he sleep with?"

"I'd say just you and Gwen. Unless you've been holding out on me."

"Lawrence and I were already engaged that

year," I said. "Not that I would have slept with David otherwise. Or more accurately, not that he would have slept with me." I finished pouring my tea. I took a cautious sip. It was plenty hot but not unswallowable. "You sure about Gwen?"

Effie hooted like an owl getting its belly feathers tickled. "I'm sure she didn't even sleep with Rollie before they were married."

I told one of my patented half-truths. "I was only wondering if she was engaged then or not, Effie. I'm no more interested in her sex life than I am in mine."

We didn't get back to Hannawa until late in the day. We unloaded Gordon's books then headed through the rush-hour traffic toward my bungalow. It was six o'clock by the time I got home. I immediately went to the basement and checked my files. The information I needed wasn't there. I called Eric at the morgue. "Stay put until I get there," I said.

He whined like a third grader. "But it's Friday."

"It also might be Christmas," I said. "Stay put!"

I filled James' food bowl and headed for the garage. I was downtown in twenty minutes, storming through the newsroom like a category five hurricane. I was so anxious to get to work that I didn't even take time to make a mug of tea. Which worried Eric to no end. "I will be able to get out of here sometime tonight, won't I?"

"If the microfilm gods are with us," I said.

Today we save stories on CDs. But a lot of the older stuff in the morgue is still on microfilm. I told him to pull out all of the film for 1956 and 1957. I sat him in front of the machine and pulled a chair alongside. "We're going to start with 1956," I said, "and check backward from the end of December."

Eric wisely asked the pertinent question. "Check for what?"

I pretended he was the ignorant one and not me. "The society pages. For the engagement announcements. For the engagement of Gwendolyn Moffitt and one Rollie Stumpf."

Newspapers don't have society pages any more. The sexual revolution saw to that. *The Herald-Union* now has a section called Hannawa Life. Despite its gender-neutral title, it's clearly geared at women. In addition to the stories on lowering your cholesterol, finding the right pre-school, and exercises you can do while pushing a supermarket cart, you'll find the same old stuff we ran before

Bella Abzug started waving her big floppy hat at us in the sixties: weddings, anniversaries and engagements, lots and lots of engagements.

We went through the December papers. The November papers and half the October papers. Then there it was, Saturday, October 13, 1956:

> Mrs. and Mrs. Calvin W. Moffitt of Hannawa announce the engagement of their daughter, Gwendolyn Leigh, to Mr. Rolland H. Stumpf, son of Martin and Gladys Stumpf, of Pittsburgh, Penn.
>
> Both Miss Moffitt and Mr. Stumpf are seniors at Hemphill College. They plan a June...

I leaned back and rubbed the long hours of travel out of my neck. "You can go home now," I said to Eric.

He was uncharacteristically concerned. "You sure?"

I swept him away with my fingers. I watched

him hurry to the elevator, swigging his Mountain Dew as he maneuvered through the mostly empty desks in the newsroom.

I thought about walking down to Ike's. But I went home to James instead. And that Rubbermaid tub of Lawrence's clippings Dory gave me.

Monday, June 11

Eric usually gets to the morgue a good half-hour before I do—or so he tells me. This morning I was the early bird. I handed him the clipping.

He glanced at the four men in the photo above the story before letting it flutter to his messy desk. In one well-practiced motion he clicked on his computer and cracked the plastic cap on his breakfast Mountain Dew. "Who are those goofy looking dudes?"

I'd looked at the photo so many times over the weekend that I'd memorized where each was standing. "Left to right they're Herbert Giffels, Rollie Stumpf, Don Rodino and Elgin 'Bud' Wetzel. They're the 1957 state collegiate debate champions."

"I figured they weren't football players," he said.

"You have a keen eye, Mr. Chen." I leaned over his desk and handed him the clipping a second time.

From the look on his face you'd swear it was five in the afternoon and not nine in the morning. "I suppose you want me to find them for you."

"You only have to find three of them," I said. "We already know where Rollie Stumpf is."

The significance of the photo finally dawned on him. "Ah—the woebegone spouse of Gwendolyn Moffitt-Stumpf."

"That's right. The other three could be anywhere."

I got to work marking up the Sunday edition while Eric worked his on-line magic. It took him only fifteen minutes to determine that Don Rodino was dead. "Nothing fishy though," he said. "Vietnam 1965. Navy pilot shot down over Hanoi."

Just before noon he found Herbert Giffels. In a cemetery in Zanesville. "Must have been a car accident or something," Eric said. "Wife died the same day. September 20, 1983."

The search for Elgin "Bud" Wetzel took all afternoon. "Here he is," Eric yawned at a quarter to five. "Beaufort, South Carolina."

"Still alive?"

"Looks like it. Apparently he's something of an expert on eighteenth century candle snuffers. He's got a website—www. wickmeister.com."

"How about a phone number? He got one of those antique things?" I asked.

And so I called Rollie's last surviving debate partner. The voice of the man who answered was deep and clear, with only a hint that he might be on the south side of middle age: "Wickmeister!"

"This wouldn't be Bud, would it?" I asked.

"It's been a long time since anybody called me that," he said.

I introduced myself. Told him I'd graduated from Hemphill a year before he did. That my late husband Lawrence had covered the state debate tournament for *The Harbinger*. "As I recall, he drove down to Columbus on the bus with you."

"I do remember somebody pestering us with stupid questions while we were trying to prepare," he said, adding a faint "heh-heh-heh" on the end to let me know he was joking.

It wasn't all that funny, but I mustered up the best laugh I could. Then I got down to business, bending the truth every whichaway as I went along. "The reason I called is that I'm writing a memoir of sorts. And 1957 was such a big year for Lawrence and me. Him writing for the college newspaper. Both of us graduating. Getting married. And that horrible murder. It was the same day as the debate tournament as I recall."

He corrected me. "The day after."

I corrected him. "Actually, the police said he was killed in the middle of night. So I guess we're both right."

The champion debater in him wouldn't let it go. "If it was after midnight, then it was the next day."

I capitulated. "You're right, of course. Anyway, I've been trying to piece everything together chronologically. When exactly Lawrence was in Columbus and when he was back here. And going through his old clippings I found the story he wrote on the debate tournament. And the photo that ran with it. The four of you with your big trophies. I figured somebody smart enough to win a state debate tournament would have a good memory."

That really puffed him up: "'Resolved...That the United States should discontinue direct economic aid to foreign countries.' Don and Herbie handled first and second affirmatives. Rollie and I handled the rebuttal. We made those Wooster College boys sound like a pack of retarded chimpanzees, I'll tell you."

A number of snappy retorts came to mind. I wisely kept them to myself. "Lawrence and I knew the boy who was killed a little—David Delarosa was his name—and we were both shaken up. As you can imagine. I've been tying to remember exactly when the bus got back to Hannawa. I know I picked Lawrence up but I can't remember if it was morning or afternoon or just when."

Bud made my ear buzz with a long, thoughtful moan. "Boy, you're making me go back a long time."

"Unfortunately it has been a long time," I said, trying to sound sympathetic. The reason I was asking him about the bus schedule, of course, was to humor my silly suspicions about Gwen: That just maybe she was the Miss Forty Below in David's letter to Gordon. That maybe David had succeeded in seducing her that Wednesday night at Jericho's. That maybe with Rollie down in Columbus she simply couldn't resist David's *ample animal charm*. That maybe she was the girl for whom David flipped the seven on his door into an L. "That L means *later*," David told Howard Shay, "It means I'm getting *laid*." So maybe Gwen was the one who knocked David over the balcony, and filled with fear and shame continued to batter his pretty face on the hard floor, long after he was dead.

"You know," said Bud, "I don't think we all

came back together from Columbus. In fact, I'm sure we didn't."

I was puzzled. "Didn't come back together? With my Lawrence you mean?"

"No," he said. "I mean the debate team. The tournament ended at four. We got our trophies and your husband took that picture that ran in the college paper. We were all supposed to go out for dinner with the debate coach, Professor Cook, stay another night at the hotel and then come back on the Thursday morning bus. But Rollie was anxious to get back. He had something waiting for him the rest of us didn't. A girlfriend. He asked Professor Cook for permission to take the overnight bus."

I was more than puzzled now. I was flat out thrown for a loop. "What time did that bus leave Columbus?"

Bud let go with another one of his irritating moans. "I have no idea," he said. "I do remember Rollie going to dinner with us. Your Lawrence, too. But I know Rollie didn't come with us afterward on our tour of the local rathskellers."

"What about my Lawrence," I asked. "He took the tour, did he?"

Bud laughed like a nervous goat. "As I recall, it was his idea."

I fought off my old feelings of betrayal and got back on the subject at hand. "About those trophies," I asked, "did you get to keep them? Or did they end up in a glass case somewhere?"

"Professor Cook got one for the case outside his office. But, sure, we got to keep our individual trophies."

"Just out of curiosity—exactly what did your trophies say?" I asked.

Either Bud was staring directly at his trophy or his memory was very good: "First Place, State of Ohio Collegiate Debate Tournament, Columbus, 1956-57."

I jotted that down. "And did they also put your name on it?"

"Not the same day we won them of course," he said. "But later Professor Cook collected them and had our names engraved."

"All four of them?"

"No. Just our separate names."

"I mean did he have all four trophies engraved?"

"I suppose he did."

"But you don't remember for sure?"

Tuesday, June 12

I called the Greyhound station as soon as I got to

work. In the sweetest voice I could muster I asked the sleepy man on the other end if he had any bus schedules from 1957 lying around. He questioned my sanity in the sweetest voice he could muster. He also suggested that I call the Western Reserve Historical Society in Cleveland. "They got a whole bunch of old train and bus memorabilia up there," he said. The word *memorabilia* stumbled off his tongue as if he'd never had the opportunity to use the word before.

I took his advice. The librarian at the historical society, out of some sense of sisterhood I suppose, spent the next four hours digging through the files. She called me back at two o'clock, just as I was heading toward the cafeteria with my empty mug. "I've got some good news for you," she said.

23

Friday, June 15

I could have driven over there Tuesday night. Or Wednesday night. But I just couldn't do it. I just couldn't face the ugliness of it all.

But by Thursday night my curiosity was back in the driver's seat. I watched the midnight repeat of Larry King on CNN—he was doing his umpteenth show on the Scott Peterson murder trial—and then I watched some silly half-hour infomercial on a gizmo that peels hardboiled eggs perfectly every time. Then I loaded James into the backseat and headed for Hemphill College. It was a quarter to two in the morning. West Tuckman was absolutely empty. As if the rapture had sucked everybody up to heaven but James and me.

I reached the college in ten quick minutes. I pulled over in front of Mueller Hall. It sits right on the corner of West Tuckman and Balch Avenue. It's where Greyhound used to have its campus bus stop. Hannawa was on the north-south route between Cleveland and Columbus. In addition to the main station downtown, the buses would make a curb-side stop here for college students. That campus stop was eliminated years ago. These days even the poorest students have cars. But in the fifties the big noisy Greyhounds would pull over right where James and I were now standing.

"I suppose you're wondering what we're doing here at this ungodly hour," I whispered to James. He was preoccupied with the glorious smells along the curb but I told him anyway. "According to the old bus schedule that the librarian at the historical society found for me, the overnight bus left Columbus at ten-fifteen. It made its way up Route 42, through Mansfield and Ashland and a dozen other towns. It reached the college at two, and then headed downtown before continuing on to Cleveland."

I gave James' leash a tug and we started up the sidewalk. "There's no way to know now if Rollie got off the bus exactly at two. But it was spring. No snow or ice on the roads. So more than likely the bus arrived on time. And more than likely he was the only one who got off. It was Easter week. Nobody would be coming back *to* the college that week. Anyway, Rollie got off the bus with his suitcase and his big first place trophy."

James found a nice forsythia bush to lift his leg on. I gave him all the time he needed. "We can't say for certain that Rollie came this way. But even if he cut across the lawn between Mueller Hall and the field house, he still would have ended up on Hester Street. And Hester is the only sensible way to get to the apartment building on Liberty Street where Gwen lived her senior year. She'd talked her father into renting it for her, even though he'd already bought her that pink Buick."

James finished. We walked on in the dark. The streetlights looked like dim, faraway flying saucers. "Rollie could have gone straight to his dorm on the other side of Tuckman, of course. But the reason he took the overnight bus was to see Gwen, wasn't it? That's what Bud Wetzel figured and I'm sure that's right. He was anxious to show Gwen his trophy. Reap whatever romantic reward it might bring."

We reached Hester Street and headed east. "It's impossible to know which side of the street Rollie walked on. He could have crossed here and walked along the north side. Or he could have stayed on this side until he reached Liberty. But it doesn't matter. If Rollie saw what I think he saw, then he could have seen it from either side of the street."

We crossed Mortuary Street and then Church Street. The big, turn-of-the-century houses along Hester gave way to two blocks of Tudor-style apartment buildings. They had brown brick façades and green tile roofs. I stopped and gave James a biscuit, a reward for his patience. I pointed my chin at the building directly across the street from us. "See that building," I said. "That's where David Delarosa was killed. Early Thursday morning. Easter week 1957. Well, you can see what I'm thinking, can't you, James?" I painted the picture for him in case he didn't. "The street is dark and empty just like it is tonight. And Rollie is hurrying along on his way to Gwen's. No doubt he's exhausted. It's been a rough couple of days and he's had a long bus ride. But he's also a man with not just one big trophy, but two. Never in his life did he think a classy girl like Gwen Moffitt would fall in love with him. But she had. She'd looked beyond his family's embarrassing working-class status. She'd recognized his potential. Just that past fall she'd accepted the modest diamond ring he'd bought with his grocery packing money. So Rollie is a tired but happy young man that morning. Then he sees it. A pink Buick convertible. As bright as neon under the street light. Parked in front of that apartment building where all the athletes stay."

In my hazy imagination I could see that pink Buick, too. I could see the anguish on Rollie's face. I could see him walk slowly to the apartment building door. I could see his cloudy eyes and the debate that was raging behind them, his anger taking the affirmative, his better judgment vainly arguing the negative. I could see his trembling hand try the heavy latch. See him wince when the latch depressed with a quiet click. I could see him slip inside and stare up the steps. I could see his fingers tighten around the neck of his trophy, the bones of his knuckles pushing hard against the stretched white skin.

I gave James a tug and headed back down Hester Street. "Now remember," I said, as if he'd seen all of the imaginary things I'd seen. "This is only a scenario. And you know what a scenario is, don't you, James? It's a theory unencumbered by evidence." I looked back at the apartment building and in my imagination saw Gwen's pink Buick make a wild U-turn and speed off into the fuzzy night. "And I don't have any evidence, James. Not any real evidence. All I have is that old letter from

David Delarosa and a whole truckload of cockamamie assumptions."

Monday, June 18

I learned long ago not to give story ideas to reporters. They smile at you like you're five years old, give you a sickly, "Oh, that's a great idea!" and then they never do them. And if by some miracle they do write the story, they never do it right. So I just keep my mouth shut and let them come up with their own brilliant ideas.

That's why Louise Lewendowski was more than a little surprised when I ambushed her in the cafeteria. "I've got the neatest idea for a feature," I began. I'd made sure I had an extra cinnamon twist on my tray.

The kolachky lady yodeled at me. "You do?"

I slid the sweet roll across the table and made my pitch. "The other day I was visiting my old friend Gwen Moffitt-Stumpf and—"

Louise took the sweet roll and the bait. "You know Gwendolyn Moffitt-Stumpf?"

I pawed the air. "Oh, yes. We ran around with the same crowd in college. We still see each other every now and again."

She was leaning forward on her elbows,

nibbling on the cinnamon twist like a rabbit. "I hear her new house is a regular palace."

"Nothing regular about it," I said. "Which strangely enough leads me to the idea I had. Her husband, Rollie, you see, has the most incredible den. It's just spectacular. And I was thinking, wouldn't that make a great Sunday feature for Louise? The dens of Hannawa's powerful men. You could do Rollie's den, the mayor's, some of the corporate presidents. Our readers would just eat it up, don't you think?"

"That is such a great idea," Louise said. I could tell by the size of her eyes that she really meant it.

And so by the time we headed back toward the newsroom the story idea was firmly planted. "I just hope they'll go for it," Louise worried. "You know how private men can be."

I was brimming with good advice. "I wouldn't go directly to the men themselves," I suggested. "Go to their wives. They'll see it as a great way to show off their husbands as well as their decorating talents. And their husbands won't be able to say no."

"You're right—that's the way to do it."

"Of course you'll want to get the men in the photos. Ties off. Feet up."

"Of course."

I pretended to have a sudden brilliant thought. "You know who you should get to shoot it? Chuck Weideman."

Louise's eyebrows disappeared under her bangs. "Weedy?"

"Absolutely. He's been shooting the city's bigwigs for a million years. He wouldn't be the least bit intimidated by them or their wives. I bet he'd get some terrific candids. They might even start your story on Page One."

Louise was not exactly known for her hard-hitting journalism. I'm sure she could count the number of Page One stories she'd had on one finger. "You think he'd do it?"

"He just might," I said.

We reached the newsroom. I felt like a skunk. A very happy skunk. "If you do go ahead with the story," I said, "I'd appreciate it if you didn't tell Gwen it was my idea. I wouldn't want her to think I was taking advantage of our friendship."

Louise gave my shoulder an empathetic squeeze, like it was a fresh roll of toilet paper. "Of course, Maddy."

An hour later I slipped back to the photographers' studio, the windowless bunker where the paper's photographers pretend to work. Weedy was busy playing solitaire on his computer.

Weedy has as much professional integrity as anyone else at *The Herald-Union*. He'd also sell his own grandmother into white slavery if it meant a Page One photo credit. And of course that's why I put that bug in Louise's ear about him.

I sat on his desk and spun his monitor around so he'd pay attention. "Weedy," I said, "you know I'm not the kind of woman who wallows in frivolity."

"Indeed, I do."

"Or plays bullshit games."

"If you say so."

"So if I were to give you a tip—as murky as it sounded—you'd take my word for it?"

"Abso-fucking-lutely."

"Good. Because if Louise Lewendowski asks you to shoot a story for her, I would strongly recommend that you don't try to pawn it off on somebody else."

Weedy winced. "And why's that?"

"Just happily accept the assignment and keep my name out of it. Okay?"

He studied my face. "Okay."

I handed him the Post-it I had pinched between my thumb and index finger. "And should you by chance find yourself in a room with a mantel full of trophies, discreetly see if there's one with this engraved on the front."

He read the Post-it aloud: "First Place, State of Ohio Collegiate Debate Tournament, Columbus, 1956-57." He put the tiny square of sticky paper in his shirt pocket. "Not to sound like the glory grubbing bastard I am, but what exactly might I gain from this despicable act of subterfuge?"

I allowed myself a grin. "Either nothing—or just maybe the most important photo you've ever taken."

Thursday, June 21

When I got to work I found a big sack of kolachkys on my desk. Good gravy! I could have danced around the morgue like Ginger Rogers. I divided the kolachkys into three piles. Six for me, six for Eric—a necessary bribe so I could enjoy my six—and twelve for Weedy. I headed straight for his desk with his share.

"Good news for Morgue Mama?" I asked, dangling the bag in front of his face.

Weedy did have good news for me. The features editor had given Louise the go-ahead and he'd been assigned to do the photos. In fact he was going to do two of the shoots that afternoon:

Mayor Flynn in his den. Rollie Stumpf in his. I dropped the bag in his waiting hands.

The rest of the day was absolute torture. I marked up that morning's paper. I had lunch at Ike's. I dug out the files Doneta Deetz needed on the 1927 Apple Creek Bridge disaster—the county engineer was warning it could happen again if commissioners didn't come through with the budget increases he'd requested—and I watched the elevator for Weedy and Louise.

Finally they appeared, at ten minutes after four, carrying big red cartons of McDonald's French fries, giggling like a couple of fifth graders returning from a field trip to the local mental hospital. I wanted to charge at Weedy like a bull, screaming "Well? Well?" Instead I got busy clipping meaningless squares out of the sports section with my black-handled scissors. Out of the corner of my eye I watched Weedy flirt his way through the newsroom. With Carol Voinovich. With Cheryl Presselo. Even with Margaret Newman. I watched him wash down his fries at the water fountain. I watched him turn toward the morgue. I watched him wipe his greasy fingers on his pants. Reach into his shirt pocket. He finally reached my desk. He smiled and handed me the Post-it. He headed for the men's room. I pulled my reading glasses to the end of my nose, lifted my chin and read. Scribbled below the inscription I'd given him were these three words: *No such trophy.*

I didn't know whether to be delighted or depressed. I did know that I needed more information before going to Detective Grant. "Eric," I said sweetly, "how about I buy your supper tonight?"

Thirty minutes later we were sitting in my Shadow outside the office building in Brinkley where Rollie Stumpf had his insurance agency. I had a fish sandwich inside of me. Eric had a Whopper inside of him. He was still protesting.

Right at five the three women who worked in Rollie's office hurried out to their cars and drove off. "I'm not good at this kind of thing," Eric whined.

"Nobody is," I assured him. "Now go!"

So Eric went inside. My instructions to him couldn't have been clearer: Under the guise of seeking information on insurance rates for his pickup, he was to scour every desk, table and shelf for that debate trophy.

Eric was back in fifteen minutes with a thick stack of brochures. "And?"

"No debate trophy," he said.

"You look everywhere?"

"He's got plaques and awards all over the walls. Couple hundred of them. All for selling lots of insurance."

"You're sure you didn't tell him you worked at the paper?"

"I'm sure."

"Anybody else in there besides Rollie Stumpf?"

"Nope."

"You didn't give him any reason to be suspicious?"

"I just looked like an idiot looking for cheaper truck insurance."

"And no debate trophy?"

"Not unless he keeps it in the bathroom."

"You didn't look there?"

"Maddy. Get a grip."

24

Monday, June 25

Detective Grant and I started up the pathway. The brown matted grass that covered the hill when I was there in March had been replaced with a thick growth of green sprinkled with yellow buttercups. It wasn't any easier passing the spot where Gordon was killed than it was three months before.

We followed the rim of the landfill to the old dump. It was only eight in the morning but Andrew J. Holloway III and his students were already busy digging.

There had been quite a nasty debate in the weeks after Gordon's death whether to continue his garbology project. The new chair of the archaeology department—some woman from New Jersey who was absolutely gaga over old Buddhist temples—wanted nothing to do with it. But Gordon's students raised such a fuss that the dean persuaded her that it would be politically incorrect to drop the dig so soon after Gordon's murder. So it was handed off to Andrew, who accepted it eagerly.

"Well, here we are," Grant said to me. His arms were folded menacingly over his chest. His feet were planted far apart. His chin was jutting out.

I just had to laugh. "You look like Yul Brynner in *The King and I.*"

He self-consciously put his hands in his pockets and shifted his weight onto one leg. "I hope you didn't invite me out here for a dance lesson."

"Not hardly," I said. "I want you to arrest Rollie Stumpf."

"For Professor Sweet's murder, I gather?"

I dug the letter from my purse and handed it to him. "For David Delarosa's, too."

His huge eyebrows shot up. The corners of his mouth went down. He opened the letter in slow motion, as if it might be filled with anthrax.

"It's from David to Gordon," I said as he read. "Written the Christmas break before David was killed." I told him who I thought Miss Forty Below was. "David could have been talking about any number of girls at the college. But I don't think Gordon would've been too upset about David trying to seduce any of them. And Gwen and I were the only two women in our crowd engaged at the time."

Grant peeked at me over the top of the letter. "Any chance you were Miss Forty Below?"

"I wondered about that, too." I told him about the night at Jericho's when David tried to *protect* me from Shaka Bop. "But there's that line about the tiny chip of ice. Gwen had a diamond. I didn't. My Lawrence couldn't afford a plastic ring from a bubble gum machine. It had to be Gwen."

I then told him all I'd learned about the debate team trip to Columbus. About Rollie deciding to take the overnight bus. About Gwen's pink Buick. About my own middle-of-the-night walk down Hester Street.

"Do you have any proof that Gwen went home with David Delarosa that night?" he asked.

I admitted that I didn't. That I'd left Jericho's before midnight. "But some of the others might. Effie or Chick Glass or maybe even Shaka Bop. After his scuffle with David, I'm sure Shaka kept his eye on him the rest of the night."

Grant was not impressed. "It might be hard to get a conviction based on a fifty-year-old recollection of a guy picking up a girl in a bar," he said.

That's when I told him about Rollie's trophy—or more accurately the absence of his trophy.

This he considered seriously. "And you think after bludgeoning David Delarosa, he threw it in a garbage can and it ended up here? And all these years later that's what Professor Sweet was looking for? And Rollie Stumpf killed him before he could find it?"

"Actually," I said, "Gordon was looking for something else."

"Oh yes," he said, "proof about Jack Kerouac's cheeseburger."

"You know about that, do you?"

"Of course I know about that."

"Well, then you can forget about it," I said. "Because Gordon was actually digging for a cocoa can full of pine cones." I told him about my visit with Penelope Yarrow. The collection of cocoa cans I'd bought from Gordon's nephew.

"Digging up an old dump for a can of pine cones—why the hell not?"

I didn't care for his attitude. "It really doesn't matter what Gordon was looking for. It only matters what Rollie thought Gordon might find. A dented, bloody trophy that would lead right to him."

I started across the dump toward Andrew. Grant followed me like a nervous penguin. Which

I liked. "I have to admit you've dug up some interesting stuff," he said.

"Well, thank you."

As quickly as he gaveth, he tooketh away. "But it's all a tad circumstantial, isn't it? You have no real proof that the trophy is missing. And no proof that it's buried out there."

"True enough," I admitted. "But you've got to admit Rollie sure had a motive. For both murders. And from what I understand, he doesn't have an alibi for the evening Gordon was killed."

"Neither does anybody else—as you know."

I was not going to let his pessimism deter me. "But we are off to a promising start, aren't we?"

"There is no we, Mrs. Sprowls. There is only me. Cautiously taking one step at a time." He promptly tripped on one of the archaeological stakes hidden in the high grass.

He was a big man. I was a little woman. I let him get up by himself. "I should have warned you about those," I said.

We reached the hole where Andrew was digging. He crawled out and slapped the dirt off his knees. He hadn't known we were coming. He was nervous. Uncertain. Andrew the boy instead of Andrew the man. Detective Grant got right to the point. "Andrew, did Professor Sweet ever tell his students to be on the lookout for an old trophy?"

"Not that I ever knew."

"If anybody knew, it would be you, wouldn't it?" Grant asked. "The two of you were very close."

For all Andrew knew, Detective Grant was there to arrest him. "We discussed the dig every week—as I've told you."

Grant let him stew. "To your knowledge was a trophy ever found?"

Andrew's head quivered no.

I piped in. "How about cocoa cans? Find any more of them?"

"We always find cocoa cans," he said. "Why?"

Grant shushed me before I could explain the cocoa can scenario to Andrew. "You'll let me know if you do come across a trophy, won't you?"

Andrew assured him that he would.

"And you'll keep this under your hat? Won't talk to any reporters or nosy librarians or anybody else about this?"

Andrew assured him that he wouldn't.

Grant glowered at him like an angry, Old Testament God. He shook his hand and started for the parking lot.

"That's it?" I squeaked, hurrying after him.

Grant stopped. He put both of his big hands on my shoulders. He bent low. Until his eyes were six inches from mine. "I think your role in this investigation has come to an end, Mrs. Sprowls. You've rooted around and—"

I was furious. "Rooted around?"

"Admittedly not the most flattering imagery," he said. "But you do get the point, don't you? You've given us an intriguing lead. We appreciate your help. Now you're going to wait patiently while we evaluate what we've got."

"Evaluate? Heavens to Betsy! What you've got to do is dig!"

"One thing I am not going to do is dig," he said. "Do you know the field day the media would have if I mucked up a scholarly archaeological dig and found nothing?"

"*The Herald-Union* especially," I conceded.

He wasn't finished. "Or the money it would require? The man hours? Over a bit of adolescent braggadocio in an old letter? I've just tiptoed through one minefield with that Zuduski murder."

I gave him my best Morgue Mama: "So you're going to let two murders go unsolved because you're a little gun shy?"

He was not the least bit intimidated. "And

that's the other thing. Gordon Sweet was shot. I'm supposed to be searching for a 9mm semiautomatic pistol. Not an old debate trophy."

We walked in silence to our cars. But I wasn't giving in just yet. I leaned against his door and wrapped my arms around the wall of shapeless blubber where my waist used to be. "Maybe there's a way we can dig without actually digging," I said.

He winced at the word *we*. But he listened.

Tuesday, July 3

I picked up the phone on the first ring. It was Dale Marabout. I swiveled toward the newsroom and wiggled my fingers at him. "Morning, Mr. M."

"You think you can get away?" he asked. "Detective Grant is holding a *meeedia* conference at eleven." Dale always pronounced media that way. In the old days when people still read newspapers, public officials held *press* conferences. Now that most people get their news from the bobble heads on TV, the powerful p-word has been replaced by the milk-toasty m-word, out of some warped sense of fairness I suppose. "Word is it's about that little murder of yours," Dale said. "I thought maybe you'd want to tag along."

"I've got oodles to do—but I guess I can get

away for a bit."

Of course I could get away. I'd known about Grant's media conference for two days. I'd come in two hours early that morning to get my clipping out of the way. And I pretty much knew Dale would invite me along. Although I was prepared to go by myself if he didn't.

So at ten-thirty Dale and I met in the parking garage and drove down the hill to police headquarters in his old station wagon. We got Styrofoam cups of coffee—Hannawa's finest never heard of a tea bag apparently—and found a pair of empty metal chairs in the Media Room. Tish Kiddle and her crew were there from TV21. So were a couple of the Cleveland stations. All in all about a dozen reporters.

Grant slipped in right at eleven with the department's press officer. There was also a pair of burly uniformed officers. Dale pointed his chin at them. "In case Tish's hairspray can turns out to be a bomb," he whispered.

Grant fiddled with his notes. Took a test-sip from his glass of ice water. Slowly surveyed the reporters gathered before him. Scowled at me. Then he began the most impressive display of verbal gymnastics I'd heard since Lawrence tried to explain his serial infidelities to me: "I'm Chief Homicide Detective Grant. G.R.A.N.T. I'm going to talk to you this morning about our investigation into the Friday, March 3rd murder of Professor Gordon Sweet. Admittedly it has been some time since we last updated you on our progress, and I wanted to assure you and the public, and especially the Hemphill College community, that we have not ceased in our desire to give this case the highest investigative priority."

He gave a couple minutes of background for the sake of the out-of-town reporters. Then he got down to the nitty-gritty: "In the weeks since the murder we have been pursuing a number of leads. And as of this morning, while we have made some progress, we unfortunately still have not identified a motive for the murder. Nor have we identified a probable suspect."

He gave the reporters a few seconds to get all that down, then continued: "We have in recent days, however, discovered a possible link—and I emphasize possible—between Professor Sweet's murder and the April 1957 murder of Hemphill College junior David Anthony Delarosa." He spelled Delarosa for us and then gave a brief account of his murder.

Then he finished with this cryptic gem: "Specifically, we have identified an object that may or may not be helpful in satisfactorily resolving both murders. I cannot because of the ongoing nature of our investigation be more helpful in identifying the object we've identified. But I think I can say with some certainty that this object does not link the late professor to Mr. Delarosa's murder as much as it links the murder of Mr. Delarosa to the late professor's. Now if any of you have questions, I'll try my best to be equally opaque." Grant chuckled at his joke. The reporters only moaned.

I'm sure that Dale was the only reporter in the room familiar with both murders. He had the first question: "Is the object you've identified the missing blunt instrument used to bludgeon David Delarosa?"

Answered Detective Grant: "Unfortunately, I cannot confirm that for you at this time."

Dale quickly followed up: "And when you said identified, does that mean you've found the object? Or merely identified it?"

Answered Grant: "Identified. I. D. E. N. T. I. F. I. E. D."

"So you haven't found it yet?" Dale asked, as other arms began to shoot up around him.

Grant answered with a question of his own: "When, Mr. Marabout, did I say we were looking for anything?" He pointed at Tish Kiddle before Dale could ask another question.

Tish came out of her front row chair like a Pop Tart out of a toaster. She held her pen and reporter's notebook high, as if she was actually going to take notes. Her question—if that's what you want to call it—was exactly what you'd expect: "You said you wanted to update us on your progress. But it sounds to me like you're really updating us on your lack of progress. Can you possibly explain to the frightened citizens of this community why you haven't found the killer yet?"

Dale made a U-turn in front of police headquarters and started back toward the paper. He began to pepper me with questions about the investigation: Did I know what the mysterious object was? Were they looking for it in the Wooster Pike landfill? Did the police finally have a suspect?

"It wasn't my media conference," I reminded him.

My reticence made him furious. "Jesus, Maddy! Just who are you working for anyway?"

"Truth, Justice and the American Way?"

He punched the steering wheel instead of my nose. "Never heard of them."

That was Dale's cute way of admitting I was right to keep my lip buttoned. And I couldn't give him any of the inside poop I had, could I? "I know you've got a story to write," I said as we pulled into the parking deck. "But Detective Grant wouldn't confirm anything I told you anyway. I'd only be getting myself into hot water without helping you one damn bit."

Dale pulled into his slot on level three. He swiveled toward me. "Make you a deal," he said. "I'll let you read my story before I zap it to the desk. And if there's any little thing you can amplify a bit."

I pressed my shush finger across his eager smile. "I'll make you a deal. You write your little story and after it runs, I'll personally see it gets filed away in the right morgue file. How's that?"

And that's how it ended. We took the elevator to the newsroom without saying a word. Dale went to his desk. I went to mine.

There was no guarantee the plan I'd cooked up with Detective Grant would work. But at least it was finally in the works: That night TV21 would dutifully report that the Hannawa police had identified a mysterious object that might link the two murders. The story Dale was writing for tomorrow's *Herald-Union* would certainly get a big, black, above-the-fold headline. Charlie Chimera would be pissing and moaning about the police department's ineptitude all afternoon on the radio.

The police meanwhile would go to work on Rollie Stumpf. They'd put him under surveillance. They'd visit him at the office. They'd hint that they had more than they did. What Rollie would do was anybody's guess. Maybe he'd confess. That was our hope. Or maybe he'd panic and do something foolish that gave him away.

I did know what I'd be doing. For the first time in four months I'd be doing absolutely nothing.

Wednesday, July 11

The week that followed was simply torture. Detective Grant didn't call me once. Andrew hadn't returned my calls. Dale was paying me back and enjoying it. Every time I asked him how things were going with the murder investigations he'd shrug and say something smart like, "Maybe there'll be something about it in tomorrow's paper."

So I was out of the loop and you can just imagine how I felt about that. Then on Wednesday morning Gwen called me at the paper. "I just felt like giving you a buzz," she said.

"Well, I'm glad you did," I said.

She rattled my eardrum with a huge, over-rehearsed sigh. "I just hope you're having a better summer than I am," she said.

"Things not going well?"

She told me about the wrong shade of blue on the Tuscan tiles she ordered for her guest bathroom. About the trouble she was having with her maid service. About her ongoing search for a pet therapist who understands the delicate temperament of dachshunds. "Then there's that business with the police," she said.

"About Gordon, you mean?"

"Yes—and that silly stuff about David Delarosa. They've talked to us three times in a week. Me once and Rollie twice."

I commiserated. "They've talked to me about it, too."

Her second sigh was better. "I don't know what they think we can tell them. Rollie wasn't even here that night."

This was not the time for me to tell Gwen everything I knew about Rollie's early return to Hannawa, or David's letter to Gordon. This was the time for me to play dumb and listen closely. "That's right," I agreed. "He and Lawrence were in Columbus at the debate tournament."

"And you and I were with Gordon and Chick at Jericho's." She hesitated. "That was the same night David and Sidney got into it over you, wasn't it?"

I told her it was.

Now she confided in me. "You know how worried I've been, Maddy. That maybe Chick had something to do with Gordon's death. Because of the way they fought at the Kerouac Thing."

"We've all had that worry," I said.

"But now that the police think there's a link to David's death, well, who knows, maybe it was Sidney after all."

"What about Effie's alibi for him?" I asked.

"Maybe Effie had no choice," Gwen said.

Sunday, July 15

The concept of Sunday morning, unfortunately, means nothing to James. He whimpered me awake at seven, as he did every day, demanding that his breakfast be served immediately. I filled his bowl with nuggets and sprinkled the top with stinky liver treats so he'd eat it. Then it was my turn. I put a mug of water in the microwave for my tea. I poured a bowl of cereal. I retrieved my Sunday paper from the driveway while the pieces of petrified bananas and strawberries softened up in the skimmed milk.

We'd finally run Louise's feature story. On Page One, too. There was a big photo of Mayor Flynn lounging in a big leather chair, surrounded by his collection of Democratic donkeys. Below the photo was this headline:

SOME DANDY DENS
Where City's Movers And Shakers Get Away From It All

I read Louise's predictable cutsie-wootsie lead—*Even the Energizer Bunny has to recharge its batteries once in a while*—and then turned to the jump page to see if they'd run a photo of Rollie Stumpf. Boy did they. It was a huge, three-column shot of him standing in front of his mantel full of trophies. He was flashing a forced jack-o-lantern smile. I could just see Gwen on the day of the shoot standing behind Weedy screeching, "Smile bigger, Rollie! Smile bigger!"

"I bet he's not smiling this morning," I whispered to myself.

I scanned the story for the part about Rollie's den. He got several paragraphs, right after Worldstar Hydraulics CEO Vernon P. Welty. There was this self-effacing quote by Rollie:

> "Sometimes I can't believe it's mine," said Stumpf, the son of a steelworker who today runs one of Hannawa's most prestigious insurance agencies. "It's bigger than the entire house I grew up in."

And this rather sad quote from Gwen, which I'm sure she spent a week of rehearsal getting just right:

> "My husband is the busiest man in the world, so he doesn't get to spend as much time in here as he'd like," said Stumpf's wife of 48 years, Gwendolyn Moffitt-Stumpf. "But I've made sure he

`absolutely loves the few precious moments he does get."`

After breakfast I took James for his walk. It was one of those July days you dream all winter about but hate when they finally arrive. It was only nine o'clock but the temperature was already pushing eighty. When we got back to my bungalow, James went straight to his rug for a nap. I took a shower and put on the worst tee shirt and jeans I could find.

I had big plans for this particular Sunday. My backyard is a disaster. It has been since Lawrence and I bought it over forty years ago. The lawn has more dandelions than grass blades and the flowerbeds are solid clay. For years I've been dreaming of turning it into one of those beautiful English gardens you drool over in the magazines. In my mind I can picture the cobblestone walkways and serpentine beds of perennials. I can picture a comfy teakwood bench beneath a vine-covered trellis. I see roses. I see zinnias, and marigolds, and bright yellow mums. I can hear my imaginary garden, too. A trickling fountain. Tinkling wind chimes. The buzzing wings of hummingbirds. I figured today was as good as any to start.

The first thing I did was get my kloppers from

the garage and go to work on the dead limbs hanging from my pin oak. When that was finished, I scrubbed out the crud in my bird bath. When that was finished, I de-thistled my day lilies. When that was finished I made myself another mug of tea and curled up on my new glider. Gardening is always easier between your ears than on your hands and knees.

While I was busy deciding where my future herb garden should go, the phone rang. And rang and rang. "Damn it," I growled at the unknown caller, "can't you see I'm not here?"

The ringing continued. I gave in and trotted inside. It was Detective Grant.

"I figured I'd better tell you before you saw it on the news," he began. "Rollie Stumpf overdosed on drugs this morning."

"Good gravy! Is he dead?"

"Not yet."

"Please don't tell me it was intentional."

"He left a note."

"Good gravy! Where was he? And where was Gwen?"

"Gwen was in the kitchen. Rollie was in his den."

"Good gravy! Don't tell me that."

25

Wednesday, July 25

Ike was wearing a beautiful gray suit. I was wearing my navy blue funeral suit, the one I wished fit better. "You up for all this?" he asked as he helped me down my front steps.

"I'm okay," I said. I had my arms around a crock pot full of baked beans.

Ike put the beans in his trunk. We headed for Greenlawn, the leafy, upscale suburb north of the city. The morning rush hour was long over. There was only a dribble of traffic on Cleveland Avenue now.

Why was Ike coming with me? In March, I'd asked Eric to go with me to Gordon's funeral. And he was a pain in the ass the whole time. This time I wanted a little maturity at my side.

We pulled into the Umplebee & Meyer Funeral Home. It was, as you might expect, Hannawa's most prestigious. Its white brick façade was trimmed with oodles of columns and fancy cornices. It looked like the bottom layer of a wedding cake.

Ike parked his modest Chevrolet next to a big boaty Lincoln. We headed for the entrance, elbow to elbow like an old married couple. A pasty man in a baggy black suit held the door for us, his right eye studying Ike's brown skin, his left eye studying my white skin. We followed the organ music to the chapel. There had to be a hundred chairs set up and ninety of them had to be empty.

The minister was already leaning on the pulpit next to Rollie's urn, ready to start as soon as somebody nudged the organist. Ike and I hurried to the front and sat behind Chick and Effie. Effie looked over her shoulder and smiled. Chick looked over his shoulder and frowned.

It was terrible seeing all those empty chairs. But I was hardly surprised. Rollie had committed suicide. He'd left a note taking responsibility for two murders—a note *The Herald-Union* saw fit to print on the front page. Still, how could you not feel bad for Gwen? She'd spent a lifetime befriending Hannawa's rich and powerful. She'd worked at it with the tenacity of a stamp collector. And now the whole kit and caboodle had abandoned her.

The only people brave enough to show up were a few relatives and a handful of old beatniks.

To tell you the truth, I'd debated about coming myself. It was, after all, my harebrained scheme that pushed Rollie over the edge. "Quit wallowing in guilt," Dale Marabout hissed at me one afternoon when I was feeling especially sorry for myself. He had a ballpoint clenched in his teeth. He was typing like a madman to meet his deadline. "Rollie Stumpf meted out his own punishment. He saved taxpayers a bundle."

I'll never know for sure, of course, but Rollie certainly must have known that he was a suspect well before Louise's feature on his *dandy* den ran that Sunday. How could he not have known? That press conference by Scotty Grant? Those repeated visits by detectives? Every day he must have worried a little more.

Gwen's first statement to the police did give me a pretty good picture of what happened that Sunday morning: Rollie got up at nine. He crawled into a sweat suit. Let the dogs out for their morning pee. Got the paper from the driveway. He poured a cup of coffee in the kitchen. Buttered two slices of wheat toast. He joined Gwen at that same tiny bistro table by the bay window where she'd served me the poached salmon and pea pods. He pulled the paper from its plastic bag and saw Louise's story on Page One. He turned to the jump page and saw Weedy's photo of him by the mantel, with all of his college debate trophies. All of them but one.

Rollie knew I'd been investigating Gordon's death. And when he saw that photo he knew for sure I'd made the link between the two murders. He knew I was not only behind that story on his den, but also the story that followed Detective Grant's press conference. And he knew one other thing. He knew he'd ruined Gwen's life. The woman to whom he owed everything.

So while Gwen called her important friends to make sure they'd seen the paper, Rollie finished his breakfast. Then he slipped upstairs. He got the bottle of antidepressants Gwen kept in her nightstand. According to the police report, there was a three-month supply in the bottle. He went back down to the kitchen. Gwen was still chatting away. He got a bottle of lemon-flavored Perrier from the refrigerator. He headed for his den. He closed the door. He sat at his enormous oak desk. He pulled out the box of expensive Italian stationery Gwen had given him one year for Christmas. His name was printed in gold across the top: ROLLAND H.

STUMPF. He wrote a note. He positioned it in the exact center of his leather desk pad. He started putting pills in his mouth. Sipping the expensive water.

The headline above Dale's story in the Monday paper said this:

INSURANCE EXEC ROLLIE STUMPF
OVERDOSES AMID MURDER PROBE

Gwen told police she did not find Rollie until a quarter after ten. By then he was already on the floor behind his desk, gasping, convulsing. Gwen said she shook him and screamed at him and then called 911. By the time Detective Grant called me that afternoon with the news, Rollie was in Hannawa General Hospital, in a coma, on life support.

Dale worked the story hard for Tuesday. I still wasn't talking to him but apparently Detective Grant was. Said the headline:

POLICE HINT MISSING TROPHY
LINKS STUMPF TO PAIR OF MURDERS

Detective Grant was smart enough not to go on the record. But Dale's story did contain plenty of quotes from a "veteran detective close to the investigation." Among them was this telling gem:

> "We cannot at this delicate juncture say with acceptable certainty that Mr. Stumpf killed either or both men," the detective said, "but the trophy is unaccounted for, and given all the interesting coincidences we're encountering, we are confidently pursuing that scenario with a cautious head of steam."

Now who in Hannawa but Detective Scotty Grant gives quotes like that?

Anyway, there was no story on Wednesday or Thursday. But Friday's headline gave me a pretty good idea where things were headed:

SUSPECT STUMPF LINGERS IN COMA

It was during this lingering that Gwen gave detectives her second statement, the one detailing how David Delarosa died.

Gwen had indeed gone home with David that

night in 1957. "When Jericho's closed David asked me to drive him home," she told them. "And when we pulled up to his apartment building he asked me to come inside for coffee. And I said yes."

Gwen was a worldly girl. Certainly she understood that coffee had nothing to do with David's invitation. Given his letter to Gordon that Christmas, it's very likely he'd been working his "ample animal charm" on her all winter. And by the time Easter vacation rolled around—and Rollie conveniently out of sight and mind in Columbus—Gwen was ready to surrender her own ample charms. "I had sexual intercourse with David Delarosa," she told detectives.

"Was it consensual?" they asked.

"I suppose it was," she answered.

Rollie showed up at David's door at three in the morning. Assuming that the bus from Columbus reached Hemphill College at two, that meant Rollie stood outside David's apartment building for a good long time, waiting for Gwen to appear, slowly coming to a boil.

We'll never know for sure, but Rollie must have been aware of David's interest in Gwen. And he must have sensed that Gwen was interested in him. There's one thing we can assume with some confidence: When Rollie saw Gwen's pink Buick in front of that apartment building on Hester Street, he knew who lived there. He knew behind which door he'd find his fiancée.

David went to the door in his socks and underwear. He stopped Rollie from coming in. Rollie was crying like a baby. "Come out, Gwen!" he begged her repeatedly.

"She ain't going nowhere," David said. He pushed Rollie into the hallway. Pushed him toward the stairway. David was laughing at him. Taunting him. "Looks like I got her first," he said. "Ain't that a god-diddly-damned shame."

Gwen told detectives that she ran after them. That she reached them just as Rollie dropped his suitcase and swung his trophy with both arms. The thick metal stalk of the trophy struck David square on the nose. He staggered backward and fell over the stairwell railing.

Rollie was in a rage now. He ran down the stairs and pounded away at David's prostrate body. Until David's face was raw. Until David's blood was everywhere.

Gwen ran down the stairway after Rollie. She tried to pull him off David. But Rollie kept bashing away. "I was afraid someone in the building heard the fight," Gwen told detectives. "But no one came. I went back to David's room and put on my clothes. I brought a pair of David's pants for Rollie. And a shirt."

"The same ones he was wearing that night?" the detectives asked her.

"Yes," said Gwen. "Rollie's clothes were covered with blood. He changed right there in the lobby. I went back to David's room again and found his wrestling bag. I put the trophy and Rollie's clothes in it. We drove around for hours. Until it started getting light. I finally stuffed the bag in a garbage bin. Behind that A&P that used to be across from the Crystal Theater. On Tuckman."

"You weren't afraid somebody would find the wrestling bag in the garbage?" the detectives asked her.

"We spent the next fifty years worrying about that," she said.

Dale's next story appeared on the following Wednesday:

STUMPF DIES, SUICIDE NOTE ENDS MURDER PROBE

There was a very interesting sidebar accompanying that story, by the way. A very sad sidebar.

It quoted an old girlfriend of Gordon's, a woman from Toledo named Penelope Yarrow Oakar, who speculated that Gordon was not digging for Rollie's debate trophy at all, but a cocoa can full of pine cones. "I hate to think he died for such a silly thing," she told Dale Marabout when he called her.

Over the weekend doctors sat down with Gwen and Detective Grant. They said Rollie was brain dead. Gwen agreed to take him off life support. An hour later Rollie Stumpf died. Dale got a copy of his suicide note. It said this:

> *My precious Gwen,*
>
> *Please forgive me for ending things this way. But there is no reason for either of us to live with my guilt any longer. I killed David Delarosa and I killed Gordon. Make sure the police understand that.*
>
> *Gwen, you gave me a better life than I deserved. I hope my gratitude always showed.*
>
> *Love Rollie*

Gwen knew Rollie killed David. She was right there. Naked as a jaybird. But did Gwen know Rollie killed Gordon? At least have a suspicion? "When they found Gordon's body out there I didn't dare think about it," she said in her statement.

"But in your heart-of-hearts you knew it was a possibility?" detectives asked her.

"I didn't even know he had a gun," she said.

The minister was still speaking—saying the things ministers always say at funerals—when a soft, fuzzy *voodee-voo-voo* oozed into the chapel. It was like the cool, haunting hoot of a mourning dove. It rolled forward through the rows of empty chairs. It took everyone by the ears and turned their heads. It was Shaka Bop, filling the doorway, in his dashiki and porkpie hat, his big shoulders bent over his silver saxophone. His song was recognizable at first—"My Old Kentucky Home"—but as he played, the old song's simple melody splintered in a thousand directions, in the crazy bebop way Rollie Stumpf always loved. It was so beat. And so beautiful.

Ike held the door for me. I carried the baked beans. There were only six cars in Gwen's long, swooping driveway. If the funeral was any gauge, there wouldn't be any more. We crossed the grand foyer to the living room, our heels banging on those horrible black and white chessboard tiles. Gwen was crumpled in a white wingback chair. She'd replaced the black wool suit she'd worn to the funeral with a summery silk pantsuit, the pink of raspberries not quite ripe. The handful of friends and family who'd bravely attended the funeral now sat motionless on a pair of opposing white sofas, like a collection of department store mannequins. Queen Strudelschmidt and Prince Elmo were asleep under the glass coffee table. Rollie's urn rested on the mantel above a marble fireplace filled with glowing candles.

I held up the crock pot. "Who needs beans?"

Shaka Bop's hands came together in a single, loud clap. "Oh, Dolly!" he said. "Could I ever dig a big bowl of those sweet morsels!"

Gwen padded toward me across the white carpet. She kissed my cheek. "Leave it to Maddy to think of everything," she said.

Effie, Chick and Shaka started to applaud. The handful of others in the room applauded, too, without knowing why. Gwen led us to the dining room. The table and antique sideboards were covered with multi-tiered trays of sugared fruits, fancy finger sandwiches and desserts far too pretty too eat. Enough food for an army. An army of fair-weather friends that wasn't coming. I found an empty corner on the table for my crock pot. Effie and Chick headed into the kitchen to find bowls and spoons. Shaka went to the wine cart and started popping corks.

We filled our bowls with the sticky brown beans. We filled our goblets with wine. We headed back to the living room, all that white carpet and upholstery be damned.

Given the two murders, and Rollie's suicide, there were a lot of subjects to avoid. We settled on Jack Kerouac's visit to the college. We laughed at how rumpled and fragrant he was after his long bus ride across the country. We laughed at how embarrassed we'd felt because of our better grooming. We laughed at what he must have thought of us, a gaggle of eager fools groveling at his scuffed shoes like he was Moses. We made Effie admit that she'd slept with him. We laughed at her detailed description of his clumsy lovemaking.

We laughed and laughed that cheerless afternoon. And Gwen laughed right along with us. Good gravy, she needed to escape for a while, didn't she? She'd just lost the man she'd lived with for fifty years. Thanks to the *Herald-Union*, everyone in Hannawa was buzzing about his confession to the murders of Gordon Sweet and David Delarosa. Oh, she needed an afternoon of laughter all right.

And not just because of the grief and humiliation hammering away at her. Ever since Gwen's statement was leaked to the media, there'd been speculation that she would be charged for her role in David Delarosa's murder. She had, after all, hurried Rollie away from the murder scene. She'd made sure that his bloody clothes and the battered trophy wouldn't be found. And even if the police didn't file charges, she still faced some very hard time—alone in her own big house. The number of empty chairs at the funeral attested to that. The mounds of untouched food in her dining room attested to that.

The afternoon faded away. One by one people found a reason to leave. By six o'clock there was just Gwen, Chick, Ike and me. "I'm afraid we'd better get going, too," I said. "But we can help you tidy up a bit before we go."

Gwen was curled up in her chair like a child. Her arms around her ankles. Her chin on her knees. "Don't be silly. My maid service is coming in the morning."

"Don't you be silly," Ike said. He started gathering up empty bean bowls and wine glasses. Which agitated me to no end. My offer to help was not a sincere offer. I wanted to get out of that house as fast as I could. Before I said the things I came to say. But now didn't want to say. I started gathering up bowls and glasses, too. Five minutes later Gwen, Chick and I were standing side by side at the huge double sink in her kitchen. Gwen was washing. I was rinsing. Chick was drying. Ike was standing behind us at the serving island, hovering over my crock pot with a silver serving spoon, eating the last few baked beans.

Gwen handed me a soapy bowl. "I'm glad you came today, Maddy. I know it had to be awkward for you."

"I was afraid it would be awkward for you."

Gwen smiled weakly. "You didn't know where things would lead."

I dunked the bowl in the rinse water. Handed it to Chick. I felt like someone who'd stupidly signed up for skydiving lessons, and was now crouched in the open door of an airplane, about to jump for the first time. "Gwen," I said. "I don't think Rollie shot Gordon."

Gwen didn't say anything. Chick did. "Maddy—this is hardly the time for your cockamamie theories."

If ever a magic genie had given me a wish, I would have used it right then. I would have turned myself invisible and tiptoed the hell out of there. "You're right, Chick. I shouldn't have said anything."

Ike's low, adamant voice shook the kitchen, like a commandment from God. "Say what's on your mind, Maddy."

I glared at him over my shoulder. He was licking his big spoon. And grinning. It was a reassuring grin that said, "Go ahead, Morgue Mama, you've got it right—and if things get too crazy, I'm here."

So I proceeded, shaking like a baby bunny. "First of all," I began, "I'm sure David's death occurred exactly as you said in your statement, Gwen. Your account certainly fits everything I've learned. And I'm sure Rollie's trophy ended up in the Wooster Pike dump. From what Gordon's graduate assistant told me—confirmed I should say—all of the city's garbage from the neighborhoods around the college was dumped out there in those years. From the end of World War II until the early seventies. That's why Gordon was confident he'd find that cocoa can full of pine cones Jack Kerouac gave him.

"Anyway, Gwen, you told police that you threw the bag with Rollie's bloody clothes and the trophy in the dumpster behind the old A&P on Tuckman. That's just a block west of the campus.

Back then we all knew the local garbage ended up at the Wooster Pike dump. Students went out there all the time. To drink beer and make out. Dig around for interesting things for their rooms." I shook the rinse water off the bowl in my hand. Held it up to the light. Dug off a stubborn nip of dried bacon with my thumbnail. Handed the bowl to Chick. "Which makes you wonder why you threw the trophy in that dumpster, doesn't it? But killers stupidly put bodies and guns and other evidence in the garbage all the time, don't they? You see it all the time in the news. And you and Rollie were certainly in a panic that night. You drove around until dawn. Good gravy! What do you do with a bag of bloody evidence? Then you saw that big metal box behind the A&P. A mound of rotting fruit and vegetables would be as good as any place." I peeked at Gwen for her reaction. She didn't have one. She just handed me another soapy bowl. "Of course you and Rollie began to worry about your choice almost immediately," I said.

Gwen's voice was no louder than a breath. "And kept on worrying for the next fifty years."

I finished rinsing the bowl and handed it to Chick. Continued my rambling soliloquy. "You'd think your sleeping with David would have ended your engagement. But Rollie needed a woman like you. And you needed a man like Rollie. And I'm sure you truly loved each other. And you were certainly tied to the hip after the murder, weren't you? So you went ahead with the wedding, forgiving and forgetting the best you could. Life got easier for you after the city built the new landfill and pushed all that new dirt on top of the old dump. Then Sweet Gordon starts digging. And the old worries came back."

It was clear from Chick's squinty-eyed scowl that he hadn't forgiven me for my unannounced visit to his house in April, and the insinuations I'd made about his relationship with Gordon. "Jesus H. Christ, Maddy! Why are you putting Gwen through this? Rollie confessed to both murders!"

"In a suicide note lacking any details," I pointed out. "Which means we have to fill in the blanks for ourselves."

Chick gave me another shot: "Lucky for us you're good at that."

I shook the hot water off the bowl in my hand. If we weren't standing right next to each other, I would have thrown it at him, the way he threw Gordon's bowl in the fireplace that night at the Blue Tangerine. Instead I handed it to him and went on, as if he'd given me a compliment. "Let's say that Rollie did kill Gordon. He certainly had a motive. Any day now Gordon's students were going to find his trophy. It wouldn't have Rollie's name on it. That would have been engraved on later. But Gordon would have known whose trophy it was and put two and two together."

"Maybe he'd already done the math," Ike said.

"Maybe," I admitted. "But if I had to bet my 401K on it, I'd say the only thing Gordon wanted to find was that cocoa can. Not Rollie's trophy. And in case you're wondering, Chick, not that order slip from Mopey's proving what Jack Kerouac had on his hamburger."

To say the least, that hit a nerve. "I never once suspected Gordon was looking for that," he fumed.

I fumed right back, quoting that awful poem he'd recited at Gordon's memorial service: "*And now that weighty question that never mattered much matters not at all!* Good gravy! If it didn't matter you wouldn't have written the damn poem!"

"It mattered," Chick said, nervously twisting his towel. "But not so much that I killed him."

I took the towel from him. Shook out the damp twists. Handed it back. Continued rinsing and explaining: "Nobody has an alibi for the evening

Gordon was killed. Not you, Chick. Not Effie. Not Shaka. Not Andrew Holloway. Not Gordon's nephew. Not Gwen. Not even me. But let's focus on Rollie. After all his success, and all the money he'd made, Rollie still worked late at the office almost every night. In fact, you had to drive to the Kerouac Thing by yourself that Wednesday night, didn't you, Gwen? And we know Rollie was working late again on Thursday, the day Gordon was killed."

I played devil's advocate now, recreating Gordon's murder as if Rollie did do it: "Rollie told detectives he worked alone in his office until eight o'clock that Thursday. He said the three women who work for him left at five. And that's probably right. I checked it out myself."

Gwen handed me the last bean bowl. "Rollie always sends them home at five," she said. "He knows they have families." She started washing the wine goblets.

I could have bawled when she spoke of Rollie in the present tense like that. But I'd gotten myself into this mess. I had no choice now but to buck up and see my foolishness through. "Andrew Holloway found Gordon's car at the ball fields north of the campus," I said. "Gordon must have met Rollie there and then driven out to the landfill with him. Or maybe they took Gordon's car. It could have happened either way, of course, but I think Gordon drove his car to the landfill. When Andrew found it, the doors were unlocked, the keys were in the ignition and Gordon's briefcase was in the back seat. It's hard to believe that even an absent-minded professor would leave his car like that and drive off with somebody else."

"Unless maybe he was forced at gunpoint," Ike pointed out.

Gwen handed me the first soapy goblet. I swished it in the rinse water and passed it on to Chick. "Okay," I said, "let's say it was at gunpoint. Why didn't Rollie just shoot him right there by the ball fields? Nobody's around there in March. No, I think Gordon willingly drove his killer to the landfill. He loved showing people the dig site. Even on a crappy evening in March he would have happily driven out there."

The goblet slipped from Chick's hands. Hit the rim of the granite counter. The delicate bowl of the goblet shattered. The stem snapped in two. He screeched at me like an entire flock of cockatoos. "First you tell us Rollie didn't kill Sweet Gordon, then step-by-stupefying-step you prove he could have!"

I helped him gather up the sharp shards of glass. "Could have but didn't," I said.

Until now Gwen's self-control had been, well, Gwen-like. Now tears were sliding down the sides of her nose, into the frown lines around her pale lips. "So you really don't think my Rollie killed Gordon?"

"No, Gwen, I really don't."

She wiped the tears with the back of her hand. Left a puff of soapsuds on her cheek. "Why would he say he did?"

I forced myself to look her in the eye. "Because he figured you killed him, Gwen."

Gwen said nothing. No one else did either. Including me. We all just stood there, with our chins on our chests, Gwen washing, me rinsing, Chick playing with the broken pieces of glass on the counter. We still might be standing there if Ike hadn't come to the rescue—if that's what you want to call it. "Give us your wisdom, Maddy. Did Rollie figure rightly or wrongly?"

I gave him the dirtiest look I could. He gave me his best smile. I turned back toward Gwen. "I don't know if you and Rollie discussed the possibility of Gordon finding the trophy when he started his dig. My guess is you didn't. In fact, my guess is you hadn't said boo to each other about David

Delarosa's death since the night it happened. What was there to say? But when Gordon's body was found out there, how could Rollie not conclude that you were the one who put that bullet in his head?"

Gwen didn't object to a word I said. She just kept washing. The same goblet. Over and over.

"Rollie wasn't just protecting you in that note," I said. "He was apologizing to you. You'd protected him when he killed David and now you'd been forced to protect him again. Remember what he said? 'There is no reason for us to live with my guilt any longer.' It was a noble thing for him to say. But of course it wasn't true. Because the guilt was yours. You slept with David. Your betrayal made Rollie lose his head. It's so ironic and so sad. If Rollie hadn't been so anxious to show you his trophy, hadn't taken that early bus home, well, three dead men would be alive today, wouldn't they?" I stopped my moralizing and returned to the evidence. "God only knows when you decided to murder Gordon, Gwen. But certainly by the night of the Kerouac Thing you had. You knew Chick and Gordon would get into it. They did every year. And this year they fought like a couple of little boys on the playground. In a room full of witnesses."

I took the goblet from Gwen's hand. Swished it in the rinse water. "When you found out I was snooping into Gordon's murder, you got worried. You knew I was the one person in Hannawa with enough history in her noggin to link his murder with David's. So you invited me to lunch. You made sure I knew how heated the argument between Chick and Gordon had been at the Kerouac Thing."

Chick bleated at me like an angry goat. "It was not that heated!"

I shushed him with my finger and went on. "And then there was that horrible trip to Pettibones. It went right over my head at the time. But your invitation to tag along with you and Rollie had nothing to do with dog toys. It was about your guilt for trying to blame Chick for Gordon's murder. You cleverly tried to put a bug in my ear about Gordon's graduate assistant, Andrew Holloway. Remember what you said? 'If Chick was going to shoot anybody, wouldn't he shoot Andrew?' Better for your conscience that I pin Gordon's murder on a kid you never met than an old friend, I guess."

Chick bleated at me like ten angry goats now. "Gordon and I were just friends!"

I handed him the goblet. "Take a pill, Chick. This is not about you and Gordon."

I twisted back toward Gwen. "And then you called me out of the blue the other day to chat about your horrible summer. Your trouble finding the right tiles for your guest bathroom. The right therapist for your dogs. Good gravy, Gwen! You knew damn well I'd pointed the police in Rollie's direction. You tried to make me have second thoughts. You put a bug in my ear about Sidney and Effie."

Gwen didn't say a thing. She just kept washing goblets.

"You've tried to put me on the wrong track from the start," I said. "But there was one interesting fact you knew you couldn't keep from me. And so you told me yourself. That you drove Gordon home from the Kerouac Thing. You wanted to make it sound as innocent as you could. Of course it was anything but innocent. You used that opportunity to seduce him. Not sexually. Not exactly. You soothed his battered ego. You showed interest in his dig. You asked him to show it to you sometime. Whether it was his idea or yours, the two of you agreed to drive out there the very next evening.

"Gordon was eager to show off his dig to anyone who showed even the slightest interest. He was especially eager to show it to you, Gwen. Gordon always had—what's a good beatnik word for it? A *thing* for you? Remember that Halloween party at the Kappa Kappa Gamma sorority house? When you both came as scarecrows? And did a lot of things scarecrows usually don't do? I'm sure Gordon was remembering that night when you suggested that you meet at the ball fields and drive out from there."

I was finally ready to describe the murder. "So you drove out to the landfill with Gordon. In his old station wagon. You followed Gordon up the hill. You shot him. Just once. In the back of the head. You stayed just long enough to make sure he was dead. Then you drove back to Hannawa."

Gwen handed me the last goblet. She started washing the spoons. "Can you actually prove that's what happened, Maddy?" she asked.

I had to admit that I couldn't. "Have I found a witness or uncovered some physical evidence that the police haven't? No, I haven't done that. But I have managed to catch you in a big lie. Of sorts."

She handed me the dripping spoons as if they were a bouquet of flowers. "Of sorts?"

"It was in the transcript of that second statement you gave the police," I said. "You told them you didn't know that Rollie had a gun. Which made me wonder why Rollie didn't shoot himself in the head the way he shot Gordon. Why he took himself out of the picture in such a messy, uncertain way. With that bottle of your antidepressants."

"Because he threw his gun away after shooting the professor?" Chick offered.

I handed him the bouquet of spoons. "Why didn't he just buy another gun?" I asked.

"Because he knew he was under surveillance?" Chick asked back.

I did not want to get in a verbal Ping-Pong game with Chick. I moved on before he could serve another impossible-to-answer question. "I was quite ready to believe that Rollie committed both murders. Then I got to thinking. About the murders. About human nature. Gordon's murder was very tidy. A well-planned execution. In the middle of nowhere. David Delarosa's was messy as the dickens. In the hallway of an apartment building. It's a miracle no one else saw it or heard it. Whoever killed Gordon was exercising a boatload of self-control. Whoever killed David Delarosa was acting out raw spontaneous rage."

Chick was playing with the broken glass again. "Those murders were a half-century apart, Maddy. Couldn't somebody who went loony in 1957, kill somebody cool as a cucumber now?"

"Oh, I suppose it's possible," I admitted. "But not likely. Sidney may call himself Shaka Bop these days, but he's the same old Sidney. Effie's the same Effie. You're the same Chick. God help us, I'm the same Maddy. Sweet Gordon was Sweet Gordon until the day he died."

Gwen's quivering lips struggled into a melancholy smile. "Rollie the same Rollie? Me the same me?"

I turned my back to Chick. Spoke to Gwen as if she and I were the only two people in the room. "I went back over all the clippings I have on you. It's quite a bundle. Then I went to City Hall and had a nice long lunch with my old friend Rosemary Hicks. She's head clerk in the records department. Been there for years. Back in the eighties, when we had all those awful rapes, you organized those self-defense courses for women. Rosemary is just like me. Never throws anything out. You not only organized those courses. You took every one of them yourself. Including the gun safety course. It was held at the indoor shooting range at police headquarters. I found the sergeant who taught that course. He's retired now. Dick Drake. He had some old records, too. And a good memory. You passed the course with flying colors. The gun you bought for the course was a 9mm semiautomatic pistol. Like the one used to kill Gordon."

Gwen wiped her hands on her expensive silk jacket. "I told Rollie to sell that gun years ago. I guess he didn't."

"The first and last time he didn't do as you said, apparently."

Gwen reached between Chick and me. Swept the broken glass into her hands. "I suppose you've discussed all this with Detective Grant?"

"Of course—and I wish you would, too."

She motioned for me to open the cupboard under the sink. "I've already told him everything I can."

I opened the cupboard. She deposited the glass in the wastebasket. It was a cheap plastic one. Just like the one under the sink in my little bungalow. "I guess that does it for the dishes," she said.

"Except for Maddy's crock pot," Ike said. He started pulling the ceramic pot out of the metal liner.

Gwen quickly stood up. She reached into the dirty dishwater. Twisted the stopper. The suds began to swirl. "Maddy can wash it when she gets home—can't you, dear?"

"Yes, I guess I can." I let the rinse water out.

Dried my hands on Chick's damp towel. I took my crock pot from Ike. Tried to blink the tears out of my eyes. "I'm so sorry about all this, Gwen."

There were tears in her eyes, too. "So am I."

I tried to give her a good-bye hug but she pulled away.

As Ike and I were leaving, I saw Chick give her a kiss on the forehead. Heard Gwen beg him to stay a while longer. "Sorry babe," he said. "Time for me to split, too."

26

Monday, August 6

It had been a long day. Mondays always are. Not only did I have to fend off requests for information from a dozen well-rested reporters, I had to mark up both the Saturday and Sunday papers. There was one front-page story from Sunday's paper that I clipped for myself. It was a terrific piece. Dale Marabout had spent the whole week on it. The headline was terrific, too:

GWEN & ROLLIE

Sad, Secret Lives Shrouded By The Sweet Smell Of Success

Dale couldn't report the whole story, of course—that it was Gwen, and not Rollie, who murdered Sweet Gordon—but he could recount their long climb to wealth and prominence. He could explore the long-ago sins that eventually destroyed them. He could ponder Gwen's future.

Anyway, right at five I scooped up my purse and the shopping bag I'd kept under my desk all day and headed for the parking deck. I drove down the hill and parked in front of Ike's.

Ike sang out like he always does. "Morgue Mama!"

I sat where I always do, at the table by the cigarette machine. It has the best view of the street. Not that there's ever anything on the street worth seeing.

Ike's coffee shop is always empty at that time of day. He brought me my Darjeeling tea and a handful of those little Ghirardelli chocolates. He brought a mug of black coffee for himself. He said just the right thing. "What's in the bag?"

I pulled it out. Put it on the table between us.

"So that's what caused all the fuss?" he asked.

It was the cocoa can, of course. The one Jack Kerouac gave to Gordon for safekeeping. One of Andrew's students had found it just that past Thursday. Andrew could have kept it for himself. He was close to Gordon, too. But he brought it to me. I pried off the lid and showed Ike the tiny pine cones. He took one out and studied it like it was a precious jewel plucked from the sarcophagus of an Egyptian pharaoh. "So how's your disposition today?" he asked. "More endurable I hope?"

I took the pine cone from his fingers. I put it back in the cocoa can. Snapped on the lid.

"I know I've been a real B lately."

He laughed. "Lately?"

I laughed. "More than usual, I mean."

He unwrapped one of the chocolates and playfully slid it to me, as if he were feeding a rabid raccoon. "Don't be so hard on yourself, Maddy. You did what you had to do."

That was true enough. I did do what I had to do. Two days before Rollie's funeral I'd had lunch with Detective Grant at Speckley's. Over meatloaf sandwiches I told him about the gun class Gwen took. About the gun she bought. About the motive she had for killing Gordon. Why Gordon was eager to take her to the landfill. Why Rollie would take the blame before taking those pills.

Of course Grant already knew all that stuff. "More than likely you're right," he said. "But evidence-wise it adds up to zip."

I bristled like a porcupine. "Common sense-wise it adds up to murder."

He calmly buttered another roll. Gave me half. "It's all circumstantial, Mrs. Sprowls. No gun. No other physical evidence."

"I thought you folks convicted people on circumstantial evidence all the time?"

For some reason he was amused by that. "That we do. But we've also got Rollie's suicide note. No way in hell the prosecutor's office goes after Gwendolyn Moffitt-Stumpf when her husband's already confessed."

"Have you tried to get her to confess?" I asked.

"Every which-a-way," he said. "How about you?"

And so I made those beans, mustered up my courage, and after Rollie's funeral confronted her. And she showed me the door. With nothing more to show for my effort than my dirty crock pot.

Ike unwrapped two more chocolates. "There's still a chance her conscience will get the best of her, isn't there? Call Detective Grant and admit she did it?"

I patted his hand. I liked it that he was trying to lift my spirits. "I suppose, Ike. But more than likely Gwen intends to live with her guilt. She's good at that. And she still has Rollie's money. Her big house and those awful wiener dogs. But at least she knows that I know. That has to be some kind of punishment."

Ike kept trying. "What about the other murder? Maybe the police will charge her for her part in that. That would be some consolation, wouldn't it?"

"For me or for the police?"

"Both maybe?"

I took a nibble out of my chocolate, as if it was a knotty little crab apple. "Detective Grant made it clear they have no plans to rattle Gwen's cage. And in case you're wondering, Ike, neither do I."

Ike's voice was softer now. His eyes were moist with concern. Probably something more. "I know this has been plenty rough on you," he said.

I quickly saved us from an awkward moment. "I'll live," I said.

His cool eyes and smile were back. "You were right about things, weren't you? The connection between the two murders? The trophy? Even this little can of pine cones?"

"Not everything, Ike." I pried off the lid again. I carefully emptied the pine cones onto the tabletop. Among the pine cones was a small piece of paper, folded into a square. I unfolded it and showed Ike the words printed across the top in fifties-style script: *Mopey's Diner.* I jerked it away from his eyes before he could read any more. Held it face down against my blouse.

"Now don't play with me, Maddy. Was there cheese on that famous burger or not?"

I smiled wickedly. But I could not have been more melancholy. "Either way, Chick Glass wouldn't be very happy with the answer, would he?"

"No," said Ike, "I guess he wouldn't."

Ike's is different than most other coffee shops these days. He doesn't mind if people smoke. He has a cigarette machine. He has ashtrays and packs of matches on the tables.

"Ike," I said, "strike a match for me."

He did. I held the restaurant slip to it.

"Dolly Madison Sprowls," he said as the slip curled and disappeared in the ashtray, "you are the cruelest woman alive."

"But lovable, Ike?" I asked.

To receive a free catalog of Poisoned Pen Press titles, please contact us in one of the following ways: